A MARRIAGE OF CONVENIENCE

Recent Titles by Janet Woods from Severn House

THE STONECUTTER'S DAUGHTER
AMARANTH MOON
MORE THAN A PROMISE
CINNAMON SKY
BROKEN JOURNEY
THE COAL GATHERER
EDGE OF REGRET
WITHOUT REPROACH
HEARTS OF GOLD
SALTING THE WOUND
STRAW IN THE WIND
PAPER DOLL
LADY LIGHTFINGERS
MOON CUTTERS
DIFFERENT TIDES
FOXING THE GEESE
WHISPERS IN THE WIND
A MARRIAGE OF CONVENIENCE

The Tall Poppies Series

TALL POPPIES
SECRETS AND LIES
I'LL GET BY

A MARRIAGE OF CONVENIENCE

Janet Woods

severn House

Welcome to the world Mave Rose Hampton.
born June 2017

This first world edition published 2018
in Great Britain and the USA by
SEVERN HOUSE PUBLISHERS LTD of
Eardley House, 4 Uxbridge Street, London W8 7SY
Trade paperback edition first published
in Great Britain and the USA 2018 by
SEVERN HOUSE PUBLISHERS LTD

British Library Cataloguing in Publication Data
A CIP catalogue record for this title is available from the British Library.

ISBN-13: 978-0-7278-8780-1 (cased)
ISBN-13: 978-1-84751-895-8 (trade paper)
ISBN-13: 978-1-78010-958-9 (e-book)

This is a work of fiction. Names, characters, places and incidents are either the
product of the author's imagination or are used fictitiously. Except where actual
historical events ~~~ ~~~~~~~~~~ ~~~ ~~~~~ ~~~~~~~~ ~~~ ~~~ ~~~~~~~ of this novel,
all situations in ~~~~ ~~~~~~~~~~~ ~~~ ~~~~~~~~~~ ~~~ ~~~ ~~~~ ~~ ~~~ actual persons,
living or dead, ~~ ~~~~~~~~ ~~~~~~~~~~~~ ~~~ ~~~~~~~~ ~~~~~~ ~~ ~~~ncidental.

All Severn Hous ~~~~~~~~~~ ~~~~~ ~~~~~~~~~~~ ~~~~~~~~~~~~~~~~~ ~~~~~~~~~

Severn House ~~~~~~~ ~~~ ~~~~~~~~ ~~~ ~~~~~~ ~~~~~~~~~~~~ ~~~~~~~ [FSC™],
the leading inte~~~~~ ~~~~~~~~ ~~ ~~~ ~~~~~~ ~~~~~~~~~~~ ~~~~~~~~
All our titles th~~ ~~~ ~~~~~~~~ ~~~~ ~~~~~~ ~~~ ~~~ ~~~ ~~~~~~ ~~go.

MIX
Paper fr
responsible
FSC
www.fsc.org
FSC® C01

Typeset by Palin~~~~
Falkirk, Stirlingshire, Scotland.
Printed and bound in Great Britain by
TJ International, Padstow, Cornwall.

One

Lady Florence was dead.

The old lady departed peacefully and with a secretive smile on her face, her passage to heaven oiled by the last drops of brandy left in the cut crystal decanter on her bedside cabinet.

Her death had been nicely timed, for it was autumn and there had been some drenching rain after a particularly dry summer. It had softened the top soil so the gravediggers could shovel the earth from the grave without fear of the sides caving in lower down, where the earth was still firm.

James Archibald, Lady Florence's pompous, pot-bellied legal representative had travelled the twenty miles or so from South-ampton using a private carriage. He gathered the six servants together. 'Apart from you, Ellis, Lady Florence has left each of you a bequest, the sum of which has not yet been disclosed.' But along with the good came the bad as James Archibald found his second wind and puffed out, 'You will all work out a month's notice. Lady Florence's executor has been informed by messenger and I imagine he'll arrive in time for the funeral and stay here for as long as it takes to wind up the estate.'

The servants muttered amongst themselves and the attorney raised his voice.

'The house will be boarded up until her nephew is informed of his aunt's demise and we receive instructions as to the fate of the building. You will be paid at the end of the month, and be warned, you will forfeit both wage and legacy should you decide to leave prematurely and without permission.'

Grace doubted if Lady Florence would have put such a condi-tion in her will. 'Perhaps we should wait to see what the executor has to say about it before you impose conditions on us.'

'It's a bloody liberty, if you asks me. What if we're offered another position?' the cook muttered. 'And what about Sam?'

'Sam? There's nobody by that name in the staff book.'

'Lady Florence took him in and he looks after the donkey and the horses of visitors while they're here.'

'Who pays him for that?'

'The visitors I reckon. Lady Florence provided him with his meals and gave him a bed in the stable loft. He does odd jobs as well.'

'Tell him he must leave, the visitors can look after their own horses. Brian can look after the donkey.'

'It's not my job to tell him.'

'You are speaking out of turn to your superior.'

'Out of turn? Whose turn to talk is it then, pray? There's only one windbag here that I can see?' Jessie grinned at her husband . . . though whether she and Brian were truly wed was a matter for conjecture, Grace thought.

Uncertainty flitted across Archibald's face. 'I imagine exceptions can be made.'

A sniff of indignation came from the cook and she folded her meaty arms on her chest. 'Warning us, did you say earlier; are you calling us dishonest?'

'No . . . I didn't mean that at all. One or two of you might be tempted to leave earlier when you are needed here, and I'll be in trouble if the inventory isn't up to date.'

Grace sighed. 'There's nobody to chastize you until the nephew arrives from the continent, Mr Archibald. By that time the inventory will be completed. If anything is missing we can put it down to household breakages . . . they do happen on occasion.'

Archibald loosened his collar and gazed around him, clearly flustered. 'It will take at least two months to sort out, and just when I was about to retire. Where's Pawley? Somebody fetch him, please? He was responsible for keeping the household accounts, I recall.'

Grace stepped forward. 'Mr Pawley is no longer with us.'

'You mean Pawley has died as well?' Blood drained from his cheeks and he pressed his hand against his chest. 'Oh dear . . . oh dear.'

'Bring a brandy for the gentleman, if we have any, Jessie,' and Grace led him to a chair. 'Sit down, do, Mr Archibald. Mr Pawley is still alive, as far as we know, and I see no reason why you shouldn't retire when, no doubt, Lady Florence's executor is highly skilled and extremely diligent.'

The attorney took a sip of the brandy, smacked his lips and the colour began to return to his face. 'And your position is?'

'I was Lady Florence's companion. Mr Pawley was discharged some five months ago and she asked me to take over management of the household and the books.'

His voice rose an octave. 'But you're a female.'

'Good lord, I hadn't noticed that before,' Grace murmured, turning it into a cough when the attorney levelled a stare at her.

'What's your name, young lady – how old are you?'

Why did men think females were useless for anything but housework, embroidering cushion covers and bearing children? 'My name is Grace Ellis and I'm twenty years of age.'

'Where did you train for the management position?'

'I kept the household and business accounts for my father until his death two years ago. I was also able to manage Lady Florence's . . . "affliction". I do have some knowledge concerning the preparation of herbal remedies. Who better to administer to a woman than another woman?'

'Under a man's guidance, of course.'

Grace felt like tearing his ears off. 'As you indicate, Mr Archibald. Lady Florence was very ill at the time and had a hacking cough and a fever. Her death came as a blessing, for Mr Pawley's transgression grieved her.'

He cleared his throat. 'Indeed. There is no need to furnish me with the details, young lady.'

'I'm sorry, sir, but I daresay I will be looking for employment soon, so the more people who are made aware of my skills, the more likely a successful outcome will result.'

'Very enterprising of you, my dear.'

'That goes for the rest of the staff, of course. Winter is not far away and it's a bad time to look for work.'

'Indeed.'

'May I ask why wasn't I treated like the rest of the staff?'

'With regards to?'

'The staff legacies.'

He flapped his hand at the rest of the staff. 'You may go about your business.'

When the door closed behind the staff, he turned to her. 'Ah, yes,' and he shuffled from one foot to the other. 'Lady Florence had her reasons, of which you will learn in due time.' He patted her hand in a familiar manner and left it there. 'Don't you worry, my dear, I'm sure we can find a little spare cash about the house. A favour for a favour, I aways say. Perhaps you and I can do a little business together. Tell me, Miss Ellis, what was the nature of Lady Florence's affliction? I've heard rumours she had some fine medicinal brandy tucked away in her cellar. Perhaps I'll take a few bottles home, for she won't be needing them now.'

Tugging her hand away from his, Grace shuddered. The odious little rat! Lady Florence liked a drink, as did many people, and she sometimes became slightly merry. Grace amended 'sometimes' to 'often', and then she admitted to herself the truth. Her mistress had been in her cups much too often, and sometimes to the point of collapse. Grace had done her best to look after her but it wasn't her place to tell Lady Florence what she should or shouldn't do.

Lady Florence had told her, 'Grace, my girl, a brandy or two has a mellowing effect and helps me to resurrect the ghosts of my past. If I've learned anything from my life it's that I don't regret one damned thing, especially the men. The dear creatures can give a woman so much pleasure. But then, with you being a doctor's daughter, you would probably measure men and their various parts through a more anatomical manner . . . hmmm?'

Trying to appear worldly, Grace had mumbled something and turned away, embarrassed.

'No good trying to hide that blush,' the woman had teased. 'Have you ever seen a man's shaft when it's in good working order? Such a silly looking appendage, but ah . . . put it to work and it becomes so warm, vibrant and pleasurable. But there, my dear, I shouldn't shock you. I recall the virginal state as being tedious; what say you?'

Although she'd blushed Grace agreed with the sentiment. Keeping herself tidy in case a suitable man with marriage on his mind happened to come along was becoming more unnecessary as each day sent her sliding a little bit further down the social scale into servitude. She'd allowed Lady Florence to have the last word since she hadn't wanted to encourage the woman – which didn't mean she didn't think about what went on between men and women, and often!

Now, outside of her warm circle of thought Mr Archibald intruded with an impatient humming sound in his throat. She couldn't imagine his manly appendage giving any woman pleasure since his stomach would get in the way. But then, she knew nothing about such matters except the information gleaned from her father's books, and those hadn't mentioned any emotional content to the act of procreation.

'Are you listening, Miss Ellis?'

Grace gave him a faint smile as she scrambled to pick up the thread of the conversation.

'You'll have to discuss Lady Florence's condition with her doctor, sir. I'm not qualified to diagnose it, especially on her death, but I would have thought it was brought on by her advanced age. No doubt the doctor will provide you with a death certificate.'

'Quite so . . . I'm surprised you were placed in such a responsible position, and at so young an age.'

'As you indicated before, Mr Archibald.'

'Come, come, Miss Ellis, don't get haughty with me. You know very well I'm referring to Lady Florence's disposition.'

'Disposition?'

His sigh had an edge of exasperation to it. 'I understood Lady Florence could be difficult.'

'From whom?' Grace had never found her to be difficult. She'd been straightforward, generous, sometimes acerbic and often vulgar. Grace was sorry the old lady had died, but she knew Lady Florence wouldn't have encouraged her to mourn, but to turn her mind to her own future. What would she do now? She had a little put by because since she'd entered the household eighteen months previously she'd saved nearly every penny she'd earned. And she had prospects, just that morning, Jessie, the housemaid had offered, 'Come to Australia with Brian and me if you can't find anywhere else to go. We can always pool our money. We're going to search for gold. It will be such an adventure, luvvy, I can't imagine you working in a mine, though. You could always start a school for the miners' brats.'

'I'll bear it in mind,' she'd said, even though the idea didn't really appeal to her. They'd both laughed at the thought of the diminutive Grace yielding a pickaxe.

'Perhaps you could start a school. You're good with children and the afflicted.'

Grace had been encouraged by the offer for she'd never really got along with Jessie and her husband. Sometimes their manner was disrespectful towards Lady Florence, and Grace had caught them listening at keyholes more than once when their mistress had visitors. They had also been the friends of the disgraced Pawley.

Afflictions in Lady Florence's household usually meant a splinter in the thumb, grit in the eye, a sore tooth, which an application of cinnamon would usually cure, or an aching joint relieved by a gentle rub of wintergreen ointment on the site of pain.

Her father's illness had been incurable, brought on by his excesses. His death had been instant and the certificate stated he'd died from a sudden brain seizure. How would the death certificate word Lady Florence's affliction? Grace had told the doctor that Lady Florence had been short of breath of late.

He would be kind, for the man had been one of the old lady's lovers, or so she'd said. Passed away peacefully in her sleep would be appropriate, she imagined.

Grace's mind drifted into the future. She might be able to buy one of those medicine carts in Australia and go from town to town, selling lotions and potions and medicines.

No . . . she was a woman alone and to take up such a scheme would be to place herself in constant danger from felons, high-waymen, or worse, wild animals. Where would she sleep, eat, bathe – buy her supplies of herbs and feed for the horse? She could ride a horse, but not expertly, and she could manage with a cart attached, also not expertly. Mostly she used the donkey cart when she needed to go into the town.

'Will you kindly stop dreaming girl. Tell me, why I was not informed of these staff changes?'

Jerked back to the present, Grace said, 'I couldn't say, sir. Most likely Lady Florence would have informed you on your quarterly visit, which is long overdue since she was expecting you at the beginning of September. From my observations she may have had good reason to mistrust Mr Pawley.'

'What reason?'

'Pawley wouldn't take instructions from Lady Florence and sometimes swore at her. I understand he left when Lady Florence told him she was going to write to her financial manager and ask him to do an audit.'

What Grace didn't tell him was that several amounts of cash had been secreted away by the old lady. She didn't trust the attorney either, and she thought it best for the executor to sort it out.

And she'd noticed that Archibald had already counted the cash in the old lady's pocket, which had been left on her dresser and overlooked by Grace. When he thought nobody was looking, he'd tipped most of the contents into his waistcoat pocket, leaving just a coin or two, so the theft wouldn't be obvious.

'Dear, dear,' and the attorney's lips pursed. 'I do wish I'd been informed of this sooner. You had better fetch me the books so I can see if I can make anything of them. And bring the key to the wine cellar as well.'

'I'm afraid I can't. When Lady Florence noticed a discrepancy she called in her financial adviser. John Howard collected the books and took them away with him. I've been keeping a list of the household accounts in a notebook though, and have all the receipts. Would you like to see those?'

'You might as well hand them to her executor to deal with since I won't be able to collect her signature for payment. The key to the cellar?'

'Missing, I'm afraid.'

He raised an eyebrow. 'Missing!'

She nodded. 'That's what I said. Now . . . with your permission, sir, Jessie and I will see to Lady Florence We are just about to prepare her for her lying in.'

'Doesn't the undertaker do that?'

'Lady Florence wouldn't like strangers to handle her. I promised I'd take care of that task.'

Colour crept under the man's skin. 'Quite.'

'I've also taken it upon myself to inform the undertaker of her demise, and they should be here shortly. Lady Florence chose her casket and made her arrangements some time ago. Her wish is to lie in state in the morning room, so people can pay their respects. I hope you don't mind me going ahead with the arrangements as Lady Florence instructed.'

'On the contrary, it's a relief to find someone efficient in charge. A woman with such good sense is a rarity and I'm much relieved. Are you sure the key to the cellar is missing?'

'Yes . . . I've looked everywhere for it. I've also tried all the other house keys, and the door is too solid to kick it down.'

Grace sighed when he left her to it. 'A rarity, huh!' she snorted, and rang the bell for Jessie to return.

For once Lady Florence was unable to complain about her aches and pains, but lay there, silently. She was as cold as a lizard in winter. Hands, brown mottled by age, were held together in an attitude of prayer – a gold cross on a gold chain bound them together. She waited for the undertaker, her eyes partially open and gleaming from under slitted lids. They flickered in the candlelight but were focussed inwards.

Jessie was reluctant to touch the corpse. ''Tis said the departing soul of the dead might steal the spirit of those in attendance, so it can live its life over again.'

'Nonsense,' Grace scoffed but she didn't push it because as she removed the woman's rings she noticed her fingers were already becoming stiff.

She slipped the rings into her apron pocket.

It wasn't the first corpse Grace had seen and she wasn't squeamish. All the same, when they turned the dead woman over and she made a gurgling noise the pair of them jumped, poised for flight.

Jessie whispered, 'Are you sure she's dead?'

'Why don't you ask her? She might tell you.'

When Jessie gave a nervous giggle, Grace grinned and drew on the threads of knowledge she'd gleaned from her father's books and from snippets of loose talk when he'd entertained others of the medical fraternity. The subject of bodies and the ailments they suffered from was interesting rather than macabre, she thought, as she padded the apertures of Lady Florence's body so she wouldn't begin to smell unpleasant.

Her father had mostly been matter-of-fact about such matters. 'I wish all my students were as diligent as you,' he'd said once, and then he'd sighed and spoiled the compliment. 'A pity you weren't my son instead of my daughter. However, we might be able to turn you into a useful midwife in time.'

'Where's the soul?' she'd asked him, crushed by his casual down-grade of her from beloved daughter into inferior female.

'The soul . . . hmmm . . . now, let me see. That's a mystery to us doctors. Nobody can explain the soul but it's invisible, and it's supposedly bestowed on us by the Lord to keep us civilized and make us wise. Otherwise we'd be like the beasts in the field.'

'But where does the soul go when people die, Papa?'

'As I said, it's a mystery. You must ask the reverend, he knows about such things . . . or thinks he does. Some scholars think it's part of the heart, others that it's stored in the brain.'

Jessie jumped when Lady Florence rattled again, and Grace grinned. 'It's the juices in her body . . . like when you're hungry. When we die our insides turn into a gas that helps to dissolve the flesh.'

'Ugh! All that brandy inside her must have fermented and she thought she'd have a last fart. How do you know all this?'

'My father was a doctor.'

Grace tried not to laugh. When she'd first been employed she'd been shocked by the way servants talked so freely and crudely about such matters. Now she was used to it.

The undertaker's cart arrived with the coffin in a crunch of wheels on gravel and the slow plod of a horse.

Grace's former employer looked like a baby in her shroud and her bonnet, the ribbons tied in a neat bow to one side. She was lifted from the bed by two of the four men and then gently laid in the satin lined box, her head on a small pillow. They took her downstairs to the morning room, where her final bed was placed on a table covered with a black cloth. Grace strewed some dried lavender around the corpse.

'A perfect fit, like a sprat in a jar,' the senior amongst them said, and with a rather irreverent smile, he handed her the gold chain and cross and used one he removed from his pocket. 'You keep that, Miss Ellis. You have to be careful because something valuable is likely to be stolen by the mourners so we use one of our own. 'You've done a good job with her, lass. We'll be back in three days, lessen you want one of my men in attendance. It will cost more though.'

'Thank you, but no, we can manage and there is a man in the house if one is needed.' Grace tucked a sheet trimmed with lace across Lady Florence's shoulders. 'You may go if you wish, Jessie. Thanks for your help.'

'Good . . . because seeing the mistress like that is giving me the willies.'

Lady Florence lay in state for three days while people came and went. The mourners and the staff talked in whispers. It was to everyone's relief when the undertakers came to close the coffin, and Grace noted that the chain and cross was missing. She hoped it wasn't one of the staff.

'Would you wait outside for a moment?' Grace said, though she could still hear them conversing in hushed whispers as footsteps lightly crossed the hall.

Grace shut the noise from her mind and she gazed at the woman's pale face. Tears tracked down her cheeks and she allowed herself a sob as she dried them on her apron. 'There . . . you look lovely, just like a child sleeping in a cradle. *Requiescat in pace,* my Lady,' Grace whispered.

'A housemaid who knows some Latin, whatever next?'

She spun round, her heart thumping. A tall man with grey eyes stood between her and the door.

Her first thought? Surely it wasn't the devil arriving to collect the old lady's soul? Her glance went to his dark curls, searching for signs of horns. There were none. For certain he wasn't an angel though. His face was too sharply angled, his gaze too steady, his mouth too firm. But then, she'd never seen an angel, and neither did she want to see one just yet.

Altogether, there was a wickedly confident look to him. A fallen angel perhaps, she thought when he smiled.

'I know very little Latin. Who are you?' she blurted out, feeling all sorts of fools for being caught talking to a corpse, while at the same time being drawn to the stranger as though he possessed some magnetic attraction. She was annoyed with him – with herself, and for no reason she could think of.

A card appeared between his fingers like magic. 'LéSayres,' was written across it in bold dark letters. She murmured. 'Do you have a first name?'

'Dominic.'

When no more information was forthcoming, she asked him, 'Are you Lady Florence's nephew? We understood you were abroad.'

'He is abroad. I'm John Howard's business partner. And you are . . .?'

She too could play that game. 'Ellis . . . Grace Ellis.'

A barely discernable, but slightly appreciative smile flitted across his mouth. He was about as relaxed as a cat ready to pounce on a mouse. 'Ellis . . . ah yes . . . I remember. You must be the daughter of Dr Harold Ellis. John told me that Lady Florence thought highly of you.'

The compliment pleased Grace and she smiled. 'Lady Florence was a lively old lady, if a little eccentric. I liked her. Did you know my father?'

'I knew of him.'

She asked him before he got round to asking her, for she was almost sure he was going to. 'Did he . . . owe your business any money?'

He crossed to the coffin and gazed down at the occupier, amazing her with, 'You mustn't hold yourself responsible for your father's debt, Miss Ellis. His estate was disposed of amongst his creditors satisfactorily. We must not overlook his good points either. He was a man well-respected in his profession, and he carried out a great deal of charitable work – more than he could ever have been recompensed for had he been of a mind to charge a fee.'

She was grateful for that touch of praise. 'Thank you.'

'The pleasure is mine.' She tensed when he said, 'As to your question, I had other business with your father.'

Interest piqued, she gazed at the curve of his back. Soberly attired in a short, black cape and riding boots over dark-blue trousers, he carried a hat with a curled brim. As he turned away she caught a glimpse of his dark-blue damask waistcoat, which was topped by a white cravat secured by a gold pin. He was elegant and confident in his attire. 'May I ask what that business was?'

He turned, making a graceful arc on his feet so she imagined herself being swept into his arms and danced around the floor. Adroitly he changed the subject. 'This is neither the time nor place. I'm sorry Lady Florence died before I had a chance to meet her. John Howard spoke kindly of her. Where will you go from here; have you given it any thought?'

'I've been invited to go to Australia and dig for gold with two of the other servants.'

His dimple deepened and his smile widened as his glance swept over her. 'And will you?'

'It's a bit too adventurous for me. I would rather not leave England, but I may have no choice.'

'There's always a choice for a presentable young lady like you, Miss Ellis.'

The only alternatives Grace could think of was to find a husband, throw herself on the parish, or . . .? She thought the unthinkable. It slid across her mind like slime and her skin crawled. No, she couldn't . . . she'd rather die! 'I can't think of one at the moment.'

'No relatives?'

'None. One minute I was living happily with my father in a nice home, and the next moment I had no roof over my head, no means of support and nobody to fall back on. One of my father's acquaintances recommended me for this position, which was kind of him.'

'It was my partner, John Howard.'

'I vaguely remember him. He came for dinner once or twice when my father was alive. And I saw him here at Oakford House on one occasion. His fingers ached and I put some salve on them. It was he who rescued me from the workhouse. He gave me the coach fare and a letter of introduction to Lady Florence. He had a stern expression on his face, but it was a kind gesture. I suppose I must still owe him for the coach fare.'

'I doubt if he'd miss a few shillings, and if he did he wouldn't be rude enough to remind a lovely young lady like you of the debt. It's possible I may hear of another opportunity that would suit you when you leave here.'

Grace turned fierce eyes upon him. 'Bear in mind I will not consider anything . . . socially unacceptable.'

For a moment his grey eyes widened, and then they filled with amusement. 'That depends on your interpretation of what is acceptable and to whom?'

She wanted to laugh too. She gazed at him, intrigued, wondering if he was married. Her face heated but she refused to place her palms over her blush to conceal it. Instead, she murmured, 'It's warm in here.'

'Warm enough to wake the dead?'

'Watch out if it does. Lady Florence has a fine temper on her if her rest is interrupted prematurely.'

He chuckled when she gave a soft giggle, 'I beg your pardon, Mr LéSayres. It wouldn't do for me to encourage your peculiar sense of humour on this sad day.'

'But you haven't heard my proposition yet.'

What was she thinking of, flirting in the presence of the dead? Not that Lady Florence would have minded. She'd enjoyed the company of men, and were she to be believed had entertained many lovers after her husband had died. That was before she'd become incapacitated and too demanding, so her servants kept leaving her employ. 'I don't know if I dare listen to it.'

A discreet cough signalled the presence of the undertaker, who smiled when he noticed the chain and cross was missing. The lid was screwed down and they stood to one side as the coffin was lifted and carried outside on the shoulders of four men.

'Did you say you have a proposition for me?' she blurted out.

'Be patient, Miss Ellis, for the moment you must curb your curiosity.'

'The fact I was displaying any is an assumption on your part.'

His smile came and went like quicksilver. She had to be satisfied with that small victory because the hall clock struck eleven.

Only Grace would attend the funeral, the rest of the staff would remain behind to prepare the cold collation and sherry for the mourners.

She waited until most of the mourners were on their way then joined the rear of the small procession and followed after the glass-sided hearse, pulled by two plodding black stallions. Tears filled Grace's eyes. The coffin was decorated with an arrangement of yew tree branches, needled with dark green, the vivid red berries dramatic with their sticky black eyes.

Grace drew in her breath when a cloud of yellow hammers flew out of the stubble. Field workers were spreading dung to encourage a good crop come spring. They removed their hats and bowed their heads in respect as the cortège passed.

Dominic LéSayres lingered until she caught up with him. He handed her his handkerchief, concern in his steady gaze. 'Will you allow me to walk with you, Miss Ellis?'

She nodded since he couldn't get up to any mischief here, even if he wanted to. 'Yes . . . Mr LéSayres, you may.'

They walked for a while without saying anything, then he said, 'The countryside is colourful at this time of year.'

'The days are drawing in and the nights are growing colder. I wonder what winter will bring.'

'I'm sure it will offer some excitement in its season. Did you notice that the chain and cross was missing from Lady Florence's body.'

'The undertaker told me that mourners often take a keepsake at such times, so he uses an inexpensive substitute.'

They looked at each other and smiled.

Two

The guests had departed and the staff had retreated to their quarters, there to mull over the events of the last few days and ponder on what their futures held.

Dominic intended to do what he could to find alternative employment for them, to which end Miss Ellis's insights and observations could be useful. His brother might take a couple of them into his household.

Apart from his company, dinner was a miserable affair. The cook dished up a stew of stringy meat along with dumplings followed by a soggy bread pudding in a sea of lumpy custard.

The two of them populated a dining room, where they shared a large table, a relic of when Lady Florence used to entertain. A candelabrum sent shadowy fingers to probe into the dusty corners.

She apologized for the meal. 'It was a wild rabbit Brian snared. It must have been old.'

'Is that what it was . . . a rabbit?'

Without a trace of a smile her head tipped to one side and she said quite seriously, 'I can't guarantee that, of course. It may have been a stoat or a squirrel, or even a wild pony from the forest.'

'A pony?' He stared at her for a moment, wondering if she was gulling him or just bordering on insane.

'Perhaps not, I doubt if the cook would have been able to fit it in the oven,' she said.

Amused, Dominic began to laugh. 'You nearly had me there. You're an unusual young woman, Miss Ellis, and a delight to the eye I might add.'

'Thank you, Mr LéSayres. Remember, you're here to conduct business not to pass personal comment on my appearance, however much I might enjoy it.'

Now there was an ambiguous sentence. The girl had sparked an interest in him, and he wanted to know her better. 'Do you enjoy it?'

'I'm a woman, of course I do, but your presence isn't social, it's business and I'm a servant, and therefore, a poor host. If I were a lady I would compliment you on your waistcoat and your gold watch chain. I'm sure Lady Florence would have enjoyed your company, though.'

'As I am enjoying yours . . . what position did you hold before you entered the service of Lady Florence?'

'My position in life was that of being my father's daughter, sir, at least . . . when he remembered he had one. I was not required to earn a living and there was very little difference between my duties then and now. Unfortunately, when he died, he forgot to leave me enough money to survive on and he would have preferred a son.'

'If it's any consolation I'm glad you were not his son.'

She shrugged. 'To suggest I need consolation over the matter is unkind. I like being female.'

Dominic liked it that Miss Ellis didn't display any false modesty, but he smarted a little from her put-down. He shrugged. 'I feel as if I've shrunk to a height of six inches.'

Her eyes widened. The colour was nothing more than dark in this light but he remembered them as being brown – not a dull old donkey brown but a delicious, glistening honey-brown guarded by the longest of dark lashes.

'I'm sorry, Mr LéSayres, I didn't set out to belittle you. It's been a long time since I entertained anyone. I have forgotten my manners and I hope, now that you've corrected me, that you'll forgive me.'

How could he ignore such a pretty plea, especially when she smiled so entrancingly?

'I cannot resist that smile. Of course I will forgive you, Miss Ellis.'

'Then I'll try to avoid tripping over the six inches in height that I've reduced you to. I might squash you flat, then what would you do?'

He laughed.

'I'll make us some coffee when I take the dirty dishes out, or would you prefer tea? The fire is alight in the drawing room.'

He wasn't surprised that her job here wasn't clearly defined, considering the upheaval of the last few days. 'I would prefer coffee, and also that the servants do the job they're paid to do.'

Crossing to the bell pull, he gave it a jerk. Half a minute later Jessie appeared and looked from one to the other before saying, 'Yes sir?'

'You may clear the table, Jessie.'

Jessie glanced at Miss Ellis and then towards him again. She sniffed. 'Usually Grace—'

'I'm aware of what Miss Ellis usually does, but while I'm here she is at my disposal, and will be taking coffee with me after dinner while we plan for the house to be closed down. We will use the drawing room for that purpose.'

'Yes sir,' Jessie said, and curtsied, throwing his delicious little companion a mean look at the same time.

In her turn, after Jessie had gone, Grace Ellis pursed her lips at him, making herself look kissable rather than angry. Her voice rose. '*Disposal?*'

'A bad choice of words, Miss Ellis, and I apologize. Rest assured, I have no intention of disposing of you . . . I promise.'

'In that case I will accept your apology.'

He was the guest, and in his honour she'd exchanged her servant gown for a bluebell-coloured taffeta that had faded into its folds and rustled when she walked. Dominic appreciated a woman who used the power of her femininity, even if she was unaware of the fact.

They went across to the drawing room and he gazed around the place with an assessing eye. This room was untidier than the dining room due no doubt to the guests Oakford House had catered for this day. It wasn't a large house compared to the one he'd grown up in, but it was of comfortable proportions for a family with six bedchambers, and attic rooms for the servants. It stood on two acres of land in a good position in the countryside surrounding the town of Ringwood, and fronted on to the main highway that snaked through the New Forest.

From the upper floors there was a view over three fields. Then a partial view of the church behind a copse, near enough to add to the view and far enough so the bells didn't annoy. The copse was rapidly losing its bounty of gold and ruby leaves. Beyond was a glimpse of the cemetery Lady Florence now occupied.

Although it had a slightly neglected appearance, the warm, red-brick house sat solidly in its spacious grounds. It would sell easily if tidied up, and for a good price. The ornamental spires at the front gave it a faintly bizarre, slightly Gothic appearance.

Inside, the house seemed to have attracted everything to it. Ornaments nudged each other on the tables and mantelpieces and the dust was a sticky fixture in the spidery corners. There was enough staff to keep a house of this size clean if they worked for the common good, but he could see that the bulk of the work fell on the shoulders of the delightful Miss Ellis, while the key staff took advantage of her need to be useful to someone.

They would be set to it on the morrow, counting the contents. He must sort things out with the staff first, and as quickly as possible.

He stood near the fireplace and gazed down at his unlikely host while the shadows leapt and danced around the room.

'Would you be seated, Mr LéSayres. You're giving me a crick in the neck.'

Dominic chuckled. He was not quite as tall as his brother, but tall enough to be an inconvenience to shorter people on occasion.

He sank into the chair opposite her and stretched his legs towards the fire.

'You mentioned earlier that you have a brother. Is he as tall as you?' she asked.

Dominic casually added an inch or two to his own height. 'About the same.'

'Is he younger or older?'

Dominic didn't like gossiping about himself or his family, but on this occasion it was harmless social chat. 'My brother Alex is older by a year or so. He and his wife live in Dorset and have an infant son. I'm his godfather.'

He nearly laughed at the pride in his voice, especially when she murmured, 'An honour indeed, what is the child called?'

'It's Nicholas after his LéSayres great-grandfather, and Ambrose after Vivienne's father, Reverend Fox.'

'Am I to assume Vivienne is the boy's mother?'

She was rewarded with a smile. 'You are.'

Jessie brought the coffee tray in and set it on the table. 'Will there be anything else, sir?'

'No . . . it's been a busy day for all of us so thank the staff for their cooperation.'

'We will have to make up a guest bedchamber,' Grace said with panic in her tone.

Jessie gave a thin smile. 'Already done, second left at the top of the stairs.' The door closed firmly behind Jessie and smoke billowed down the chimney into the room.

Grace offered him a coffee along with a wry glance. 'I'm sorry, with everything else going on I forgot about your bedchamber.'

'I wouldn't have thought it your task, but that of the maid.'

'I imagine Ella will be washing the dishes, I usually help her with it before getting Lady Florence ready for bed. Jessie doesn't understand how hard it is for invalids to carry out everyday tasks.'

'Oh . . . I imagine she's well aware, but does as little as she can get away with,' he said, using his hand to fan the smoke away. 'Who's in charge of this household?'

'It used to be Mr Pawley, but now he's gone . . . I don't know.'

'You were closest to Lady Florence, and she gave you a

position of trust. With your permission I'll make it clear to the rest of the staff that you're in charge.'

'I'll do my best. Lady Florence had a good, active mind, and she appreciated my help. Would you like a brandy, Mr LéSayres?'

At his nod she crossed to the decanter and held it up to the candlelight. 'There doesn't appear to be much left. Somebody must have drunk it. Mr Archibald, I expect. He said he wanted the key to the cellar so he could take a couple of bottles home with him.'

'I thought he was staggering a bit on the way to the funeral. Did you give him the key?'

'Certainly not! The brandy's not mine to dispense. Would you like what remains in the decanter in your coffee? There's only a tablespoon, hardly worth soiling another glass for.'

'That's a contradiction if ever I heard one.'

Her smile warmed his heart. 'Do you think so?'

Sipping at the brandy she handed him, he smiled. 'This is good liquor; do you know who her supplier is?'

'It's one of her former acquaintances, a smuggling man called Rafferty Jones. He and Lady Florence had known each other since childhood, or so she said. He came to see her when she was lying in state. You probably didn't notice him.'

'Let me think . . . he was about forty and wore black breeches and a blue jacket. His eyes were dark and he wore side-whiskers. He stood to one side of the potted plant and you stood at the other side.'

'I stayed in the room with him in case he stole something.'

He spluttered, because this innocent girl didn't have the slightest idea of the nature of the trouble she was courting . . . a smuggler? 'You must not place yourself in danger by consorting with criminals.'

'Oh, I don't consort with them. Rafferty Jones doesn't say much, though he looks fierce despite being very shy and respectful.'

'How is the brandy despatched from here?'

'It's picked up by the wine merchant Jones & Son. I understand they are related. It comes in small kegs and is decanted into bottles, labelled and corked in the cellar, or so Lady Florence told me.'

'Miss Ellis, I beg you not to get involved with the business of smuggling.'

'I'm not involved. It's what Lady Florence told me. I wouldn't dare tell anyone else. She was full of tales, and she told me all sorts of things – things I didn't want to know about, and sometimes didn't believe.'

Her laughter made the hair prickle on the back of Dominic's neck when she said, 'Would you really beg me? You don't look to be the type of man who would beg for anything.'

'I would not like to see you hurt. A lovely young woman like you, all alone in the world, can become prey for many men, especially those on the wrong side of the law. Although you've escaped the fate of many young women, as far as I can see it's more like luck than design.'

She leaned forward and gazed at him, the candle flames reflected in her eyes. 'You're a proud man, but a kind one nevertheless, Mr LéSayres . . . and not at all what you seem.'

'And how is that?'

'You are quiet, but you're used to exerting your authority, and without raising your voice. No . . . you wouldn't beg, but you'd expect people to act on your word, and without question.'

She was right, but this woman with her air of independence would never do as she was told.

Her mouth had a graceful curve to it and the air vibrated with tension around them. She needed to be kissed, and he needed to kiss her. 'Forgive me for what I'm about to do.' Dipping his finger in his coffee he ran it along her lips, dewing them with moisture. Then he kissed her.

For a moment she stiffened, and then for just a moment she responded, her mouth clinging to his. A few seconds later she pulled away and gave a soft, trembling laugh. 'That's the first time I've been kissed.'

'And I.'

She experienced an irrepressible need to flirt with him. 'That's a bag of moonshine, Mr LéSayres. You are much too good at kissing to be a beginner.'

'How can you know that when you have nothing to measure it against? Perhaps we should try it again as a comparison . . . just to see if I'm able to make a better job of it, you understand.'

'I understand very well.' She stood, laughter in her voice. 'Clearly, and on those grounds alone, perhaps we should not. Goodnight,

Mr LéSayres. I'll leave you with the candle since I know my way round the house in the dark.'

Dominic didn't know whether to laugh, or put her across his lap and smack her behind.

He lost both opportunities when she turned and scurried off, her footsteps pattering across the hall and up the stairs. A door opened, and then closed again. A few scuffling noises reached his ears, when he imagined her gown slipping from her shoulders and pooling around her ankles in a most erotic manner. A few minutes later he heard a key turn in a lock.

She was taking no chances, and that amused him.

Staring into the firelight he thought about her, smiling between sips of his coffee. Such imaginings didn't contribute to an easy slide into sleep though.

After a while he began to relax and tiredness crept through him. Time to retire for the night. He placed a spark guard around the fire and, picking up the candle, he headed up the stairs.

The door to his allotted room opened with a creak. In the dark reaches of the upper corridor a provocative whisper floated, 'Sleep well, Mr LéSayres.'

Dominic chuckled. He was acting like a besotted youth instead of a grown man, who would have interpreted her husky whisper as an invitation and followed it to its source. But she was still young and untouched and was following her instincts without any real intent. It would be a shame to ruin her. Then again, someone would eventually, so it might as well be him.

But not tonight.

'And a sweet sleep to you, Miss Ellis,' he whispered.

Three

Grace was up at first light and had washed and dressed before she remembered she didn't have to assist Lady Florence to prepare for the new day.

At a loose end she tidied her bed and went down to the kitchen, where she revived the fire in the stove with several new coals and a vigorous stir of the poker through the hot ashes. Soon flames began to snap and crack.

She placed two kettles of water on the hob.

When they began to boil Grace made a pot of tea for the staff and set the other kettle aside to keep the water hot. She thought to take a jug of hot water upstairs and placed it on the marble-topped stand outside the guest room with a dish of soap that she'd made herself. By the time he rose the water would have cooled a little.

It was unusual to have time on her hands at this time of day. She might as well get the temporary accounting book completed for Mr LéSayres since she had the accounts ready in alphabetical order, and enough money in the strongbox to cover the total amount that would be paid out. She kept them in the morning room at the front of the house. Hardly anybody disturbed her there, and daylight adequately illuminated the paper she was working on.

She took through a cup of tea, savouring the fragrant steam that rose from the clear brown liquid as she sipped it. After a while, and lost in her calculations, she became aware she was being watched. At the same time Dominic LéSayres said from the doorway, 'You look extremely efficient for this time of morning, Miss Ellis.'

She jumped, and then slipped him a smile. 'How long have you been there?'

'About five minutes. You were certainly absorbed and I didn't want to disturb you. What are you doing?'

'I'm completing the accounts for goods purchased after Mr Howard took the books away. I'm just entering the outstanding ones for Lady Florence's funeral expenses. The tradesmen will be knocking at the door for payment soon.'

'If they do, refer them to me and I'll settle up.'

'It was Lady Florence's custom to pay them all at the same time, on the third Tuesday of every month, that's the day after tomorrow. She used the morning room and liked to take a glass of ale and gossip with them. Lady Florence was a great believer in habit. She said it breeds trust in people.'

'Then let's not break that trust. Ale and gossip it will be.' Three strides brought him to her. He leaned over her shoulder, his breath flirting with her ear and ran a forefinger lightly down the column of figures. 'Unlike Mr Pawley, you have a neat hand, and an aptitude for figures. Do you usually do the accounting?'

'I took it over when Mr Pawley left. Nobody else in the house had the education to work with numbers, except Lady Florence, and her sight was beginning to fail. I used to keep my father's books, at least as best I could since he was careless with money. You will need these figures in the coming days, I think.'

'Yes I will.' He gazed at her nearly empty cup.

'It will be rather informal but can I fetch you a mug of tea? I've only just made it.'

He placed a hand on her shoulder as she went to rise. 'No . . . stay where you are, Miss Ellis; I know where the kitchen is and will help myself. I'm fairly domesticated and can even manage a simple meal should the need arise.'

'I'll remember that if I'm ever in the position to employ a cook.'

He lowered his voice and grimaced. 'Promise me you won't hire the cook who works here.'

'The meals are usually better than that. Lady Florence's death has had an unsettling effect on everyone.'

'Yes . . . I should have thought. May I bring you another cup of tea?'

She handed her empty cup and saucer over with a smile. 'I take mine without milk.'

'So do I.' He was back in a couple of minutes. Placing her cup and saucer in front of her he perched on a high stool, with one leg providing a prop against the floor and the other heeled on a rung halfway down. His long fingers curled around a blue and white mug that had appeared after the summer fair. It was decorated with a crude portrait, supposedly George III. No one in the house had ever claimed it as their own.

They gazed at each other while they sipped the tea. His eyes were assessing, but not in an offensive manner. This morning they were a silvery grey colour and they had a faintly faraway expression, so she wondered if he really saw her but was pondering on a problem.

She realized he did indeed see her when he said, 'Am I disturbing you?'

He was hard to overlook, and yes, he was disturbing her, but in a way that made her feel slightly flustered and totally aware of herself. He probably knew that. 'Of course you're not. Lady Florence was an early riser and I usually readied her for the day at this time.'

'Old habit dies hard.'

'Yes. I must admit I feel at a bit of a loose end. I keep expecting her bell to summon me.'

He gave a faint smile. 'There's something sad about a house when the inhabitant dies. It seems to lose its joy at first. Then the contents are reduced to numbers on a sheet of paper and it becomes impersonal. Dust fills the empty spaces while it's waiting for someone else to live in it and give it another life to live.'

'You're talking about soul. I used to try to discuss the existence of such with my father.'

'And?'

'He didn't believe in such things. He told me the soul didn't exist, any more than fairies, elves or ghosts, and if I wanted to know about such myths I should consult with the local reverend, since he was a first-class liar.'

He laughed. 'And did you?'

'I didn't see the point of standing through one of his private sermons, since the reverend and my father were the best of friends and both of them thought they were right about such matters.'

'Men often think their wisdoms are absolute truths,' he offered apologetically. 'My stepmother, Eugenie – though she was our governess then – used to take me and my brother into the garden on warm summer nights to watch the stars emerge. She told us if we saw a shooting star it was a soul on its way to eternity and if we looked hard enough we might see our mother's soul smiling at us.'

What a lovely sentiment, Grace thought, though she didn't disturb his emerging memory by talking. His voice was low and pleasant, but clear.

'One night, Alex, who is my elder brother, told me he saw our mother in a white gown riding a white horse through the stars. I was envious, and desperate to see her too. So I lied. The next night I told Alex I saw her in a silver carriage with flames coming from the wheels, and it was pulled by six black horses. She wore a silver gown and a gold crown covered in rubies, and was leading an army of ghouls that were going to roast my brother on a spit and eat him alive.'

Her eyes widened and her hand crept upwards to cover her heart. 'Oh, my goodness, such a bloodthirsty imagination . . . what did poor, doomed Alex say to that?'

A smile crept across his face, making him appear villainous. 'One thing Alex has plenty of is confidence. He accused me of lying. Then I accused him of lying. Then he punched me and I punched him. We were rolling around calling each other names and happily killing one another when our father came out of his den. He took us both by the collar and gave us a good shaking. He said the next time we mentioned our mother it had better be with more respect else he'd thrash us.'

She sucked in a breath.

'Oh, don't feel sorry for us. Despite his faults Pa's threats were always surrounded by empty air. One thing we were always sure of was his love and support. He'd die rather than deliberately hurt us. Before we went to sleep that night he encouraged us to reconcile our differences. I swapped half of my imaginary horses for half of my brother's imaginary horses, and we had a fine time chasing the ghouls from the house with our wooden swords. By morning the argument had been forgotten. But sometimes, when I see a star shooting across the sky I wonder if my mother's soul has a connection with mine.'

'Then the soul must exist for you because you believe in it. Just to look at the sky when darkness falls inspires me. The sky is so deep and . . . and . . . mysterious. Do you ever wonder what the soul consists of?'

He raised an eyebrow. 'Apart from animal, vegetable or mineral, do you mean?'

She laughed. 'You're hiding yourself by being pragmatic. Why do men hide their real selves when they're getting close to feeling emotion.'

'Ah . . . emotion as related to soul, you mean? Perhaps a man's emotion displays itself more physically than a soul connection. He likes to know he's appreciated, to examine what he feels and make sure his heart is properly engaged and secure, and it's not just some pretty face and a carnal dream he's lusting after.'

True love condensed into a teaspoon of incandescence, she

thought. There was a romantic hiding inside that quiet exterior. 'What about the emotions of despair, anger, envy . . . love even?'

'Ah, love . . . you have me there, lady. I've loved, and have been loved, perhaps, but I've never been in love, therefore I'm reluctant to shine any light of wisdom on the subject. This conversation is getting rather personal for such an early hour.'

'Yes, you're right, Dominic. Will you show me which one is your mother's star?'

'I might . . . one day.'

Dominic LéSayres was a sensitive but complicated man. There was a touch of the lone wolf about him – a depth she couldn't quite fathom. He'd given her just a glimpse of himself, like a view through a keyhole. Then, as if he'd realized he'd revealed too much, he'd raised his guard.

He stood, tall and relaxed, and then bowed over her hand. 'If you'll excuse me, I'll leave you to your tasks while I exercise my horse, else he'll be restless all day. I'll be about an hour.'

'Enough time to finish what I'm doing and have breakfast cooked ready for you when you get back.' She picked up a basket. 'I'll walk with you. The chicken coop is behind the stable and I'll need to collect some eggs.'

Dominic plucked his hat and gloves from the hallstand and followed after her. He hadn't missed the unconscious use of his name. The girl trod lightly, her feet dainty on the stable cobbles, her hips adopting their own rhythm so he felt like dancing alongside her.

The air misted into the distance, though not so heavily that the horizon was completely obscured; the plants were dewed with it and the spiders' webs drooped along the hedges like lacy collars. They were weighed down with sparkling globules and the leaves sheltered an army of ginger spiders, crouched and waiting for the sun to absorb the damp before seeking out their prey.

His horse stamped impatiently, raising a few sparks on the cobbled stable yard and he neighed a shrill greeting, his head jerking up and down. He gave a couple of small, but powerful bucks as Dominic saddled him.

Grace hastily stepped back when the horse turned an aristocratic eye her way. Argus, for that was his name, arched his neck towards her displaying an expanse of yellow teeth and pink gums, and he whuffled noisily, his lips flapping. She laughed.

'Easy, Argus,' he soothed. 'You mustn't scare the lady.'

'He's a handsome animal.'

'I won him from a soldier in a card game. I think the soldier was relieved to get rid of him; it took six months to train the wildness from him.'

'He doesn't strike me as being particularly tame yet.'

'He's a strong animal and needs plenty of exercise. But he still has his moments of independence. I think he was badly treated when he was young, and he remembers it at times. Argus won't allow anyone else to groom him without making a fuss, which is a nuisance at times.'

'I understand our stable lad, Sam, managed to groom him.'

'Yes, that took me by surprise. I'll see how he went about things when I come back. Perhaps my brother will be able to find work for him in his stable.'

'Sam would appreciate that. He loves horses and they seem to love him. My father said stallions can be dangerous if they're not . . .' She pressed her hands against her rapidly returning blush. 'I must go and fetch the eggs.'

He grinned, lifting his eyebrow as he finished what she'd been about to say. 'Gelded?'

She recovered quickly, lips pursed. 'I intended to say . . . if they're not handled well. Enjoy your ride, Mr LéSayres.'

'You called me by my first name earlier.'

'Then I must apologize for earlier.'

She was quick-minded and he'd always liked women with some bounce to them. 'Why . . . don't you like my name?'

'Yes, I do like it. It's a strong, saintly name, one you'd find hard to live up to, I should imagine.'

'You're only fifty per cent correct. I'm certainly strong.'

She waited for further comment but when he didn't give her one she struggled on. 'We, meaning, you and I . . . are too familiar with each other for such a recent acquaintance.'

'Do you think so? We have answered to the names we were christened since birth, so why should you object if I call you Grace? Does it trouble you?'

'Yes . . . no . . . I don't know. It's convention, I suppose.'

'I'm not conventional and it's quite apparent you're not either. My parents didn't go to the trouble of giving me a saintly name for it to be ignored.'

'But why did they call you after a saint?'

His grin widened. 'I didn't think you'd let that pass. I was named after a maternal great-grandfather. By all accounts he wasn't a saint either. I call the other servants by their first names and they don't seem to mind.'

She gave an exasperated little huff. 'Your pardon, sir, and no, they don't object. I had forgotten my lowly status in this house. I should like to point out that, although the other servants are called by their first name, they do not reciprocate by calling you by yours.'

'Point taken.'

'Good.' She reinforced it so he wouldn't forget. 'You are also Lady Florence's guest . . . well, not quite her guest, since she's moved on and I doubt if she'll be receiving visitors. Actually I'm quite bemused by the nature of you as a visitor. I do know that guests, whether on business or social footing, should not occupy themselves by kissing all the servants, and a servant shouldn't take it upon herself to greet every visitor to the house with a kiss.'

'Be fair, Gracie, I've only kissed one servant, and that's you. How many visitors have you kissed?'

'None, sir, I am not that forward and neither do I intend to be.'

'If it would make you feel more worthy of accepting such a liberty from me, then you can list me in your tidy mind as a businessman. My business is finance in its many guises and I'm desperately in need of a competent clerk. Take the position and from now on I promise to be more circumspect.'

She crushed her sudden flare of enthusiasm underfoot. She doubted if she could trust him, or herself, come to that. On reflection, she knew she didn't want him to be circumspect. She didn't want to be circumspect with him either. And she desperately needed to know she had employment to go to, else she'd be spending Christmas in the poorhouse . . . an unattractive proposition.

'Couldn't you have just asked me? Is this the opportunity you said you had in mind for me?'

'Partly; I'm still working on how much value I could expect to get for my wage before I offer you a contract.'

'You're a philanderer, Mr LéSayres?' she said, pushing aside the urge to hug him tight. 'Your contract will get you nothing more than a kick in the seat of your breeches. As for my worth, when a contract is presented I shall calculate my own to you.'

He laughed at that. 'Don't you like to get value for your money?'

'Of course I do. Working in a household where I must earn enough to keep myself fed and clothed has taught me thrift. In fact, I have saved nearly everything I've earned so far.'

'Which wouldn't be much.'

'I consider it to be quite a useful sum, since it started out as nothing but a halfpenny, and I earned that singing in the street.'

Interest came into his eyes. 'You begged on the street? Do you realize the danger that put you in.'

She nodded. 'It was only a song or two. Then I was offered the job at Oakford House. I daresay you'll think I'm a trollop now.'

'Not at all, I think you're an enterprising young woman who is full of surprises, and you're a lady after my own heart.' He tipped up her chin and kissed her until she melted like winter frost on a pane of glass.

Pink-faced she fanned the heat from her cheeks with her hands. The hens kicked up a raucous din with each egg that was laid. Grace opened the coop so those who'd already done their duty could roam free and scratch in the dirt. First though came the cockerel, its feathers a glossy bronze like Dominic's riding boots as it strutted around its small domain to organize the hens and cock-a-doodled the house servants from their beds at dawn. It was such a magnificent creature. So was Dominic.

The position he'd offered her was one she could only have dreamed of the previous week, but to even consider working for Dominic was madness. She could feel the excitement gathering force inside her, so she wanted to leap in the air and shout. It was an effort keeping her buoyant mood contained. 'I will think on it.'

'As you wish, but only a fool would turn down such a position.'

'I said I will think on it,' and she took a deep breath and plunged in. 'Should I decide to work for you I will expect the same wage as a man would earn, and if I do allow myself to trust you and become your clerk, you must never kiss me like that again, Dominic LéSayres.'

His mouth twitched. 'You expect me to pay you a man's wage when you're such a little dab of a sparrow? Already you are laying down conditions.'

When he mounted the fidgety Argus and settled himself in the saddle the fabric of his breeches tightened firm against his thighs. She closed her eyes and stamped on her imagination. When she opened them again the fact that she was standing upright and without support, surprised her.

She saw the clerk's position sliding away and said hastily, 'Well, perhaps I might accept less.'

His horse tossed his head and gave an impatient little snicker that sounded like a laugh.

'Once you make a stand never back down without a fight, my Gracie. Tell me why you think you're worth such a sum?'

'Because you've offered me a position, so it's obvious you consider me to be competent enough to employ.'

She drew in another deep breath, though was more reluctant to voice it. 'You have conveniently forgotten the other condition.'

'The one that forbids me from kissing you in the manner I did? If you insist, Gracie mine. No doubt I can find something equally pleasurable to replace it with. A glimpse of your smile each time we run into one another perhaps.'

'Or laughter from me when I see you coming and run in a different direction.'

'You flirt most delightfully.' Tipping his hat, Dominic left her in a forward thrust of energized horsepower, fighting off the pleasurable feelings roiling inside her.

Four

The days were lost in a flurry of counting.

Lady Florence's room was left until last, mainly because the other servants didn't want to go in the room where death had visited. On the first breezy day Grace removed the bedding, washed it, squeezed it through the rollers of the mangle, and then hung it on the line to dry. It was now in the linen cupboard, neatly pressed and indistinguishable from the other bedding.

November came in with a gale that blew the remaining leaves from the trees and swirled the smell of bonfires into the air.

The room was still musty but at least it now lacked the personal odour of its most recent occupant. Grace threw the window wide. Superstition in the area demanded that the windows of the room of the newly dead should be opened to let the spirit escape otherwise they would haunt the place. She hoped she'd been in time. Not that she believed in ghosts, and she doubted if Lady Florence's spirit would harm her even if she did believe in them. Even so, goosebumps trickled down her spine.

She mentally shook herself. 'The strongbox is in that cupboard, and so are her jewels,' she said, handing Dominic the keys. 'I've replaced the gold cross and the rings that were on her fingers for part of her mourning period. They are on the top.'

Dominic lifted the exquisitely lacquered box out from its den. Gently he set it down on the table and gazed at her. 'Do you know what it contains?'

'Lady Florence called it her treasure. She was thrifty but she tended to hide money in odd places, and then forget about it. There are several hiding places I know of, and probably some I don't know of. I've made a list of those I do know.'

He took the paper from her and his gaze ran down the list. He shook his head and gazed at her. 'The chamber pot is used as a hiding place? I find that unbelievable!'

'Oh, it's quite clean since it's never been used. Lady Florence uses . . . used the maid's room next door for private purposes, and the door into the corridor was kept bolted on the inside.

'Are you certain this *container* hasn't been used, Gracie?'

She couldn't resist it. 'I can't say I've inspected the contents recently, but there's one way to find out, Mr LéSayres.'

'After you, Miss Ellis.'

'No . . . you may do the honours.'

Reaching under the bed he took a grip on the handle and pulled the china pot out. He lifted the lid gingerly.

'Boo!' she said as the lid cleared the rim. He jerked back and banged his hand on the underside of the bed.

When she laughed, he rubbed the spot and offered her a threatening look that made her laugh even more.

The chamber pot contained several coins wrapped in paper money. The loose floorboard under it yielded five gold sovereigns.

By lunchtime they'd amassed a tidy amount of money. Lady Florence hadn't spent much of her monthly allowance on herself, though she'd been generous with others. Grace had been allowed to see what the box contained on one occasion. There had been no coins then. Lady Florence had lifted out a tray of jewellery, a diamond tiara and a necklace and earrings. She'd made Grace try it all on. It was heavy and cool against her throat, and sparkled prettily in the candlelight.

'They belonged to my mother and I brought it into the marriage as part of my dowry,' she'd said. 'I have no daughter to leave it to, just a nephew.'

Grace turned to Dominic. 'I think that's about it and if I remember anywhere else she might have used to hide valuables, I'll let you know.'

'Don't underestimate the powers of observation of the rest of the staff.' He placed the key in the lock. 'Before we examine the contents of this chest I need to inform you of something.'

'Which is?'

'Lady Florence left instructions that, with the exception of the furnishings, the contents of this room was to be your legacy. Of course, you might wish to ignore items like the chamber pot.'

'Surely not.' She stared at him, unease wriggling through her like a worm, and thinking that it must be his twisted sense of humour. She pandered to it with a smile.

'There was an addendum added the last time Mr Howard visited here. Do you want to see what's in the box?'

She nodded. 'I suppose I must.'

'The thought doesn't seem to excite you, though I expect it will be to your benefit if you decide to take advantage of it.'

'I'm struggling with the reality of it, Dominic. Sorry . . . Mr LéSayres.'

He sighed. 'Just call me by my first name, it's much easier.'

'Dominic then. We've already found a fortune.'

He smiled, probably because she'd used his name, or perhaps

because a fortune in her mind when set against one in his consisted of vastly differing sums. Odd that she always thought of him as Dominic. Her resistance toward him seemed to be waning – probably because he'd behaved like a gentleman since she'd set personal limits.

There was a piece of paper on top of the tray, sealed with a blob of red wax.

'The addendum was witnessed by my partner, John Howard,' he said. 'That's his seal. I'll send Mr Archibald a note to come and verify that the sum enclosed is correct, if you'd like.'

Dismay filled her. 'Surely you cannot think I've stolen the contents?'

'Not at all, it's so you can be certain I haven't. Perhaps you'd like one of the staff to check the amount instead.'

Grace remembered the times she'd surprised Jessie or Brian lingering within earshot when she'd been in conversation with Lady Florence, or more recently, with Dominic . . . how often had they avoided her eyes, or stopped talking when she entered a room. 'I don't think I want the staff to know my business, since they gossip so. I trust you. I mean . . . I think I do, and I certainly trust myself. It would ruin both our reputations if the box was empty.'

'It isn't empty; the weight gives it away.' A wry smile came her way. 'Thank you anyway, I'll look on it as a compliment but as you've ably demonstrated in the past, you have quite a sting in your tail at times.'

The floorboard creaked outside. Swiftly, she crossed the floor and threw the door open.

Except for a few dusty shadows haunting the landing the space was empty.

'You're chasing shadows, Gracie.'

He was right. 'You've made me doubt the people I work with and I don't like feeling that way.'

'A little caution won't harm you. Shall we open the box together or would you rather do it alone?'

'Do you have a list of the contents?' she asked.

'I haven't brought it with me, but I do have a good memory. I'm aware of most of them.'

She challenged him. 'Tell me.'

Grace lost the contest before they really started when he said, 'There's twelve troy ounces of gold and an equal amount of silver.'

'What's a troy ounce?'

'It's a system of weighing precious metal. Using the avoirdupois method, which is common calculation, sixteen ounces would equal one pound. In troy weight it would be twelve.'

'So that provides an answer to the question: which weighs heavier, a pound of lead or a pound of feathers? They both weigh the same.'

'Do they?' and he chuckled. 'You will find it easier to treat the two methods of weight as separate entities.'

'I think I will put that puzzle aside until I have learned more about the troy measurement. Have you seen the jewellery?'

'No . . . but John Howard said it's old-fashioned and heavy, and includes a tiara, necklaces, brooches, rings etcetera.'

She made a face. 'I'll never wear it.'

'The jewellery can be broken down and sold for its value in precious stones and metals, though a better idea is to keep it as an investment. There is also a letter of credit to an account in the Bank of England for two thousand guineas.'

Her mouth nearly fell open. 'Two thousand guineas?'

'It's a generous sum,' and he ran his forefinger roughly down the stack of coins, as though he was angry with them. One of the golden towers collapsed and the coins slid across the dressing table. 'With this added in it the sum could almost double.'

Grace reached for the nearest chair and sank into it. 'It's too much.'

'More than you expected?'

Something in his voice made her gaze sharply at him. 'Of course it is. I expected something personal to remember Lady Florence by, a brooch or a figurine perhaps. The most I hoped for was the same sum as the others received. With an amount like this I might be able to buy a small house in town to live in, one that isn't too expensive to run.'

And with roses rambling round the door and a little lily pond with golden fish. And from it she'd walk to Dominic's office every day and it would be wonderful to work for him.

And admire him from afar.

The second tower of coins was demolished into a pile of

expensive rubble. 'I would have thought that living here would have made you more ambitious in your pursuit of the life you had before you became a drudge.'

She winced. 'I never considered myself to be a drudge. As for being ambitious, that's an odd word to use. If I was ambitious it was because I was educated. Becoming a servant didn't occur to me because I wasn't brought up to it. Both occupations are worthy ones if the person takes pride in their work.'

'I wasn't criticizing. I've cleaned a few floors in my time, and cooked a few dinners. Our stepmother used to make a work schedule every week, and we'd rotate the jobs. The house wasn't always clean. There were corners where the broom never reached and we locked the door on the dust. The rooms we used regularly got all the attention. You must miss the home you grew up in.'

'Not very often, since I didn't have the time. My step down on the social scale brought an increase in my activities. Looking after an invalid was time consuming, and left little time for leisure. Even if I'd had enough money to purchase the house I grew up in, I wouldn't have bought it. It was too big for one person, and cost too much to run. So does this one.'

'Yes . . . I suppose it does. Grace, I have to tell you something – something I should have discussed with you before this, but I was bound by Lady Florence's instructions.'

She engaged his eyes. 'What is it?'

'There's a condition attached to the legacy, I'm afraid.'

'Which is?'

He gazed at her for a moment, expression inscrutable, and then said, 'The money is to provide you with a dowry.'

She smiled at that. 'As to that, I suppose the legacy can remain in the bank until I need one. I've never been comfortable with the notion of buying a spouse.'

'That's only half of the condition,' he said, his expression morose as he reached out to tuck a stray lock of hair behind her ear. He took her hands in his. 'Don't think I'm happy about saying this, but there's more to the condition than that. Lady Florence's wish was that you should marry her nephew.'

She gazed at him for a full minute, her expression unbelieving, then colour rushed into it and she gave a strangled scream. 'What have I done to become a condition in somebody's will? It makes me feel liked an animal trapped in the boundary of my cage, looking for a way out. I'm speechless.'

She was not speechless, as was demonstrated by her next sentence.

The words were forced out – brittle words, so they snapped off in short sections like twigs in a gale or a dagger stabbed into her chest. 'Not only does she provide me with a dowry, she *dares* to chose that odious parody of a man to be my husband. Brigadier Maximilian Crouch, I recall his name is.'

'She suggests you might be good for him. Even if you refuse the marriage the contents of her wardrobes will be yours, excluding any jewellery or cash.'

'I don't want the contents of her wardrobes. They're a testament to her vanity. Besides that, her nephew would hardly want a wardrobe full of ladies' gowns.'

Dominic gave a wry grin. 'From what I hear I wouldn't rule that out, my dear.'

She stared at him for a moment and then she blushed and averted her face.

'I'm sorry if I embarrassed you, Gracie. Forgive me.'

But it seemed she was just warming up.

The long sigh she gave was followed by a short, frustrated scream. 'So if I want the legacy she'd have me marry a stranger. Her seemingly generous gesture will simply pass from her hands into mine and then back into the family coffers. In other words I will be earning my own dowry but without actually being paid it. In fact, she is insulting me, treating me like a—'

Hastily, he said, 'Getting in a temper and letting fly with bar room language will not encourage anyone to think better of you.'

She gasped.

He placed the sealed letter in her hands. 'This is addressed to you.'

She stared down at it, and after a while he asked her, 'Aren't you going to open it?'

'No, I don't want to read her pathetic excuses, for it will only serve to make me think less of her. And I don't want her clothes. I'd rather walk around undressed . . . or, in rags, at least. What she is trying to do is turn me into a . . . a *woman of fortune* for her relative. I'm surprised you think so little of me that you'd act as a messenger.'

Coming from her sweet little mouth the stark meaning of the words shocked him, and although he had to admit the thought of seeing her naked held a lot of charm, he had to admit that she was right in her assessment of the situation.

She mocked him. 'Oh dear . . . did you think I wasn't aware of such words? I'm not a delicate bloom raised in a hothouse, I'm a doctor's daughter, remember? Tell me, Dominic, what if I refuse Maximilian Crouch?'

'Then no one person will receive the main legacy, not even her nephew. All of her money will go to charity.'

It was an onerous burden to place on a young woman's shoulders, and Dominic felt for her. He could almost see her simmer as she thought the matter through and looked for someone to blame. He was the closest.

Her voice grew stronger as she found the courage to hurl some scorn at him. 'You led me on and paid me attention, and you made me like you, when I didn't want to. God only knows why I enjoy your company so much. I imagined . . . well, never mind, fool that I am. I suppose your conceit allows you to believe that all types of females sigh over you, and without you even noticing them.'

'My dear Gracie, believe me, I notice every woman who flutters an eyelash at me, and also those who don't. Let's not allow this to become personal.'

'It's not funny. How could you be so conniving and cruel, Dominic LéSayres? Damn it, you were her adviser.'

'No . . . John Howard was.'

She shot to her feet, shoved the paper into her pocket and glared at him. 'You should have told me about this earlier.'

He flinched and his mouth set into a taut line. 'It would be better if we discussed this issue rationally.'

'Issue . . . issue! This is the rest of my life you're talking about. For whom would it be better, may I ask? It's easier said than done when the outcome of it will affect me rather than you. Didn't anyone consider I might not want to become the bride of Brigadier Crouch?'

'It seems not. Calm down, Grace. Nobody has consulted him yet. He may have wed, or he might refuse the condition.'

'There is a possibility he might pressure me to obtain the money.

There is a possibility . . . Lady Florence may have placed me in danger.' Her eyes widened and colour rose to her cheeks. 'Did you say he might refuse to wed me? Why, what's wrong with me?'

'Nothing . . . except when you turn into a shrew. I'm not accustomed to people shouting at me. You should learn to control yourself if you intend to work for me.'

'How can I work for you if I'm married off to Brigadier Crouch?'

'You do have the right to refuse the condition, Grace. If you don't want to be married off, then don't be. Most women I know would jump at the chance to be respectably wed to a man of means. You could stay on as the mistress of this house. I doubt if he'd bother you much since he would be going about his soldiering for most of the time. I've heard the war is practically over now though, and Napoleon is exiled on the island of St Helena. You need only to run the brigadier's household, bear him a child or two and play host.'

Her voice rose and she gave a little shiver. 'Oh, is that all I have to do. Obviously you haven't met him. He's an old man of at least sixty years, and he has a moustache that looks like a grey caterpillar.'

His mouth twitched at the corner. 'I didn't think you'd met him.'

'I haven't. Lady Florence told me. Sometimes she was indiscreet when she drank strong spirits, and she told me he preferred the company of men, but I didn't think . . . well, I daresay you know what I didn't think. Her ambition in life was to see him settled in a suitable marriage and with a family. I was given no reason to believe she'd chosen me for that particular responsibility. She suggested once or twice that marriage would knock the foppish nonsense from him, and I agreed with her because it's one of those statements that didn't need to be explored. But I didn't think she meant marriage to me.'

Dominic looked as shocked as Grace felt. Lord, what had she said? Young women of breeding were not supposed to know such things, let alone talk about them . . . but then, perhaps he'd used his own interpretation of her words.

A growl gathered inside her. So that's what he thought of her, that she was a vixen. He was probably right. She gulped back a retort to stop her anger from spilling over again and choked out, 'I'm sorry.'

He took her hands in his, turned them over and kissed the palms. 'You're forgiven. I'm sure we can work something out between us.'

He was treating the problem as though it were nothing . . . a tease. 'It's you who needs to control himself. I've told you not to do that.'

He chuckled. 'You'll be striking me next.'

'If that's what it takes to reinforce the notion that you cannot take advantage of me every time you feel like it.' She lashed out and her hand slapped against his cheek as though she was swatting a fly.

They stared at each other, and there was shock in his eyes. Then he touched his stinging flesh, his fingers gentled the site of his pain as his words reflected the damage she'd inflicted on him as more emotional than physical. A sudden bewilderment grew in his eyes that made him appear vulnerable so she wanted to snatch him to her and hold him tight.

'That hurt, but I imagine I deserved it,' he said. 'Will you accept my apology?'

He was an expert at making her feel guilty. Of course he hadn't deserved it, and she owed him an apology, not the other way round.

Her lips were trembling as she gazed at him, tears gathering in her eyes. Eventually, she brought herself to say, 'Of course it hurt, it was meant to. It was unforgivable of me and now I despise myself as much as I . . . like you.' She drew in a deep, shuddering breath. 'I'm sorry . . . it's me who should ask your forgiveness.' She touched her finger against the reddening mark on his cheek.

'You are overwrought, and that was my fault. Go and compose yourself,' he said calmly, and he handed her his neatly folded handkerchief.

Dashing her tears away encouraged more to flood down her face and replace them. Damn him . . . her eyes would turn red, she thought.

She burst into tears, and then she turned and hastened away from him to the room she called her own – though for how much longer, even that was in the lap of the gods.

Locking the door behind her and feeling like a child she threw herself on the bed and sobbed into the pillow.

Five

Grace didn't immediately join Dominic for dinner, though the smell of cooking wafted deliciously through the house and set her mouth watering. She was wondering which of the chickens had been sacrificed when Jessie came up to fetch her.

'Mr LéSayres desires your company for dinner.'

'Tell him I'm in no mood for *his* company, I'll have my dinner in my room.'

Jessie had no sympathy to spare for her. 'I'm not running up and down the stairs pandering to the likes of you. Either come down to the dining room or go without, but I warn you, the man is in no mood to be trifled with. He said you have ten minutes before he comes up to fetch you. If I were you I'd do as you're told.'

'You're not me, and I'm in no mood be trifled with, either. I'll box his ears if he's not careful. Tell him—'

'You tell him. By the way, you should be careful of him. Gentleman he might be but he's got a way of looking at you that tells me he's sizing you up. Has he made any advances yet?'

'I don't know what you mean,' she lied, because it wasn't really Jessie's business.

'Of course you do. You're young and impressionable, but you're not daft.'

Grace shrugged. 'Even if he did approach me in an unseemly manner it wouldn't do him any good.'

'Tell me that when his unseemly hand is under your skirt giving you an unseemly tickle. Men are right sneaky creatures. I'm telling you . . . he's just biding his time. You can only lead a man along for a short time before they lose control over themselves. Then there's no stopping them. If she'd lived, your mother would have told you that.'

Her mother wouldn't have been so vulgar, Grace was sure. 'I'll be careful.'

'Good. Cook is going to take up her new position tomorrow

and Ella will be going with her. If you don't come with us to Australia – and I've done my best to persuade you. I'll give him this, I don't know what you'll do. For all his superior manners, he found employment for those staff that needed it, just like this man said he would, and he's hired a carriage to take them to their new abode. Reckon he'll do the same for us. Send us off in style to board the ship.'

When Brian and Jessie left she'd be alone here with Dominic, except for young Sam, who regarded his new employer and his horse with a certain amount of worship in his brown eyes, and his master's horse with reverence.

Already shocked by Jessie's blunt warning Grace placed her hands over her ears. 'I don't want to hear any more.'

Jessie pulled them down. 'Now, listen to me, girl. The man has a right persuasive look to him and a way with women from all accounts. We've heard a thing or two . . . gossip, mind you, but there's no smoke without fire.'

'What sort of gossip?'

'This and that . . . some say they wouldn't be at all surprised if he turned out to be a married man.'

Gracie felt as though the house had collapsed around her. Her initial anger was replaced by more rational thoughts and they crowded in on her. Dominic hardly ever discussed anything personal from his background. She had never asked him if he was married, so she couldn't say he'd lied to her, one way or the other. All he'd done was flirted with her, as other men had on occasion. That didn't mean he wanted to take her to the altar.

No . . . but he'd like to take you into his bed.

Her voice thickened in her throat. 'Thanks for telling me, Jessie. You're leaving sooner than I thought.'

'We've stayed longer than we should have, but it was worth it for the extra wage. We have a ship to board.'

'You're still going to Australia to dig for gold then?'

'Brian's cousin has bought the claim next to his and they'll work them together.' She lowered her voice. 'There's room for you if you want to come. They're short of women over there . . . especially those who have any quality. You'll need to have some money behind you for the ship's passage, and to set up your school.'

Two thousand guineas floated before her eyes. It was tempting
. . . but no. She didn't like the way she'd have to earn it.

'I've saved all my wages since I've been here, so if need be
that should cover it.'

'Don't forget about your legacy? Mr LéSayres said we'd be
getting twenty pounds apiece.'

Grace hadn't given the legacy much of a thought up till today,
and she hadn't discussed her situation with anyone. Now there
was panic fermenting inside her. She felt trapped and supposed
there would be no legacy for her unless she married Maximilian
Crouch. If the choice was to wed a miner in a far away land,
she might as well stay here in a place familiar to her, and marry.
The difference would be a comfortable house to live in rather
than being mistress of a dirty tent with spiders walking in and
out as they pleased. She wasn't the adventurous type and digging
in the dirt for gold sounded highly speculative.

She mumbled, 'Thank you for the offer, Jessie. I'll think about
going with you, but Mr LéSayres has offered me employment as
his clerk and I think that might suit me better.'

'Well, there's generous of him. But don't set your cap at him.
He has family responsibilities.'

'What makes you think he has commitments?'

Her heart lurched when Jessie said, slightly maliciously, 'The
messenger saw him with a woman in Poole a few weeks ago
when he was delivering a message. A lovely young lady he said
she was, very elegant, and they seemed familiar with each other.
He signed for the message with just his family name, LéSayres.
It saved the messenger from riding all the way from Poole into
Dorchester with it, which shows he has some respect for the
ordinary folk. Besides, I asked him just yesterday whether
he had a family, and he gazed at me with that thoughtful look he
has when he's considering his answer, and then he smiled and
said, "Yes . . . I do have a family", before he walked off.'

It felt as though a brick had fallen on to Grace's head.

'Now, I must go before he comes looking for you. I don't
want to end up in the middle of a barney.'

Grace's hands went to her hips and she tossed her head. 'I'm
not scared of him. Which hen will we be eating? I don't think
I can eat Sophie, she's so sweet.'

'Mr LéSayres fetched a brace of rabbits back from his ride this morning, a clean shot through each head so they didn't see it coming. We ate Sophie the day before yesterday.'

'And you didn't tell me.'

'The last thing Sophie needed was you weeping over her when she faced the hangman's noose. Tomorrow it's Henrietta and Jane's turn, stuffed with chestnuts and roasted with vegetables. There will be apple pie with custard for a pudding. I must admit, I'm getting sick of eating chicken.'

'I expect they're more sick of us eating them. It makes me feel guilty.'

'That's because you gave them all names, as though they were people.' Jessie grinned at her before leaving. 'You're too soft, Grace. If we don't eat them they'll die of starvation, or the foxes will get them.'

It wasn't long after Jessie left before Grace heard Dominic's heavier tread on the staircase. It sounded quite menacing and her stomach quaked, though knowing her imagination was out of control.

Despite telling herself she wasn't scared, Grace pushed a heavy footstool in front of the door, but not so close it would prevent the door from opening. She jumped when a firm knock landed on the panel, and she pressed her ear against the door that led to the corridor.

The doorknob rattled and Dominic's voice was as smooth as silk against the panel. 'Come out, Gracie Ellis, I need to talk to you.'

'Liar . . . you just want your own way.'

He rattled the doorknob and said against the door panel, 'I have a key.'

So had she, but why should she be obliged to lock doors against this man?

Metal scraped against metal and there was a solid clunk as he unlocked the door.

Grace retreated into the connecting dressing room. Locking the door between them, she opened the one into the corridor – her escape route.

'Come out of there else I'll come in.'

She didn't answer. The sound of the connecting door being

unlocked was followed by a crash and a succinct curse when he tripped over the stool.

Taking in a deep breath and hoping he hadn't hurt himself, she flew out of the door into the corridor and scurried down the stairs before he had time to collect himself. She rang the bell for the dinner to be brought in.

Not long afterwards Dominic limped into the room, seating himself opposite her.

'You're late,' she said, her heart lurching like a cart in a pothole.

'Then please accept my apology. I was attacked by a ferocious foot stool.'

A giggle gathered force inside her. 'Were you injured?'

'One of my shins is bruised and I have a hole in my hose.'

Guilt overcame her giggle. 'I'm sorry.'

'No doubt I'll recover.'

'No doubt.' They gazed at each other without speaking for a while, and she gave a breathless huff of laughter. 'I *am* sorry, truly I am. I shouldn't have hit you. I was in a bit of a dudgeon.'

'Yes . . . I noticed.' He lifted her hand and kissed her knuckles. 'You have quite a punch on you.'

'It was only a slap. It does less damage and has better shock value than a punch because it's noisy.'

'Since when have you been an expert on the art of pugilism?'

'Two men thumping each other with their fists is hardly an art.'

'You'd be surprised how much of an art it can be.' He smiled as he poured some white wine into her glass and then placed a hand over hers. 'Will you forgive me for upsetting you?'

She summoned up only a small amount of scorn because when she was with him her bad mood seemed to dissipate as soon as it flared up. He brought out the worst as well as the best in her. 'I'm not your responsibility, Dominic.'

'I know . . . but why do I feel that you should be. I'm just following my instincts.'

It was a remark so casual it nearly robbed her of breath. She tried to push him further into the personal. 'Why do you feel like that?'

'Because you're a young woman in my employ, and you have nobody but me to offer you some fatherly advice.'

'I'm not in your employ yet, since we haven't agreed on terms. Besides, I'm still considering going to Australia.'

'Is that wise? The place is populated by criminals and is barely habitable by all accounts. You will have nobody to turn to should your expectations prove to be false. I beg you, Grace, do not embark on such a perilous venture.'

Beg? She was surprised he cared enough about it to beg. 'It's wiser than marrying a complete stranger. And may I point out—'

'That I am not your father, your uncle, brother or any other adult that could be responsible for you. Yes . . . yes, I'm quite aware of that, but I've heard that the southern continent is filled with deadly creatures such as snakes and spiders and their venom can kill almost instantly. Most of Australia is unexplored and it's believed that the deserts stretch for thousands of miles. Water is scarce in more places than not and people perish from the lack of it. Were your father still alive I'm sure he'd caution you against taking such an imprudent step.'

'My father was the least prudent person I've ever known. He lived for the day.'

'And you're paying the price for it. Perhaps his lack of fortune when he died should warn you that money, however earned, is easily spent when one is bent on pleasure. My own father was similar in his habits and disposition to yours, and it compelled me to realize the value of money.'

Grace didn't want to discuss their respective fathers. 'We were talking about Australia, I believe, and not the nature of my father. If you think he'd step out of his grave in support of your argument – even though he'd probably agree with you – then you're very much mistaken. He was reckless and I am not, since he encouraged me to think for myself, and my disposition leads towards caution.'

He shrugged. 'That's debatable, since you cannot see through the eyes of others. Besides, the gold coming out of Australia is of no great volume at the moment and the main export is the fleece from sheep farming. Earning a living there will be hard. In the main, the population is drawn from convict stock, soldiers and settlers, and the native population. It's a vast country, mostly unexplored.'

Grace shuddered as she thought of the snakes and spiders, though she found his discourse fascinating. 'How do you know all these things?'

His shrug was a mixture of pride and modesty. 'It's my business to know. I'll worry about you if you go.'

To which she wistfully thought, it might be nice to have someone who worried about her. 'Would you truly?'

His hand covered his heart, a somewhat childish, but heart-warming gesture. 'Do you doubt it?'

'That's sweet of you, Dominic. Would you worry if I married Crouch?'

He slanted his head to one side and considered for a moment, aware he'd allowed himself to be shunted into a corner. Grace Ellis was hardly out of childhood, yet she managed to get under his skin without even trying. Would he worry about her? Yes, damn it! He would. The brigadier was too old for her, certainly, and he was a career soldier set in his ways. As for the brigadier's private life . . . it wasn't that private if the talk was anything to go by.

Even if it was gossip Grace's position within the household would be untenable and she would be shunned. Were Grace his daughter, would he marry her off to a seasoned soldier who was forty years her senior? Certainly not!

'I would always wonder where you were and what you are doing.'

Her smile came, a little on the smug side, as though it was the answer she'd expected . . . or hoped for. Her next words bore that out. 'Why would you when you didn't even know me a few weeks ago?'

She wanted a reason to lighten the atmosphere their argument had created, so he gave her one. 'It's because you're as enchanting as a spring morning as well as being naïve, Gracie dear, and you would become a target for every red-blooded male who set eyes on you.'

Honeyed eyes reflected the candlelight flickering in their depths. They widened as she looked at him. There was a sweep of her eyelashes as she closed her eyes, and then they swept open again, quivering slightly. Her eyes grew even wider and her voice was so soft that for a moment or two afterwards he wondered if he'd heard her properly.

'Men like you, Dominic?'

Most women he knew enjoyed a compliment so he looked over his glass at her. 'Regretfully.'

'Why regretfully? Do you have wicked thoughts?'

Dominic swallowed his wine down the wrong way and snatched up the table napkin when he began to splutter.

She didn't seem to notice him choking to death beside her but carried on with the conversation. 'My father told the reverend there was no such thing as wicked thoughts. He said nature designed us just as we are, faults included. I'd much rather heed my father, then I wouldn't need to pray for forgiveness every time I did something wrong. The reverend advised him he was feckless and had brought me up to be a heathen.'

He began to laugh. 'It would have served you better had the good reverend provided you with a roof over your head.'

'Only one man did that, and that was Mr John Howard. And he asked for no reward. I had only met him once, I recall, and that was when I was a child and I thought he was stern, so that was a kind thing for him to do.'

She peered at him. 'Perhaps I'll marry Mr Howard instead if he's available . . . at least I'll be able to spell his name. Maximilian Crouch is awfully tricky; I can't even pronounce it properly. And the family name reminds me of a frog waiting to leap at me from the pond.'

'John Howard is widowed . . . and he is a little on the mature side.' Dominic doubted that John could leap from a pond with any great ease though, and began to wonder what the cogs of her brain were greased with as he struggled not to laugh all over again. He couldn't imagine his sedate business partner married to such a lively young woman.

'Are you all right, Mr LéSayres? You sound rather hoarse?' she said, and so sweetly he began to laugh. Pouring water into a glass she handed it to him with a beaming smile. 'Be careful you don't choke.'

Dominic shook off the remnants of his laughter and pulled on a more sober mien as he briefly analyzed his feelings towards Grace. This young woman was running rings around him, and he was disinclined to put a stop to it.

Why?

He liked her and enjoyed her company . . . he liked her too much. He loved her company and he loved her. The stray irrational thought stunned him.

His thoughts were interrupted by a knock at the door and Brian entered carrying a tray. He held out a square of folded paper. 'The messenger delivered this yesterday and I forgot about it. Sorry.'

'No matter, I doubt if it's urgent. He read the missive and then folded the paper. His glance went from one to the other. 'I'm reminded that I need to attend a business meeting in Poole tomorrow. Brian, tell Sam I'll take him with me and he can settle into his new home. No doubt you can manage without me for a couple of days.'

'That we can, sir. Jessie and I will be departing next week. Jessie thought you should be reminded so you can calculate the money we are owed in advance.'

They had obviously read the note from John Howard, and he wondered if they'd take the opportunity to leave while he was absent. But did it matter? Grace could manage being on her own for a day.

But what if she decided to go with them?

So be it . . . it was a choice only she could make.

'Your dues are ready, and a cab has been booked to collect you and take you to Southampton. I'll settle up with you this evening, and will collect your signatures before I go into town. Is there anything else, Brian.'

Brian cleared his throat and Dominic watched the man's gaze flicker towards Grace. His voice had a truculent, hectoring sound when he said, 'Are you coming with us or not, Grace? Make up your mind.'

She looked down at the table, and then at Brian, and Dominic noticed something in her that he hadn't seen before, a stubborn streak. She wouldn't be pushed.

'I haven't had time to decide one way or the other. Sometimes I think I will, and then caution sets in.'

She wasn't usually so indecisive, and Dominic thought it a good time to place a little pressure of his own on her. 'You can use the donkey and cart for the next few days in case you have last minute business to conduct, Brian.' And he reinforced his own claim to her. 'You might as well know I've advised Miss Ellis that going so far away would be foolhardy, especially since there appears to be the suggestion of a marriage of convenience on the table.'

'To Maximilian Crouch, I believe. The old lady must have been insane to suggest such a match. If it's a marriage for her you're after I'm sure my brother would oblige her. Of course, no cash transaction would be involved, so neither of them could be accused of marrying for convenience, though a little advance to help the newly weds along would be welcome, no doubt.'

Grace flinched. Having her business discussed as though she wasn't present, was galling.

Dominic said, 'This isn't really your business, Brian.'

'Beggin' your pardon sir, but neither is it yours. We'd planned for Grace to come with us. Jessie is expecting a baby in about six months. Grace knows about doctoring and she's delivered babies before. Besides which, if we add her legacy to ours it should tide us over until we can get ourselves established . . . as if we were family.'

Grace's head jerked up. 'You never mention a baby to me before?'

The man averted his eyes. 'Well, Jessie's not sure yet.'

Dominic's immediate thought was that Jessie seemed to him to be a little past childbearing age. He tried to remember the notation of age on her employment record. He recalled she was about forty-five.

Grace's small pot of savings might be the main reason they wanted her. Once that was spent he imagined Grace would be discarded somewhere along the way.

'Would it be fair to suggest that Jessie wasn't with child when you first planned this venture.'

'Yes but—'

'There are no buts about this, Mr Curtis. It's wrong of you to use the coming infant to pressure Miss Ellis with, since responsibility for the infant belongs entirely with you and your wife. I also need to make you aware that I have offered Miss Ellis a position as my clerk, and with advantageous conditions as an added incentive. I expect her to accept. Now, may we eat, please?'

Dominic caught a gleam of annoyance flicker in the man's eyes as he placed the dishes containing the food in front of them and departed, his mouth a tight line.

Grace began to serve the food, and afterwards she looked directly at him. 'Remind me of the advantageous terms, Dominic . . . this is the first time I've heard mention of them.'

'An inflated salary and furnished rent-free accommodation situated just a pleasant five minutes' walk from my establishment . . . oh yes, and a maid of all work to look after your needs.'

She tucked a stray strand of her hair into her braid, and he could see that having a maid appealed to her. 'I'm wondering . . . why would you go to all that trouble?'

'Isn't it enough, Gracie?'

She'd live in a hole in the ground if he asked her to. 'It's exceedingly generous of you and you know it is, so you needn't look so bruised.'

Bruised? He grinned. A good verbal skirmish came a close second to making love and together, they could be quite powerful. 'Shall I fetch the contract and call Brian back in to witness our signatures?'

'Certainly not.'

'Why, when you know you're going to accept my offer?'

'You're much too sure of yourself. I may have conditions of my own to add after I've read the document through. I might decide I want to look after Jessie and her baby.'

He pierced a piece of cabbage with his fork and lifted his eyes to hers. 'You're a contrary little madam. When you want a baby to care for just let me know and I'll arrange it.'

'Dominic LéSayres! How dare you make such a suggestion?'

He gazed at her for a moment, and then shrugged. 'How dare *you* think of something so outrageous, Miss Ellis? My mind was travelling innocently along the lines of adoption of an orphan, or a position as a nursery maid. However, your idea certainly has merits.'

'Oh, my pardon! I beg you not to pursue this conversation any further. Eat your cabbage, else it will fall into your lap.'

He did as he was told and his glance became a mixture of exasperation and amusement. 'To save you further embarrassment, and working along the lines that I obviously cannot be of personal service, what would be acceptable to you?'

She opened her mouth to protest, and then closed it again.

'For instance, do you need a dog to guard you and a ginger cat to chase off any mice that creep out of the wainscot to menace you?'

Head to one side she regarded him, and then a soft little giggle sent his grumpy mood skittering away. 'You're so thoughtful at times. I've always wanted a dog, but it must be small – and I would prefer the cat to be a tabby.'

He couldn't decide whether she was being sarcastic or if her pleasure was genuine. There were several tabbies living in his brother's barn, and one of the gamekeeper's ratters had dropped a litter before Dominic had left. No doubt his brother would be relieved to get rid of a pup.

He dispelled a quick squeeze of homesickness by clearing his throat. But why was he pandering to Grace like this when scores of people could do the same job just as easily as she? 'Tell me . . . how long do you want the cat's tail to be?'

'Fifteen inches, at least.'

'I've never seen cat with a tail as long as you require, my dear. You might have to settle for less.'

Her smile was irresistible. 'I like you, Dominic LéSayres, even when you're wearing your serious face. Eat your dinner before it gets cold and you begin to suffer from the gripe.'

He did as he was told, and though the meal had lost some of its heat he retained an inner glow from her unexpected and inelegant compliment.

Not usually given over to fancy he was poised for the next delicious mouthful with a forkful of dangling rabbit meat when an insidious little voice inside him suggested: if you wed the girl yourself she wouldn't cost quite so much.

'A silly idea,' his more logical side advised out loud.

Her eyes came up to his. He loved the way she looked in the candlelight, her eyes glowing like those of a sleepy cat. Her gown had collected a small tear.

'What's a silly idea?' Her smoky voice sent warm trickles into places better left undisturbed at the moment.

'It was a passing thought, nothing serious.'

So why did he feel so breathless? He never did anything important without serious consideration, and here he was on the verge of proposing marriage to a young woman he hardly knew.

When the tip of her tongue emerged to moisten the delectable pink curve of her mouth his own tongue dried. What was it she'd said earlier about wicked thoughts? At the moment he seemed to be on the verge of bursting into flames.

He hoped the grin he sent her way wasn't too easily interpreted as lecherous intent.

Closing his eyes he inhaled a deep, calming breath, murmuring as he exhaled it, 'If only I hadn't promised to behave.'

She placed a finger across his mouth. Her touch was as gentle as the fan of a butterfly's wing as she outlined the curve, leaving his lips sensitized beyond belief. 'But you did promise, Dominic, and I trust you to behave like the gentleman you so obviously are.'

Damn it! This woman was a contrary creature, and she wasn't playing fair.

But then, neither was he, and at least she was playing.

His eyes narrowed as he gazed at her, contemplative. She was fast becoming his nemesis.

When the rabbit slid from his fork and plopped into his gravy she couldn't quite stifle her laughter.

Six

Grace and Jessie were in the laundry room alone when Grace broached the subject of Jessie's condition. It had been puzzling her.

'Brian said you were with child.'

A sharp glance came her way. 'Did he now; what of it?'

'You haven't mentioned it before.'

Jessie lowered her eyes. 'I don't have to tell you everything.'

'But I remember you had your menses a couple of weeks ago, and you complained about getting the cramps. I gave you something to relax the pain.'

'You're mistaken.'

Grace knew Jessie was lying. 'Has your stomach felt uneasy in the mornings?'

'Why should it; do I look as though I'm sick?'

'I think Brian is mistaken.'

Hands on hips Jessie swung round and said, 'A lot you know . . .' and then she sighed. 'It was Brian's idea. He said you were soft hearted and it might help you make up your mind if we told you I was with child. When I told him you wouldn't agree, he said you didn't have to agree.'

Although a thought began to niggle at Grace, her sympathy for Jessie overrode it. 'Perhaps you could adopt an orphan when you get to Australia. I've heard there are plenty of them in need of parents.'

Jessie shrugged. 'Brian wants a brat of his own . . . that's why he wants you to come with us.'

'What's that got to do with the problem?'

'He reckons he could talk you round . . . and well, I wouldn't mind so much if it were you. Everyone would think the child was mine if you carried it in secret.'

Jessie's child? Half his . . . carry it in secret? Grace stared at the woman, hardly able to believe what she was hearing. She coloured when realization slapped her, and she gasped. 'Does he really think I'd agree to take part in such a scheme?'

Jessie gave a bitter laugh. 'Saving yourself for the right man, are you?'

Goosebumps rioted up Grace's spine and she pressed her hands across her ears, not that it muffled them from much noise. 'I'm surprised you'd go along with such a dishonest plan.'

'It's no more disgusting than being tied to old Crouch for his money, or becoming an amusement for a man who will abandon you when he tires of you. Still, I suppose some wealth comes with that first option. Not that it will happen. The moneyed classes marry money, not servants.'

So why was she more inclined towards becoming the mistress of Dominic LéSayres? It was not that he'd proposed such an event, but he would eventually.

Grace felt like slapping Jessie for exposing such thoughts inside her but held the urge back. Her family pedigree was perfectly sound, with a baron or two on her mother's side. But Jessie was right. Money was a definite motivator. Beside that, after she'd struck Dominic and observed the wounded expression in his eyes she'd promised herself she'd never slap anyone again, however sorely tried she was.

Jessie shrugged. 'I told Brian you wouldn't agree to it. You've been brought up as gentry, not in the gutter like Brian and I have. There were times I was forced to sell my wares else we'd have died of starvation.'

Grace turned away, shocked. 'It's a pity you didn't leave your vulgar practices in the gutter, where they belong. I don't want to hear any more.'

'Oh, that's all right for the likes of you. You've never gone hungry, or had to suffer the attention of some stranger's hands pawing at your body, or worse, and just so you could have a hot meal in your stomach.'

Revulsion shuddered through Grace at the thought.

'Brian and me vowed we'd be rich one day, however long it took. Now, with the old lady gone our dream is a step nearer. Everything was there for the taking. I've never had a friend to talk to before. That's why I wanted you to come. Besides, you're educated and could teach me to write, like you did Sam. Then I could be employed as a nursery maid and get married to Brian, properly.'

The speech was edged with a false note, an underlying pitiful whine, as though it had been rehearsed.

Grace fought back a flare of sadness for Jessie and for Brian. She no long trusted them. 'If I followed the course you're suggesting it would ruin my life. I cannot go with you under any circumstances now.'

Jessie shrugged. 'It makes no difference to me, girl. I just didn't want you to have to fend for yourself. We can soon find somebody else. Which reminds me, you'd best go into town and shop for the next few days.'

'I can't, I've got some work to do for Mr LéSayres today. Besides, that's usually your job.'

'Not this time. Mr LéSayres won't be in residence for the weekend and I'll be sorting out things and packing our trunks. We'll be taking it to the ship while we've still got the donkey cart to use. Brian has business to do in Southampton, as well, and will be out and about. So if you think I'm waiting on you hand and foot while you play the queen bee, you can forget it.

It will be the opposite. As far as I'm concerned we're equals. You can do the cooking and wait on us for a change.'

'Mr LéSayres won't like it.'

'He won't know, lessen you tell him, and you always was a sly little puss. I wouldn't advise you to tell him, and if I were you I'd be very careful. Men aren't fussy over who or what they use to satisfy their appetites. He's well connected, you can tell by the quality of his clothes and the way he talks. Men of his ilk know how to get round a woman and they're used to having their own way, see. If you marry the brigadier you'll soon find that out for yourself. They say he's not quite right in his goings on.'

Grace gasped, and then found some courage before saying as calmly as she could, 'Why do you constantly try to undermine me, Jessie? I've had approaches made to me from men before, and I'm quite capable of turning them aside.'

'You might be able to say no but that doesn't mean they're going to listen. Don't forget you'll be here by yourself, with him, and you'd better keep out of my man's way as well.'

Grace's skin crawled at the thought of Brian touching her.

'Then I won't be by myself, will I? Take my word from it. Mr LéSayres is a perfect gentleman.'

Jessie snorted. 'He may be a gentleman but he's far from perfect.'

'That goes for all of us, Jessie.'

'By the way, where is his lordship today?'

'He's gone to see Mr Archibald.'

'What for?'

'I have no idea. Business, I expect, after all he was Lady Florence's attorney. I think Mr LéSayres was going to buy Sam a warm coat at the market to wear for the journey to Dorset. 'She picked up a scuttle full of coal, a handful of kindling and a lit candle in a glass protector. 'Now, I must get on. He's given me some documents to copy and wants them ready to take with him tomorrow. I can go shopping early in the morning.'

'Is there anything of interest in the documents?'

'They are of no interest to you, and even if they were I wouldn't tell you. Whether I take up the offer of a clerkship with him, or not, the contents of anything he gives me to do in the meantime will remain absolutely confidential. Now, go away and leave me in peace, so I can get some work done.'

'You can cook the dinner, as well.'

'I can't do everything, and you've already been paid for today's work so get on with it. Close the door behind you on your way out. I don't want to be disturbed.'

Jessie slammed it shut and a clod of soot fell from the chimney into the hearth and then puffed out of the fireplace and on to the rug.

'Curse the woman,' Grace muttered, then quickly took it back. She didn't want any harm to come to her. All the same she was bitterly disappointed by what had taken place between them.

Soon, Grace began to be absorbed by her work. In the back of her mind she was vaguely aware that Jessie was being as noisy as possible. Things thumped down the stairs. Their trunks, she supposed. Then there was a muttered conversation, followed by another door being banged. The donkey cart's wheels rolled over the carriageway, the contents rattling and then the noises faded to a blessed silence.

It reminded her that she'd probably never see Brian and Jessie after the weekend, and she didn't want them to part less than cordially. She must make it up to them. She went to the kitchen to find a dustpan and brush to clean up the soot.

She started when Brian looked up from the table. 'I thought you'd gone out.'

He grinned. 'You needn't believe what Jessie said. We had a bit more brandy than we should, and we were thinking of you and our imaginations ran riot and we got a bit silly. I never thought Jessie would take it to heart. You don't think I want to swing at the end of a rope, do you? You're not worth it.'

It did sound rather stupid. 'You don't have to be so rude, Brian.'

He shrugged. 'I'm sorry you're not coming with us, Grace. If you change your mind let me know in the morning. In the meantime you needn't be scared of me, and I hope you don't take Jessie's word as gospel. I want us to part as friends.'

She nodded. 'Thanks.'

'What's the dustpan for?'

'Some soot came down the chimney.'

'I'll clean it up, while you make yourself some tea. Jessie made some gingerbread to go with it. She knows you like it. Sit in the kitchen where it's warm.'

'I heard the donkey cart.'

'Jessie's gone to the farm to get some smoked ham to see us over the weekend. It will make a change from chicken and rabbit.' He picked up the dustpan and brush and was gone.

The kettle was hot and she filled the teapot, and then taking a slice of gingerbread she seated herself at the kitchen table. The door was closed to keep the warmth from escaping. When she heard the low rumble of voices she wondered if Dominic had arrived.

Fetching another cup and saucer she picked up the tray and crossed the hall to the morning room. There, she nudged the door open with her foot. Grace stared at the man who stood there with Brian, but not with any pleasure. He hadn't changed and his face still wore a sly smile. Her late mistress had banned him from entering the house ever again.

Pawley, Lady Florence's former secretary, had been leaning over the desk with Brian. Now they stood upright and turned to gaze at her. The last time she'd seen this man he'd been walking off down the carriageway. 'I'd heard the old lady had died and I came to offer my respects,' he said.

'To the servants? How very odd.' She placed the tray down and approached the two men. Rolling up the documents she'd been working on she hugged them against her chest. 'You were not welcomed here by Lady Florence and I'm inclined to respect her wishes in this, Mr Pawley.'

'You've got a neat hand.'

'I'm not interested in your opinion of my handwriting, and the books are no longer your business, unless you want to explain the peculiarities of your accounting system to Mr LéSayres. He'll soon be home, and I'm sure he'd be interested. Neither are they any of your business, Brian.'

'I can't understand the numbers anyway. It's all gobbledegook to me. I'd rather have a penny in my pocket than a paper one.'

Flush mottled Pawley's cheeks and his lip curled. 'You've become a bit high in the instep, missie. Be careful your pride doesn't bounce back on you one of these dark nights.'

Annoyance overtook her prudence. 'That's enough from you, Pawley. You no longer work here so please leave.'

Stepping forward he ran a dirty finger down her face, lightly scratching the surface. He took her by the collar of her dress, fisting it so tightly she had to fight for a breath. 'You should be careful, Miss Ellis. I'd hate to see that flawless skin of yours scarred for life.'

She kicked his shin as hard as she could and he hopped on one leg, cursing. He began to shake her and she began to choke.

Brian intervened. 'Release her, Pawley. We can sort out that other business later, and Jessie said there's to be no violence.'

Pawley thrust her backwards as he let her go, snarling, 'Who cares what a woman says? I know my way out, and I know my way in, even when the doors are locked. Just you remember that, princess.'

A chair captured her body safely and her breath left her with a gasp.

After Pawley had gone Brian poured her a cup of tea. 'You look pale. Drink that while I clean up the soot.'

'What was Pawley really doing here?'

Brian's eyes flickered her way, his expression slightly reptilian. 'He was passing through. He'd heard about Lady Florence's demise and thought he'd drop in. I doubt if we'll see him again.'

'The time to pay her respect was when she was alive. Mr LéSayres might have to know about him threatening me.'

'I wouldn't read too much into that. It was just hot air. I didn't hear any threats.'

'But he pushed me.'

'I didn't see no push neither. Besides, LéSayres would probably take him before a magistrate and then you'd have to go to court and be a witness, which would place a stain on your reputation. They might even say you were flirting with Pawley.'

'But I wasn't. He came here to steal what he could, and you're helping him. I've noticed lots of pieces missing.'

'The court doesn't know that, and they'll need proof.'

'But surely you . . .'

Brian smiled as he looked at her. 'I didn't see or hear a thing, Miss Ellis.'

'You mean you'd lie?'

'I mean nothing is going to get in the way of my plans, and I'll be long gone before it came to the attention of a magistrate. Besides, I owe Pawley a favour.'

'What if they found him guilty anyway?'

'Pawley would be sent to prison, or fined, something he can't afford, since he has a wife and a youngster to support. You wouldn't get anything out of it except a guilty conscience when they're starving on the street. Sometimes it's better to just let things slide, girl. It will be all over in a few days, and what I don't want is some silly girl making me miss my sailing date.'

She saw the logic in that. 'All right . . . I won't take it any further, but promise you won't take anything else.'

'Good. Just keep your eyes and mouth shut until after we've gone.'

'But if I tell the authorities then, they will accuse me of taking part in a robbery.'

He patted her cheek, causing her to recoil. 'There's a clever girl, then. Go and clean that scratch up now, before it turns bad and leaves a scar on your pretty face.'

There was an aloe plant in a pot in the kitchen. Washing the wound Grace snapped off a small piece of the plant and applied the inner jellied substance to her inflamed skin. The wound lost most of its sting almost immediately.

Dominic and Sam returned an hour later, just as she'd finished the tasks he'd set her. Sam was swamped in a greatcoat.

Gently taking her chin between finger and thumb Dominic turned her towards the light. 'Who've you been fighting with?'

He was so near to the truth that she stumbled over the first plausible lie that came into her head. 'The pen . . . I picked it up too fast and scratched myself.'

'Hmmm . . . is that all. I detected a bit of temper in the atmosphere when I came in.' As if it were the most natural thing in the world he planted a lingering kiss on her mouth and then let her go.

'My head aches, I think there's a storm coming,' she said, when it would have been much easier to tell him the truth.

'I think the storm might have been and gone, and taken the pen with it. You wouldn't lie to me, would you?'

'Depending on the circumstances, it's entirely possible.' At least that was the truth.

His smile widened and he ran a finger gently down her nose.

Deciding it would be a shame to change Dominic's mood by complaining, she took Brian's advice and dismissed the incident from her mind.

Except for the kiss. That seemed to be branded on her in flaming red letters. *Dominic LéSayres' woman.*

She ran her tongue over her lips when he began to walk away. 'Libertine.'

He laughed. 'You could be right, at that.'

Seven

It was early morning when Dominic and Sam departed, stomachs filled to the brim with the breakfast Grace had cooked for them. Sam quivered from the excitement of going somewhere new and carried his sack of worldly goods tied around his waist.

Dominic had bought the lad some warm clothing at the onset of the colder weather, including the greatcoat that reached to his ankles.

'He'll grow into it,' Dominic had said when she'd teased Sam and ruffled his hair.

Nobody knew where Sam had come from. He'd turned up on Lady Florence's doorstep three years previously, thin, cold and sickly. He could remember being in a gypsy caravan with an old man and woman and waking in a stable to discover them gone. There was a wound on his head he couldn't account for, and he couldn't remember his name.

Lady Florence had taken Sam in and made sure he was nursed back to health. Without being given a clearly defined position in the household, he made himself useful to anyone who needed an extra pair of hands, and for that he received two meals a day.

He was a shy lad who rarely spoke unless spoken to. Lady Florence had told Grace the boy had the same look to him as her late husband and he was probably his by-blow, so it was her duty to take him in. Once her mistress got an idea in her head nothing would dislodge it.

When Grace had entered the household Lady Florence had charged her with teaching a reluctant Sam his letters and numbers. When he protested she'd told him he was born with a brain, and if he didn't want to use it he could take that up with Lady Florence. After an initial struggle he'd discovered he could learn after all, something that opened the world to him.

The morning was cold, but clear. Argus danced on the spot, impatient to be off. Every exhalation of warm breath evaporated into small clouds of steam that surrounded their heads and then quickly evaporated.

The stallion didn't seem to mind its extra burden but Sam didn't weigh much and Argus was a strong horse. Besides, it wouldn't be for long because they'd ordered a hire horse from the black-smith for Sam to ride for most of the time – that would make the journey more comfortable for all of them.

Before they were gone from Grace's sight, Dominic twisted in the saddle and waved to her. The image stayed on in her mind, and she thought, Dominic treated Sam as though he cared what happened to him, and the boy responded.

Dominic would make a good father . . . but then, perhaps he already had children. Unaccountably her heart sank.

As a girl she'd daydreamed of falling in love with a handsome man, and of marriage. The first part had come true. The second seemed unattainable at the moment. Now she was grown up her expectations had fallen by the wayside one after the other, along with her status in the world.

She doubted if any of her father's friends would recognize her as the precocious child who'd amused them just a few years previously. Sometimes she hardly recognized herself. She wallowed in a moment of self-pity. She had sunk too low in society and was now just another servant struggling to exist and to be ordered about. Though she missed her previous life she didn't want to revisit her former hopes and dreams.

One thing she did know. She had fallen in love, and if Dominic wanted her she didn't think she'd have the will to resist.

What if he did have a wife and family? Then she would be

placing her foot on the first rung of a very slippery ladder. Neither she, nor anybody else – and that included Dominic – would hold her in any great respect.

She sighed. Perhaps it would be better if she went mining in Australia. But then there was always marriage to Brigadier Crouch to consider. She brightened. The brigadier might be too old to become a husband and father. Lady Florence had indicated that he didn't have much time for women.

After a sunny morning the clouds rolled over the sky. The wind turned cold just after Dominic and Sam crossed the border into Dorset and the air threatened rain.

They bought some lamb pies from an inn and washed them down with a hot toddy to warm their insides. They'd gone easy on their mounts but even so Argus had lost a bit of his ginger.

Dominic's glance fell on Sam. The lad was beginning to look weary. 'Have you the strength to carry on? Otherwise we'll rest here until morning? The journey should only take a couple more hours.'

Sam nodded. 'I'm strong enough, and the horses are good for a while longer if we take it easy.'

'You're a good horseman, Sam. Who taught you to ride?'

His face screwed up in thought. 'Couldn't say . . . I could ride when the old lady took me in, I reckon.'

'Do you have a second name?'

'Not one I can remember. Lady Florence called me Sam.'

'It might be a good idea to give you a second name. What would you like it to be?'

Worry etched across the lad's face, and then he said doubtfully, 'Reckon I could use your horse's name. Sam Argus.'

The stallion's snicker sounded like laughter and Dominic grinned. 'If I call you Argus then you'll both come running at the same time and I won't know which is which.'

'I'd be the one without a tail, I reckon. Would you give me a name then, Mr LéSayres?'

Dominic thought for a moment, searching his mind for a name that might give the lad some dignity, and identity in his occupation. 'Rider . . . Sam Rider?'

Sam's face lit up. 'That's me all right. Sam Rider. Thank you sir. It's a grand name.'

Dominic stretched the truth a bit. 'I recall it was Miss Ellis who planted it in my brain. Sam's a good rider, she said.'

'Miss Ellis is a lady with a good heart.'

Dominic seized the moment to prompt, 'Tell me about her.'

'She taught me my letters when the other servants said I was too buffle-headed to learn. We'll show them, Sam, she says to me. Your brain is as good as anyone's. It just hasn't been given any work to do and has become lazy.' After a moment of silence while Sam seemed to search for words, the lad mused, 'I reckon it wasn't so hard, at that, and she stopped the other servants from giving me a clout whenever they felt like it. She can be fierce when she needs to be, like a terrier snapping up a rat.'

'One must hope the result isn't quite as lethal.' Dominic stroked his recently slapped face reflectively and then smiled, because Sam's face had lit up like a beacon.

'A name of my own,' he said with quiet pride. 'I reckon I'll be able to hold my head up when I walk down the street from now on. I'll be someone.'

Yes, young Sam would be someone, and he deserved to have a name of his own. It would give him a sense of belonging. Dominic thought, and he'd be proud to help him on his way.

The lad fell silent when they remounted and they conversed no more for the rest of the journey.

It was late afternoon and the sky was darkening as they came over the hill and looked down on King's Acres, a tract of land gifted by a king to a lady for her favours.

To Dominic's left the sea was a crumpled sheet of pewter grey, the waves topped with whitecaps. The smell of salt and the cry of the seagulls riding the wind reminded him he was home.

He and Alex had grown up here, raised by a father who'd loved his two sons dearly, but whose gambling habit had lost them nearly every possession. It was no small matter of pride to Dominic that he'd helped his brother restore a small portion of the fortune in the early days after his father's death. Neither of them could remember their mother but she had died giving Dominic life.

The King's Acres estate was up ahead and slightly to the right. It was a solid country estate occupied by the incumbent earl and his family. The family consisted of Dominic's brother Alex, his wife, the Countess Vivienne, and his nephew, Nicholas Ambrose, the heir of the house despite him not yet reaching his second birthday.

Then there was Eugenie, who'd been stepmother to Alex and Dominic after their mother had died, and who had raised them.

Dominic was always welcome here, and had never thought to buy a home of his own, but his mind was now moving in that direction. Town property usually increased in value long term and it was about time.

Smoke flowed from the chimney pots of his childhood home and it was whipped away by a capricious wind.

Dominic reined in at the top of the hill, stuck his fingers in his mouth and whistled. Argus whickered and jerked at the reins, obviously sensing a warm stable and a feed waiting for him.

A couple of tall, shaggy dogs left the stable yard and raced up the hill. Making little yips and yaps they sniffed at Sam's ankles, tails wagging. When Dominic clicked his tongue they moved off at a walking pace so the horses cooled down gradually. The dogs escorted them down to the house.

Leaving the horses with the stable hand the pair made their way to the house and Dominic told Sam, 'You must address my brother and his wife as my Lord and my Lady, as befits their rank.'

'Yes, Mr LéSayres, sir.'

Alex didn't stand on ceremony, but he did wait for them to come to him in the hall, his smile a mile wide. 'Dom, at last,' he said, as they hugged and slapped each other 'I was thinking of sending out a search party.'

Standing back Alex winked at him and then gazed at Sam. 'Tell me, is there someone inside that grinning greatcoat?'

'May I introduce Mr Sam Rider. He has a fine hand with horses and I thought you could fit him into your stable staff. Other than myself he's the only person I've met who can handle Argus.'

'Then he has my utmost admiration. The last time I tried to ride Argus he bucked me off, arse-over-head.' Alex nodded. 'How do you do, Mr Sam Rider? If my brother has recommended you then it's good enough for me.'

Sam seemed to swell at the courtesy offered him, and gave Alex a sweeping bow. 'I'm doing nicely, my Lord.'

Alex nodded to a hovering footman. 'Take Mr Rider to the stable, where he can assist the groom. Tell him to make sure the lad is fed, look after him and find him a bed. Tell Cook there will be one extra for dinner, and one staff. He looks as though a good meal wouldn't harm him.' Alex's arm came round his shoulders in a brotherly hug. 'I'm glad you're back, Dom. We've missed you. Tell me, how can a lad of that size control that stallion of yours?'

'Sam has a way with him.'

'It's about time you had the beast gelded.'

'I'm thinking about it. I'm only here for a couple of days while I make a few arrangements. The old lady's will is turning out to be more vexing than I expected. It might have to be decided in court. Also John Howard wants to see me. How's Vivienne?'

His brother's smile grew even broader. 'Vivienne is beyond compare. You'd consider yourself lucky if you had such a wife.'

'I certainly couldn't argue with that. You were lucky I didn't see her before you did.'

Alex laughed when he saw Vivienne hastening down the stairs, a lantern held aloft and a smile illuminating her face. 'Did you hear that, Vivienne, my love? Be careful he doesn't run off with you.'

'Dominic, how lovely to see you again . . . and such a lovely compliment. You must tell us what you've been up to.'

He kissed her hand. 'First I must tidy myself up.'

'Of course you must, and you will find everything ready for you, including Alex's personal servant.' When she moved to Alex's side he pulled her against him to touch a kiss against her hairline. She was tall for a woman, yet still had to gazed up at him. 'You must allow Dominic time to rest and rid himself of the dust from the road.'

'Of course I must since he's not fit company for a lady at the moment.'

Alex had met his match in Vivienne and Dominic envied him that.

Half an hour later and Dominic was up to his chin in a tub of warm water. He closed his eyes and sighed as the tension in his body gradually dissipated. Alex's man went about his business, tutting over Dominic's scruffy discarded clothing. Fresh garments were laid out on the bed for him to wear, his boots were polished to a high standard.

The firelight was soothing and he wondered what Gracie was doing at that moment. Uneasiness touched him. There had been a sullen atmosphere at Oakford House the day before that had made him reluctant to leave. The politeness of the two remaining servants had almost been a mockery.

When Alex came in and drew up a stool, Dominic grinned at him. 'I hope you don't want me to pay you homage with a bow, my Lord.'

'In your present state of undress there's no fear of that. Tell me, Dom, where did the lad come from . . . is he a side-slip of yours?'

'Good lord, no! I've been more careful than that. Sam was part of Lady Florence's household. He was left on her doorstep a few years ago and she took him in. Apparently she believed he was fathered by her late husband.'

'On what grounds?'

'Wishful thinking, mostly. She had no children of her own.'

'What about his name?'

'Lady Florence called him Sam and I gave him the second name. He wanted to be named after my horse at first.'

'*My* horse. I won him from you in a wager, remember?'

'Was it my fault he preferred my arse to yours on the saddle?'

'You knew damned well he'd throw me off.'

Dominic grinned. 'About Sam's name . . . you're a magistrate and I wondered if you'd be able to formalize it so Sam has some sort of background. He can't remember anything much before he was left at Oakford House by gypsies at the age of eight. He was suffering a head wound. I understand Gracie has been teaching him to write.'

Dominic became the recipient of a suspicious look. 'Gracie?'

He didn't want to talk about Grace; his feelings towards her were ambivalent and his family would jump to conclusions. He must think things through, make sure any decision he reached was the right one. 'Gracie is a servant . . . and nothing to sing about.'

'You were ever a good liar, Dom, but not good enough to fool me. You're gone on this one, I can see it in your eyes.'

Dominic thought fast. He didn't want his brother to push him into anything and came up with an evasion that wasn't really a lie. 'Gracie is my new clerk, you bonehead.'

'So why did you say he was a woman?'

'I didn't. It was an assumption on your part.'

Alex spread hand came down over Dominic's face and pushed his head under the water. Dominic's legs thrashed about as though they had a life of their own. Just as he thought he might drown he realized Alex's weight was gone. He surged out of the water spluttering threats and shook the droplets from his body as he headed for the door, muttering, 'Just wait till I catch up with you, Alex.'

The valet pushed past him and got to the door first. He spread himself across it like a stranded starfish.

'Out of my way, Edward.'

Edward stayed put, saying firmly, 'You must not leave the room in that state, sir. You are undressed and the ladies are about. What would they think?'

Nothing complimentary in his present state, unless one collected miniatures, Dominic thought, looking down at his relaxed appendage. But no, it wouldn't do to scandalize the ladies.

Water flew from his hair when Dominic shook himself again.

'Shall I snip some off before you dress for dinner, sir?'

Snapped out of his reverie Dominic cupped his hands protectively over his haft. 'I wouldn't try it if I were you.'

The man chuckled. 'I was referring to your hair, sir.'

Slipping his arms into the robe the valet held out Dominic smiled, his humour fully restored. 'Thank goodness for that.'

When he was ready to present a tidy appearance to his family he went down to the drawing room and gave his stepmother a warm hug. Eugenie had been a wonderful substitute for his own mother, a woman he couldn't remember. She had also been his father's lover before their marriage, but neither he nor Alex felt any the worse off for that.

In return Eugenie said, 'Alex tells me you're only here for a couple of days. That is far too short a visit.'

'I agree but I have a complicated will to sort out.'

'Such a shame, my dear.' She kissed his cheek. 'Will your

business be finished in time to celebrate the Christmas festivities with us, do you think?'

'If the weather allows.'

Vivienne smiled at him. 'Invite your young lady . . . Gracie, isn't it? You must tell us all about her over dinner.'

Alex's expression was all innocence. 'It seems I was wrong, my dear. It turns out that Gracie is a Mr Gracie, and is Dom's new clerk.'

Vivienne exchange a rueful smile with his brother then turned to him. 'That will teach us to be presumptuous. What Alex hasn't told you is that I'm trying to find a suitable woman to introduce you to. One you can learn to love.'

'Vivienne, my dear, I have no wish to learn how to love. Like my brother I prefer to leave such things to fate. Alex fell instantly in love with you, and look how well that turned out. I'm thinking of running off with you when he's not looking.'

A blush seeped into her cheeks and Dominic winked at his brother. Dominic liked Vivienne's streak of shyness despite her outward display of confidence.

'Vivienne has already painted a picture of your bride inside her head,' Alex said.

Dominic was surprised. Were they that eager to get him settled? 'Do tell me?'

'She's tall and has dark hair and brown eyes.'

Gracie was petite, her hair was mid-brown and burnished with red. It gleamed red sparks in the firelight. Her eyes were the colour of honey, and filled with laughter. Dominic already missed her.

He scrambled to enforce his lie anyway, in case his growing affection towards the delicious Gracie Ellis faded with their current parting and became merely carnal . . . though he wouldn't object to a little bit more carnal either.

'I've been going through the house inventory with the new clerk, counting the silverware and making a record of the house art.'

'Good grief, how utterly boring,' Eugenie said faintly. 'May we ask, who does the will favour?'

'The servants have a suitable loyalty portion. Then there is Brigadier Maximilian Crouch, the old lady's nephew.'

'Good grief, is the brigadier still alive?'

'So I'm given to believe. Do you know him then, Eugenie?'

'I met him a couple of times. I was about sixteen and he was fifteen years older. He was handsome but thoroughly obnoxious and an absolute bore. He had rather a high-pitched laugh, I recall. His father bought him a commission in the army in an attempt to make a man of him. Surprisingly, he survived, and has been mentioned in despatches on several occasions, I believe.'

'He needs to wed before he inherits. I should put your name forward as a possible candidate perhaps.'

'If you do I shall poison you, Dominic.'

Their conversation was interrupted by the appearance of the nursery maid who carried the sleepy-eyed son and heir. Nicholas Alexander LéSayres was dark-haired and blue-eyed, like his father. The boy accepted a parental kiss on his downy cheeks from his parents, and then gazed intently at Dominic for a short time. He stuck his thumb in his mouth and smiled around it when he recognized his uncle. Belching out a bubble he fell asleep.

Dominic kissed the infant's delicate cheek, wondering if there was anything more precious or vulnerable than an infant . . . especially one belonging to the family. How a LéSayres miniature of such perfection could have been created by his brother was almost beyond his comprehension, though admittedly, Vivienne would have had quite a lot to do with it. The look of love in Vivienne's eyes when she gazed tenderly upon her child equalled the one she bestowed on Alex.

Longing wrenched at his gut as he pictured Gracie with their infant in her arms. His child would have grey eyes, and he'd inherit a talent for numbers so he could join his business when he grew up. He would also inherit Dominic's love of writing poetry.

He wondered if Gracie liked poetry, he'd never asked her. He might try some of his own on her. Or he might not. He grimaced. Lord Byron he was not, and she would probably tease him.

But for these things to come to pass he would need to wed. The thought of matrimony was sobering. Some men made suitable husbands and some did not. He suspected he might be in the latter group, since he'd never really considered he might find happiness with one woman – until now.

He ignored the intrusive little nudge, the one that reminded him his brother had settled to marriage after a less than faultless journey into manhood. Alex would be the first to admit he had won himself a prize in Vivienne, for she had a wit to match that of Alex, and had come with a fortune attached.

He gazed at Vivienne now, comparing her elegance to his petite Gracie, who trotted busily about like a hen in a chicken coop. Gracie amused him and he liked her company, especially in the evening when they sat in front of the fire, each sharing an awareness of the other.

Under his breath he murmured a first line of a poem as it occurred to him. '"Love should be declared in the evening".'

'Did you say something Dom?'

'He's a most handsome child, and he looks more like Vivienne every day.'

Alex chuckled. 'The last time you were home you said he looked like me.'

'That's because I needed to borrow a sovereign. In actual fact, Nicholas resembles his favourite uncle.'

'Did you pay the sovereign back?'

Dipping his fingers into his waistcoat pocket Dominic flipped a coin through the air. Alex caught it and slipped it into his own pocket. They'd been playing for the same sovereign for quite some time now.

'Since you took it upon yourself to try and drown me in the bath earlier I've changed my mind. You've developed a mean streak and I'm throwing down the gauntlet . . . swords at dawn.'

Alex's grin bordered on evil. 'I've been taking tuition so will beat you this time, just wait and see.'

Dominic laughed. 'The devil you will.'

'Let's alter the rules a bit. If you lose you get to tell me all about the clerk called Gracie.'

Dominic bestowed on his brother the most guileless of looks. 'You have a vivid imagination, Alex.'

'You're trying to flummox me, brother mine.'

'And succeeding by the sound of it.'

Vivienne gave a throaty laugh and joined in the game of teasing him. 'Describe your new clerk to us in four words, Dominic.'

'Black beard and eye-patch.'

Eugenie exchanged a glance with Vivienne. 'Hooked nose and bent back?'

'Do you ladies mean, his back is bent, or his hooked nose is bent back?'

'Both,' they said together.

Alex smiled. 'There's that . . . of course but then he might have eight legs and fangs like that creature skittering under the chair.'

Two skirts were raised off the floor in a shapely display of ankles. Vivienne gave an involuntary scream and Alex grinned when she did a stomping little dance, one designed to kill off any unfortunate spider within her reach. 'Very elegant, my love,' he said.

Eugenie gave a throaty laugh. 'It's about time the pair of you grew out of such unruly behaviour.'

Dominic raised an eyebrow. 'May I remind you that you raised us, Eugenie dear, and I could almost swear that last month you patted yourself on the back when you told us we were fine examples of young men. Oh, by the way, I delivered your letter to John Howard. Did you receive a reply?'

All eyes turned to Eugenie, who seemed flustered when she said, 'Yes . . . he has invited me to serve on the child welfare committee and interview deserving cases.'

The two men exchanged a grin. 'And will you?'

'When I decide, I will tell you.'

Eight

Dominic woke to the distant whinny of a horse and a morning that was barely there. Crawling out of bed he wrapped himself in a soft woollen blanket and dragged it with him to the window for warmth as he gazed out at the day.

He groaned when he thought of the duel he'd instigated with his brother. He'd rather build the fire up in the grate and stay in bed for another hour, wallowing in warmth. Alex had always been an early riser though and would drag him out of bed by his ears if he backed down from the brotherly challenge.

Dawn was revealing a day of bitter wind that drove the occasional handful of sleet before it. The distant horizon uncovered a frothing sea, one that would spit spume on to the shore in its never-ending quest to grind the pebbles into sand. Between him and the shore a sloping home meadow was covered in frost. In spring that same meadow would be a tumble of bright wildflowers. When they were children they used to play there, guarded by two proud lions whose stone bodies were grey and grizzled with age, and spotted with moulds of various colours. Their sole duty was to guard a short flight of steps that went nowhere. Sometimes he and Alex had scrambled on to the lions' backs, becoming knights in shining armour as they went about the business of rescuing a fair maiden from the dragon.

Dominic had dreamed of his own fair maiden the previous night. She'd called his name from a distance, as soft as a fingertip stroking a velvet ribbon, and he'd woken to a tender touch against his shoulder. Nobody had been there when he'd opened his eyes but he had felt she'd stood by his bed trying to get his attention.

Dominic . . . Dominic LéSayres.

He'd lain there, his neck hairs bristling, thinking of her. He hoped it wasn't an omen and he'd discover she'd flown the coop when he returned to Oakford House.

What would he do then?

He'd go to Southampton and find the ship she was on. Then he would fall to his knees and tell her he loved her. It shouldn't be too hard since the only ship sailing from Southampton to the hazardous southern ocean sailed on the Tuesday and was named *Bonnie Kathleen.*

The cold outside the canopy of his bed and his bare feet on the floorboards put paid to the result of his meanderings on the young lady's delights. He shivered despite the warmth of the wrapped-around blanket.

The horses came into view on the other side of the garden, creating a line of energetic dancing bodies. His brother's groom and stable lad had accompanied Sam on Argus, so the boy could learn the lay of the land, he imagined. Argus was behaving himself, though he crabbed sideways as a couple of seagulls circled the party to scream a greeting at them. Perhaps the horse was finally learning some manners. Sam had a light touch on the rein.

Dominic breathed on to the windowpane. The warmth of the breath froze immediately and a few moments later metamorphosed into a fragile melting crystal of perfect symmetry.

'As delicate as the lace of a wedding veil,' he murmured, and then he groaned with delight at the thought of the unveiling. Reluctantly putting the thought of Grace Ellis aside he turned away to ready himself for the coming duel.

Ten minutes' exercise followed by some stretching should do to warm his muscles. If Alex ran true to form he'd go straight into the attack and wear himself out trying to score.

Dominic smiled . . . then he'd have him.

Alex was already in the ballroom when Dominic went down, a smile on his face. Alex's man brought in the weapons.

'Thank you, Edward.'

'I've been practising in your absence.' Alex swiped the weapon through the air and back, looking fierce and menacing, while Dominic stretched various parts of his body that were still a little stiff after the long ride the day before.

Someone should tell his brother that practice didn't always make perfect, Dominic thought as Alex's man stood by with his weapon and attempted to read the rules of fencing.

Alex interrupted him, 'Yes . . . yes, we're both aware of *code duello*, and we don't need any seconds, so enough of that fancy stuff, Edward. It's not a proper duel and I'm not going to kill him. It's just exercise.'

'Well, just you be careful, sir, you know how good Mr LéSayres is with a sword.'

'You have my solemn promise that I will not kill him,' Dominic offered. 'Breakfast's waiting, so let's get this over with. First to get six touches in wins the golden sovereign.'

'In addition, Dom, whether you win or lose, you must tell me all about Mr Gracie,' Alex said.

Dominic grumbled. 'Why do you think you need to know anything?'

'There's something decidedly rum about your reluctance to discuss this new clerk of yours.'

Edward handed him the remaining épée, a weapon that, in

Dominic's opinion, offered a faster duel than the foil because it was lighter and every touch on the body counted, whereas the foil was restricted to the duellists' trunk.

Alex took the opposite view in the never-ending, and often quite heated, conversations about the niceties of fighting with the sword.

Dominic flexed the shining blade. He'd never fought a duel with intent to maim or kill anyone, but he could imagine the slim, shining blade sliding into Edward's paunch and the air escaping in a flatulent rush while he deflated. Not when he was duelling with his brother, of course. They wore padded jackets and the weapons had their tips guarded.

Alex struck the opening stance, body side on, right leg forward and knee bent. Dominic followed suit.

'*En garde.*'

There was a metallic shiver of sound when they clashed. It echoed around the empty ballroom and put Dominic's teeth on edge. He circled his opponent evaluating Alex's play while managing to keep him at arm's length. It seemed that his brother had not yet learned that might wasn't always better than matter.

Alex managed to register a point and he mocked, 'All this secrecy about a bit of muslin.'

How the hell had his brother found that out? He took a point off him for his deceit.

A bit of muslin? Gracie Ellis was a far cry from a scatty-headed hussy, though there was a delightful touch of the hoyden about her. And neither did she appear knowledgeable about matters of love, except in a detached sort of way. Yes, she flirted a little, but that was instinct, without knowing where, or what it might lead to. Emotionally she was enjoying the fun of it but with an instinctive wariness.

A bit of muslin, indeed not. 'Hah!' Dominic threw an oath at him and took another point for the insult to his lady-love. He went into a flurry of showy movements and steel clashed. 'How did you find out?'

'I have my sources.'

After a secretive smile Dominic realized his brother was playing him at his own game. Alex certainly had been taking tuition, but he still danced around, wearing himself out.

Alex staggered backwards, swearing and the pair went to it hell for leather, and with both scoring a point. His brother was a good, instinctive fencer, but Dominic could read his opponent. He took another point.

'Three all – to Mr LéSayres.'

Alex recovered and retaliated, and the duelling picked up speed. After a short, but fierce battle Alex scored another hard won point.

'Four to Mr LéSayres – three points to the earl.'

Alex was breathing hard but managed to score the next point quite accidentally when he slipped. 'Aha!' he shouted.

'Evens – four.'

Another point went Dominic's way.

Dominic made his brother work hard for the next point, and perspiration covered the pair of them. Alex took his fifth point. He was almost jubilant now, sure of his win.

Dominic slid his sword along that of his brother's and administered the final point, the *coup de gra*s, touching the point of the sword against the padding over his brother's heart.

'Six – five. Match to Mr LéSayres.'

Alex fell on his back, arms flung open, his breath heaving in his chest. 'You haven't lost your touch, Dom.'

Grabbing his brother by the forearm Dominic pulled him up and Edward relieved them of the swords. Hands on hips they hung from the waist, breathing heavily.

Edward offered them towels.

Dominic smiled as he caught the sovereign tossed by his brother. 'You're out of condition, Alex. I hardly had to work at all.'

'I allowed you to win.'

'Liar . . . you're wheezing like an old donkey.'

'Never mind that. Tell me about your new clerk.'

Dominic adopted a vague expression. 'What do you need to know about my clerk?'

'I need you to confirm she's named Grace Ellis and you've hired her, a woman, as a clerk.'

Dominic gazed suspiciously at him, racking his brain in case he could think of something he'd let slip. 'All right, you win. How did you find that out?'

'You forgot one small item. I visited the stable when the staff were saddling up and asked Mr Rider. He was quite eager to extol the lady's virtues.'

Dominic could have kicked himself. 'I can see you haven't lost any of your rat cunning in my absence.'

'I prefer to call it my superior intelligence.'

Alex hooked an arm over his brother's shoulder and they strode together to the bottom of the staircase, where they came to a halt. Alex asked, 'Tell me, what's the young lady like?'

'She's accomplished in the usual womanly things and comes from a medical background, since her father was a doctor.'

'And you signed her up as a clerk . . . a woman?'

'Ah . . . but she handles numbers so easily and confidently, and has good, legible handwriting to match. John Howard told me that if you throw a seed into the air it will land in the place where the best nourishment for it is to be found, and there it will thrive.'

'But a woman working in a position usually reserved for men . . . it's highly unusual, almost unheard of. It *is* unheard of.'

'Doesn't Vivienne keep your household books?'

'That's different. Vivienne is my wife.'

'Don't be so bloody pompous, Alex. Grace Ellis is a very capable young woman. Perhaps I should mention that she's the daughter of the eminent and slightly infamous Dr Ellis, who was noted for his fine doctoring as well as his, not so fine, gambling. Gracie managed his books, but she was left entirely alone and destitute and was destined for the poorhouse until John Howard found employment for her as a carer companion to Lady Florence Digby. John Howard does not merely philosophize, he puts his words into action. He paid her wage while she was employed in her former position.'

'Now who sounds pompous? Am I to take it then that this little seed has dropped into your lap in her need to be nourished? Is she aware of the danger involved in that? Are you?'

Dominic nodded, then grinned widely. 'The young lady has a unique way of avoiding my advances. If I persist she swats me like a troublesome fly, and she has a stubborn streak a mile wide. So what is your advice?'

'I would have to see the girl first, assess her merits. If you are to employ her you must control your instincts. She will come off the worse if a liaison between you became public knowledge.'

'You don't understand, Alex . . . There is no liaison yet, though I think I'm in love with her.'

'And does she feel the same way towards you?'

'She's never told me, although she did say she liked me and admired my waistcoat and watch. There is an awareness between us on occasion. Sometimes I can hear her speak my name when I'm asleep.'

Alex grinned broadly. 'Lord, you've got it bad, Dom. She's bringing out your poetic side.'

He recalled a vision of Gracie's mouth, the curves as rosy and moist as a peach ripening on the summer bough. Setting the delightful vision aside he moved to a more objective description – one his brother would understand. 'The worst thing is she grabs me by the balls every time I see her, and there's nothing I can do about it.'

'Not literally, surely.'

'Good lord, no, we haven't reached that stage.'

'If I could make a suggestion, there are other women on this earth . . . more accommodating.'

'Indeed, there is. Damn it, Alex, I don't want another woman, I only want Gracie Ellis.'

'You're willing to wait for her? Good grief, you must be in love then. I never thought I'd see the day.'

'I've resolved to pay her that respect, at least.'

'That's all very well, Dom, but seemingly reluctant women are not always as angelic as they present. They seem to know the exact time to drive a man to distraction. When they do so all resolve flies out of the window and they can surprise you.'

Dominic wondered if Vivienne had surprised her brother. Probably, since she wasn't lacking in spirit.

'It must indeed be love you're afflicted with. I can only offer you my sympathy, for I know exactly what you're going through. I would have waited for Vivienne forever . . .' Alex stared thoughtfully at him for a few moments. 'Well, perhaps not quite that long, after all there is a limit to a man's patience. Can't you just throw her over your shoulder and elope with her?'

'Would you have treated Vivienne that way?'

'Certainly not. I love her dearly and I respect her. She is all I'll ever want for in a wife.'

'I never thought you to be romantic.'

'I can be, on occasion. Of course, I wouldn't dream of making Vivienne feel embarrassed by being overly romantic.'

Dominic caught a small movement in the corner of his eye and tried not to grin as he led his brother on. 'No, of course not . . . all the same, your marital advice is welcome.'

'You have to think of your own comfort and dish romance out in small tasty portions – like caviar.'

Dominic didn't like caviar, however small the portion. 'Gracie would prefer to eat a freshly dug cockle, I would imagine.'

'I don't know if Vivienne has a preference, I must ask her.'

'Yes, you must . . . it's important to know such particularities of taste in a woman.'

Alex poked him in the ribs, proving he wasn't in the least bit fooled. 'Does this young woman eat her fish alive or dead, did you say? We could lower her into the pond so she could catch her own.'

It was the chuckle his brother gave that was catching, and the pair of them began to laugh. Alex punched him on the shoulder, and Dominic retaliated with a swipe from his sweaty towel. They wrestled each other, before they raced up the stairs like two exuberant dogs.

Quickly washing the perspiration from his body and shivering a little in the cold air, Dominic donned a pair of dark trousers. He topped it with a matching cutaway jacket and a decorative, though businesslike, waistcoat of dark cherry-red brocade. He pulled on his boots and tucked the trousers inside.

Vivienne was gazing out of the window when he reached the dining room and she turned, bringing a smile with her to brighten his day. She said, 'There you are. I didn't want to eat my breakfast alone. It looks as though the weather will stay clear for your visit with Mr Howard today, though it will probably rain tonight.'

He moved to the sideboard, and picking up a plate he turned to her. 'What will you have for breakfast, my dear?'

Vivienne sang softly, '"And she wheeled her wheelbarrow

through street broad and narrow, singing cockles and muscles alive, alive, oh".'

He laughed. 'I'm afraid we have neither. You overheard?'

She nodded. 'And you know it, Dom.'

'Everything?'

'Over the time I've lived in this house I've learned how you and Alex compete.'

'I'd just come into the hall when I heard my name mentioned, so I couldn't not have overheard. You have an affectionate relationship with Alex and I enjoy watching you together, especially when you act like a pair of twelve year olds. It makes me wish I'd been raised with a sibling nearer in age. I've always wanted a brother.'

'Now you have one, in me. When we were growing up Alex was always there for me . . . he and Eugenie. I hold them both in great esteem.'

'They both say the same about you. You are much loved in this house, Dominic. I hope your lady will be worthy of you.'

Warmth flooded through him. 'Now, you have embarrassed me enough, Vivienne. What can I get you to eat for breakfast?'

'Some toasted muffins spread with gooseberry preserve, if you would.'

'Is that all?'

'For now.'

Dominic had the same, but with the addition of some ham and eggs afterwards, for he had a busy day ahead and dinner was a long way off.

Eugenie entered with Alex, just as Dominic stood up to leave.

'You must excuse me, but I have an appointment with John Howard,' he said, and taking Eugenie's hand in his he kissed it.

'Anything of importance?'

'Business. Not overly important, but signatures on papers. More urgent is the fact that my new clerk will need accommodation and a maid.'

'There, I told you that hiring a woman as a clerk would cause problems,' Alex said, and blandly enough for Dominic to gaze suspiciously at him.

'He has told me,' Eugenie said.

'But nothing has been settled. Miss Ellis is, as yet, still unaware of my feelings towards her.'

'That can easily be sorted out.'

'I thought Miss Ellis might use my rooms in town and I could move into John Howard's house until I can find a suitable home to purchase.'

Eugenie looked horrified. 'Nonsense! You cannot put a young woman in a boarding house. It will attract the wrong attention altogether and would be a stain on her character forever more. It will also cast a slur on the LéSayres name, something you boys don't deserve.'

The boys in question grinned at each other, for before she'd become their stepmother and then her father's countess, Eugenie had been far from stainless herself.

'I absolutely forbid it!'

'It won't be for long, but the matter is urgent, since Miss Ellis needs alternative accommodation near the establishment where she will be employed. Also I need to give her an option for her future. At the moment that's a roof over her head and employment.'

'Her other options?'

'Marriage to Brigadier Maximilian Crouch and become an army widow, or move to Australia where she intends to search for gold in the company of two other servants, a couple I believe to be dishonest.'

Eugenie snorted. 'I've been given to understand that the southern continent is populated by rogues and blackguards.'

'I've heard that the brigadier's company isn't much better and his regiment is to be sent to the Antipodes within the month, to help keep order.'

That was news to Dominic, but he was uneasy because the matter of settling the will was even more urgent. What if the brigadier turned up at Oakford House? He wished he hadn't left Gracie there. 'As soon as I buy a home Grace can reside there until I've sorted things out, unless you can think of anything more suitable.'

Alex plopped a couple of poached eggs and an equal number of thick slices of ham on to his plate. 'I daresay the matter of accommodations will be resolved easily enough, and shortly. She can stay here in the meantime.'

'I'd thought of that but she cannot ride to Poole and back every day, especially on these dark winter evenings. I can always bring some transcribing home for her to do.'

Vivienne sighed. 'Grace Ellis is not a slave, and by the sound of it she's had a hard time of late. You managed without her before you met, and can do so again. She will be my guest for the short time it takes for you to afford suitable premises in Poole, and to set up home. I'll prepare that little suite of rooms next to Eugenie . . . the one that catches the afternoon sun when it shines.'

Alex smiled all around. 'That's settled then.'

'I must warn you, Grace can be . . . *lively*. The girl has a will of her own, and she might choose one of the alternative paths open to her.' An extremely worrisome thought, and Dominic frowned.

Vivienne merely smiled. 'Better you leave things to me, Dominic. I'll write to her and invite her to be my guest for a while. You can take my letter with you. If she accepts my invitation it will give us all some breathing space. After all, you haven't known her for very long and must approach the question of marriage with some caution.'

It was a comment that amused him since Vivienne and Alex had met and had married within a month or so. She'd also produced a healthy heir for the earldom with a month to spare.

'I bow to your wisdom in the matter, Vivienne.'

Really, he had no choice. Albeit that this was the family home where he'd been born and raised, Vivienne was the mistress of this house and Dominic, as well as Alex, deferred to her on all matters domestic.

Problem now solved Dominic smiled as he left the house and headed for the stable. All he had to do now was pay court to Gracie and propose marriage, and he'd enjoy doing that.

Argus had been turned out of his stall and was ready, waiting for him. He was a handsome beast, beautifully groomed so his pelt was a gleam of polished ebony and his neck arched proudly. He was also in a docile mood, and that caused Dominic to ask Sam, 'Why is he so quiet?'

'Partly because he's quartered in a familiar stable, so he feels comfortable, and also because I rode him round the field a few times to rid him of his pent-up energy.'

A word of praise brought a wide smile from Sam.

Dominic reached Poole to find the quayside as busy as a hive of bees. The tide was in and the ships rode high in the water, their masts sketching acute angles against the sky.

The fishing boats were unloading cod, filched from the Norwegian shoals in the dark of night. The British fishermen were weathered-looking, bearded and watchful as well as being well muscled. They needed to be tough, for the fishing grounds were hotly disputed.

Across the water, and despite the sandbar, the dark mass of Brownsea Island allowed leeway for the ships to enter and exit the quay in relative comfort, while the island itself protected the harbour from the worst of gales.

For a moment the crowd opened and he thought he saw two familiar figures, Brian and his wife Jessie. And they were talking to . . . it looked like Lady Florence's former clerk, whom he'd met once over a business matter. Pawley, he recalled. 'What the devil!'

It didn't matter to Dominic that the servants might choose to take advantage and leave a little earlier in his own absence. In fact, he'd expected it. Perhaps the sailing date had been brought forward. He frowned. If that was the case they should be in Southampton, surely.

When he looked again they were lost in a jostling crowd. It must have been someone else, he thought and put the servants from his mind. He had enough problems lodged in his mind.

John Howard lived on the other side of the aptly named Ladies Walking Field, where women from the poor house worked their way along lengths of rope, separating the coarse hemp from the tar so it could be reused on the sailing ships. It was a thankless task – one that would have been Gracie's fate without the intervention of a man like John Howard.

Dominic had bought two acres of land there, earmarking it for his future home. It would have a view down the hill and over the town with the harbour wrapped round it. The water was shallow here and the site could be reached by a stony lane behind a low stone wall.

The backwater was muddy at low tide, and dotted with figures digging for cockles. It reminded Dominic of the time he and Alex used to do the same. They'd come into Poole on market days in the carriage. Tucking her skirt into her waist Eugenie had shown them how to watch for the bubbles in the mud and dig down until they found the cockles. When they reached home they'd open the shells by soaking the cockles in fresh water and then drop them in hot water for a minute or so to cook. Sprinkled with vinegar they were a tasty treat.

His thoughts changed as John Howard's house came into view. Would he be able to sell his business partner the notion of having a female clerk?

It turned out that he didn't have to.

John Howard's home was situated halfway up the hill with the same view over the harbour, but from a different angle. Dominic found him in the library, a cheery fire warming the room. The man was aging well, looking distinguished as he entered his sixties. He was one of those men who maintained a full head of hair, and his head still worked well.

They shook hands, and it was then that Dominic felt the slight weakness trembling through him.

'I understand you've hired a lady clerk,' John said, as soon as Dominic was seated.

'Rather, I have offered her the job but she has not agreed yet. If she does I'm sure you'll like her. Her name is Grace Ellis. How did you get to hear of the matter when I've only mentioned it to the earl about two hours ago?'

'Servants, you know, they do love to gossip. One of them overheard it yesterday in the marketplace. Surely you're not seeking my approval.'

'I was about to inform you of my intentions as a matter of respect.'

'I trust your judgement in this matter, Dominic. I've also heard that you're paying her a man's wage. That's unheard of. Some of our regular clients will complain.'

'The gossip will soon die down. Miss Ellis will do the job well and they will come running to take a look at her. She will be worth her weight in gold.'

'Did you engage her out of the goodness of your heart, Dominic, or is your heart involved in another way?'

Since his secret was out Dominic decided to be honest. 'In the first place I hired her because she has the appropriate skills for the position. Now I'm in love with her, and I don't want to lose her. You should remember her. She is the daughter of the late Dr Ellis, and you've been paying her wage for some time.'

'Ah yes. I do remember her. She was a pretty little thing, and curious about everything. Am I still paying her wage, I hadn't noticed?'

'My dear John, you notice every bronze farthing you make, and probably still have it stashed away somewhere.'

John chuckled. 'I am not quite as tight-fisted as you imagine. As for Miss Ellis, I remember her as a truly sensitive little soul. She made an ointment for my aching fingers out of wintergreen and charged me a penny for it. It stunk to high heaven and raised blisters on my skin. I couldn't get rid of the stains. My cat took exception to the smell and he left home and didn't return for three weeks. Grace's father called her a meddlesome wench, and then took the penny. The harshness of it made her cry. She was a child, after all, and just trying to please. He didn't have much time for females.'

Dominic burned on Grace's behalf for the insult. 'Did it work?'

'Did what work?'

'The wintergreen ointment.'

'D'you know, I can't remember but I haven't had painful knuckles since, so it must have scared the pain off.'

They laughed, but dread gathered like a tiny grey rain cloud inside Dominic. 'What was so urgent that you felt the need to call me home, John. Are you ill?'

'You're astute, Dominic, but ahead of yourself. It's about time I told you, since I know you like your life to be tidy. I'm growing old and I no longer enjoy the cut and thrust of business. Therefore, I intend to retire. Since my wife died I have been lonely, so I recently proposed marriage to a lady of my acquaintance and I hope she will accept.'

Dominic remembered the exchange over breakfast, and smiled. 'Eugenie?'

'I have long admired her, but she remained faithful to your father's memory.'

'Now it's my turn to ask. Do you love her?'

'Of course I do.'

'Then I hope she accepts.'

'Eugenie has led me to believe she might . . . pending the approval of the earl and yourself.'

'She does not need our approval . . . but there, you both have mine.'

The retirement plan came as a relief, for Dominic had expected the worse. John said, 'My solicitor will be here shortly to sign my half of the business over to you. From then on it will belong to you alone, though I will be available to advise you for a short time, should you need it.'

'I will need you to give me a little time to adjust.'

'While I'm still senior partner I took it upon myself to hire a young man to manage the Dorchester branch. He is called Phillip Dupain, and though a little younger than you, he is quite capable. He can do most of the footwork. I don't know how he will react to working with a woman though.'

'In a mannerly fashion, one hopes. He probably knows by now, since everyone in the district seems to be aware of my business.'

'Yes . . . it happens. I must say such spontaneity on your part is unlike you, Dominic, but at least it proves you're human.'

'I didn't think I needed to prove it. Must we have a post-mortem before the event? After all, I have not officially declared myself to Miss Ellis, or decided if that course of action is a wise one. So far we have not come to terms over the contract.'

'Yes . . . we must talk about it. I'd already discussed such an eventuality with your brother, for I have made you the sole beneficiary of my estate, and you will be the possessor of a fortune once I am gone. I would like to know she is worthy of you.'

Dominic experienced shock at John's words. 'I would not have presumed . . . you have relatives . . . what of your half-sister in London, is she not to inherit?'

'Mrs Crawford and her son have already been taken care of with an income producing property. She is a good money manager.'

Dominic smiled. 'It must be a family trait. I must admit I'm surprised Alex didn't tell me of your decision.'

'Breaking a confidence is not part of his nature. The pair of you have an emotional streak that can be a little disconcerting when it surfaces. Look at it this way. We are born naked. We live a little, and then we depart, leaving all we strived for abandoned.'

The doorbell jangled.

'Bring your young lady to visit, Dominic. Although this might embarrass you, I've always regarded you as the son I never had, and I envied your father his good fortune in having such sons.'

'You already have met her. She is the daughter of Dr Ellis.'

'Yes . . . of course, a lively little creature, I thought the name was familiar.'

'Though I tried not to get involved, Gracie has little or no estate to tempt me with so what else can it be but love? I get the same feeling when one of my investments pay a good dividend.'

John laughed. 'You'd better not tell her that.'

'I don't know if she cares for me though, for she leads me on and then rebuffs me and laughs.'

John Howard choked out a laugh. 'You should play her at her own game.'

A knock came at the door and a manservant appeared. 'Mr Griffiths and Mr Dupain have arrived, sir.'

'Good, bring them in would you, and send the maid in with a tea tray. After that, I don't want us to be disturbed until further notice.'

'Yes sir,' the servant said.

Nine

Oakford House

The wind was a fierce and constant noise that battered against Oakford House as though its intention was to knock it down. Doors and windows rattled furiously.

Brian and Jessie hadn't returned. Grace sat in the kitchen, aware that the side door she'd left open for them was still unbolted and anyone could walk in.

Fuelling up the kitchen stove she watched the flames leap and roar. Beyond the kitchen the house no longer seemed friendly. Rather, its noises became stealthy. The wooden floors creaked, the wind moaned as though it were in pain and sometimes it gathered strength and howled through the cracks like a coven of cackling witches. A door creaked open and then slammed shut again at the back of the house and a flurry of fear raked through her.

For goodness' sake, it's only a storm, she thought.

Nevertheless her imagination conjured up stealthy footsteps, cackles of laughter, and the sound of breathing. More than once she said in a wavering voice. 'Who's there?'

Relief filled her when nobody answered.

She didn't know whether to go up to bed, or stay in the warm kitchen. A flash of lightning was followed by a loud smack of thunder directly above her, and it made up her mind. Damping down the stove she panicked a little at the next roll of thunder and ran up the stairs to her room. There she pulled the blankets up round her ears to muffle the noise of the storm and somehow, amidst the clamour of the storm, she fell into a sleep of sheer exhaustion.

Towards dawn a loud bang woke her. Grace started, her heart thumped and her senses went on alert all over again.

She crept downstairs to be greeted by a mess. Several candles guttered in melting wax, their wicks almost spent. The front door had been wedged open, the cellar door swung on its hinges, scraping across the floorboards. Mud had been tramped over the hall floor, which was flooded from the rain.

She closed the front door and locked it. Candlelight sent a soft glow from the drawing room. There, Grace was confronted by the sight of Jessie and Brian. Both were half asleep, muddy feet propped up on the delicate brocade of a chaise longue that Lady Florence had purchased recently at great expense. A wine bottle lay on its side, but it was empty, and a couple of the best crystal wine glasses held the dregs.

Taking Brian by the arm she gently shook him awake. 'What are you doing? How did you open the cellar door?'

Brian gave her a vacant, boozy smile. 'Miss me, did you, my darlin? Oh yes . . . I remember . . . Miss Grace Ellis doesn't consider me good enough for the likes of her. What's it to do with you?'

'I'm responsible for the house when Mr LéSayres is away.'

Jessie stared blearily at her. 'More fool you. We had the key to the cellar, that's how we opened it. We had to get the brandy out first, didn't we?'

'We'd better count it then.'

'Don't be such a dimwit, Grace. There isn't any brandy left to count. We've sold it.'

'Sold it? But it's not yours to sell.'

Brian glared at her in a way that made her quake. 'Stop shouting, I've got a headache.'

She deliberately raised her voice. 'And whose fault is that? Get the cellar contents back at once, please, Jessie. We'll all be in trouble if you don't. It's on the inventory.'

'How can it be when you couldn't open the door to count it?'

'That's by the by. The old lady bought it from Rafferty Jones. It's recorded as "Contents of cellar. Miscellaneous estimate". Look . . . you could give me the money you made from its sale in exchange for a receipt. I'm sure Mr LéSayres will accept that.'

'I can't return it, dearie. Most of the brandy has gone back to the merchant who sold it to the old lady. Brian and I took the last of it into Poole yesterday. We kept back a nice bottle of wine to celebrate, and it's fermenting inside us. Nice and warming on a cold day, it is. By the time Mr LéSayres finds out we'll be long gone and I doubt if he'll follow us for the price of a few bottles of brandy.'

'He'll come sooner if I send him a message. And he'll probably bring some customs officers.'

'They won't find anything because there's nothing to find except a few bottles – after all, they will expect to find something in the cellar. They'll only have your word for it.'

Brian stood up and circled her; she'd never seen him looking so unfriendly. 'You wouldn't rat on us, would you, Gracie girl? We'll give you a cut. Five pounds to keep your blathering mouth shut.'

'I'm not a thief. A better plan is that you leave the money you got for the brandy with me. I'll give you a receipt and then Mr LéSayres won't have you charged.'

Brian took a knife from his belt, a wicked-looking thing. 'I'd rather cut your flapping tongue from your head.'

Jessie poked him in the chest. 'We agreed there would be no violence. We'll be long gone before LéSayres gets back. Come with us, Grace. There's no future in being a servant, and neither is there any fun in being a clerk, unless it's your own money you're counting.'

'And she isn't counting that because—'

'Shut your trap, Brian. The less she knows about our business the better.'

Grace said, 'I have no intention of leaving England. I haven't enough money.'

Brian leered at her. 'There are ways and means for ladies to make extra money for themselves.'

'Will you please be quiet?'

Brian ignored the wisdom of his wife. 'The old lady hoarded a lot of cash over the years but she didn't get any pleasure from it. She tucked it away in various places and thought she was being clever. But the old duck was forgetful and she didn't notice it disappearing.'

Horrified by the depth of their deception, Grace told them, 'Lady Florence told me she suspected Pawley for a long time, which is why she dismissed him. He held a position of trust in the household. She had someone come in to look over the books and it was discovered that Mr Pawley had falsified them.'

'Over the years Pawley made a tidy sum, and after he left he told us where the old lady's hiding places were for a cut. It took but a minute to slip into her room when she had her afternoon sleep and you were busy.'

'It sounds as though you're proud of what you've done.'

Jessie shrugged. 'Don't tell me you've never stolen anything.'

'Not that I can remember.'

'You didn't have to steal to survive though, did you?'

'No I didn't, which is not to say I wouldn't have, had my circumstances been different. But you and Brian received a legacy from Lady Florence so you have no excuse to steal.'

'It wasn't a gift since it was owed to us. Mr Pawley said she was underpaying us and this was a way we could get what we were due. The old girl had plenty of money and we were doing quite nicely until you came along and stuck your nose into everyone else's business. Then Pawley was dismissed . . . and he took our money with him, the poxy thief.'

There was a poetic justice in that and Grace grinned. She was glad Dominic had hidden the strongbox well. 'Lady Florence's money I think you mean.'

'Pawley told us it was invested in the bank, and he couldn't get it out until a certain date, so we planned our journey for then. He said it would earn interest in the meantime, and that would make something to add to the sum. It put our plans back a bit, and then she upped and died.'

Grace turned to go. If she could reach the village she might be able to find someone to carry her message, or she might be able to intercept Pawley.

Brian caught her wrist as she headed for the door. 'Where are you going?'

'To get the eggs.'

'There's no hens left.'

'There's Edith, the white one.'

'She's too old to produce eggs. I'm not daft.'

'Sometimes, she lays an egg.'

'You were going to try and find someone to tell of what's happening here.' Brian's grip tightened and became painful. 'I'll tell you what you're going to do, you're going to stay here and cook breakfast, there are still some eggs and ham in the larder. I bought muffins from the bakery yesterday and there are some smoked kippers on the larder slab. You can boil the eggs hard, and pack us a meal for when we're on the road. Now get on with it, we haven't got much time.'

Grace's stomach rumbled and he pushed her towards the door. 'Watch her carefully, Jessie. The cab won't be here for another hour or so but we might as well eat before we head for Poole.'

Jessie snapped, 'Don't you mean Southampton?'

'Stop your nagging, woman, it was just a slip of the tongue. I'll give the house another quick search just to make sure while you're doing that.'

'Fetch them nice silver pieces from the cabinet.'

'We can't take everything, there isn't room for it. Besides, the coachman might get suspicious and mention it to someone.'

Grace sat at the kitchen table while various crashes and scuffs came from the rest of the house. She winced when glass smashed.

'Don't look at me, girl, get on with the cooking,' Jessie bawled from the rocking chair.

Grace took an iron frying pan from its hook, and wondered if she would be quick enough to flatten the woman with it.

Yes, but you might kill her.

Serves her right. She deserves it.

Go on then. Have you given any thought to what you'll do with her body?

Grace shrugged. 'Mind your own business.'

Jessie snapped awake. 'Did you say something?'

'You're going to be sorry when the law catches up with you.'

'They're not going to catch up with us. Get on and cook the breakfast, would you. We haven't got all day.'

Six chunks of ham were soon sizzling. She cut thick slices of bread, making a hole for the eggs to nestle in, and added that to the meal.

Grace dropped an iron spoon and Jessie's eyes shot open. 'Be careful, will you, my head aches something dreadful.'

'I could make you something to ease it. I will need my medication box and some red wine to hide the taste of the herbs.'

'There's some burgundy open on the shelf,' Jessie said.

Grace put the frying pan to one side to keep warm.

Lifting down her father's box of herbal cures she picked out a measuring glass and filled it two-thirds with the burgundy. She added some honey and powder to the liquid and shook it vigorously.

'What was that powder you put in it?'

Grace set the mixture on the table. 'It's powdered willowbark mixed with honey. It needs to infuse for half an hour and then be given another good shake before drinking. I've made two doses.'

She decided not to tell them that another ingredient was licorice, which might prove a little inconvenient in due course.

A little while later Brian joined them in the kitchen, looking irate. He helped himself to the large portion of breakfast, and began to gulp it down. Jessie ate the smaller half.

When he'd finished eating, Brian looked up at her from his chair at the table. 'Where's the bloody strongbox?'

Grace looked him in the eyes. 'I don't know. Mr LéSayres has hidden it somewhere. He didn't tell me where. Perhaps he buried it on top of Lady Florence in her grave.'

Giving a little scream she cringed away from him when he used his knuckles to deliver a couple of painful hits on her cheekbones. Then, as if he had opened a gate he began to pummel her; stomach, arms, legs. She fell to the floor and covered her head with her arms as china and pots and pans bounced and shattered around her.

Jessie came between them. She pushed Brian aside and helped her up. 'For pity's sake, Grace tell him.'

Jessie was pushed roughly to one side. 'The strongbox . . . where is it?'

'I told you, don't know where it is. Mr LéSayres doesn't take me into his confidence.'

A punch to the midriff floored her and she fell, clutching her stomach and gasping for air, frightened by the violence. 'I don't know.'

He took her by the hair and pulled her towards the stairs. 'It would be a shame to mark that pretty little face, but if you persist in lying to me it will be a knife next time.'

Jessie intervened, coming between them. 'Let her go, Brian. We agreed she wasn't to be hurt.'

The pressure on her scalp was released. 'You might have agreed, but I don't know who with. It certainly wasn't me. Beside, it was only a tap or two. I want that strongbox. If she doesn't tell me where it is I might kill her.'

Hugging her stomach Grace racked her brains, trying to imagine where Dominic would have hidden the box. She doubted if he'd hide it in the house.

Her stomach rumbled. They'd eaten all she'd cooked, leaving nothing for her.

Then came the sound of wheels on gravel.

Brian cursed. 'Damn it, the coach is early.'

'Put the silver in the sack. It will fetch a pound or two and we can sell that instead,' Jessie said.

'The strongbox must be somewhere. Tell him to come back.'

Grace made a run for the front door, where the shadow of the coachman loomed in the porch.

Grace was just about to scream when Brian put out his foot and sent her sprawling. Clamping a hand over her face he delivered one punch to her stomach and her knees weakened. She felt like a rag doll, all floppy and slow-witted. Somewhere in the midst of the twilight state she was in, she was dragged and bumped up the staircase. She landed face down on something soft and yielding.

A bed! *Her own bed,* she hoped, irrationally.

'See how you like this, Miss Ellis Have a nice sleep. No doubt the money man will come along and free you bye the bye. Count yourself lucky I didn't kill you.'

'Come away now Brian, the girl's telling the truth. She wouldn't have taken that beating if she knew where it was hidden.'

There was the sound of a slap. 'Keep your mouth shut, you poxy trollop.'

Grace tried to sleep but she jerked at every scuff and squeak. There was a metallic clunk, and then suddenly, there was no noise at all, apart from worn out gusts of wind that sounded like despairing sighs.

They might come back, she thought. They might kill her. The deed would be blamed on Dominic and they'd hang him for murder.

A loud sob thrust from her at the thought.

Enough self-pity!

That's all right for you to say but my brain is battered beyond redemption.

Nonsense! I am your brain and I'm far from being done with you. Now, rise from this bed and start trying to get us out of this jar of pickles.

She swung her legs out of the bed, and stood, clinging on to a bedpost, as the room whirled busily around her. At least she was in her own room. Allowing the dizziness to recede she limped precariously to the door like a drunken sailor. She seemed to have lost a shoe and gazed in perplexity at her bare foot.

Never mind the shoe, try and open the door!

Locked! She rattled the doorknob and shouted, causing her head to buzz alarmingly. 'Let me out!'

The donkey gave a loud wheezing bray at the sound of her voice. The poor creature would be hungry.

Downstairs, the hall clock struck five. It must be wrong. But no . . . it was almost dark outside. She couldn't believe she'd slept for all that time. She went to the window, with the faint hope that the cab driver was still there. It looked as it normally did, except for some storm litter.

No, she hadn't been asleep. She must have been suffering from a loss of consciousness. Her head throbbed as she tried to straighten out the muddle she was in. She explored her scalp gently with her fingertips then moved on to her ears. There was blood seeping from cuts and grazes. As far as she could tell her skull wasn't fractured, though her face felt puffy.

She moved to the dressing table. The image confronting her in the mirror shocked her. The sockets around her eyes were blackened and her face swollen. Blood crusted her hairline. It was probably a cut from the ring Brian wore.

A movement under her window caught her attention and she opened it.

The rooster came cautiously from the side of house, lifting his bronze feathered legs and placing them down again daintily, like a little dance. Edith followed, making concerned clucks like the governess Grace's father had hired for her when she'd become a motherless child.

The storm must have wrecked the chicken coop and she hoped the foxes didn't discover the two birds roaming free.

'Be careful you two. Sleep in the hayloft.'

Disorientated, she sat down again, feeling more than a little despair. Hunger and thirst roiled inside her.

There was a small amount of water in the jug that accompanied her washing bowl, enough to last her until Dominic arrived if she was careful. Scooping it into her cupped palm she sucked it into her mouth, then placed the damp hand on the site of her headache to help cool the pain. It came back bloodied and she wiped it on the towel.

The darkness deepened. There was nothing to light the candle with. Cold gradually seeped into her bones. Making a renewed effort to open the door with a metal hatpin she cried out in despair when she applied pressure and it snapped inside the lock.

She should have taken the key inside the room, for Lady Florence had liked to feel secure before she went to sleep . . . but that had been the last thing on Grace's mind.

She buried herself under a couple of blankets and curled up on the mattress, wondering what Dominic was doing.

It was a long night; the pressing darkness did a good job of scaring her and every noise took on some frightening significance. The pattering and squeaks of mice seemed to get louder, as though the creatures sensed they had a full run of the house. She wondered if they'd nibble at her if she fell asleep. The blood on her face might attract them. She imagined them crawling all over her, tearing the flesh from her bones with sharp little teeth.

There came a whimper.

'Who is it . . . help me, I'm locked in.'

It took a moment to realize it was her own voice and she was talking to herself.

Was she going mad? She began to count, telling herself she would be rescued when she reached one thousand. She fell asleep before she did.

Another day passed, and with a sickening slowness. She kept a watch at the window in case somebody happened by and she could attract attention to her plight.

She found a pencil in the cupboard and started counting all over again, wondering if she should aim for more numbers. Pausing for a moment she scribbled, 'Dominic I love u', but rather childishly she wrote it back to front for the sake of variety, so it read, 'u evol I cinimod'. After all, numbers could wait, as they would never run out. If she died here from lack of food and water and Dominic came across her skeleton, she just wanted him to know she'd loved him. For good measure she added an infinity sign of two joined circles: ∞

'There,' she said.

For the rest of the time she slept, but fitfully, waking with every noise. There was no way out of her prison however hard she battered at the doors. Even if she did find the courage to attempt a long drop to the ground from the window, it was covered with flagstones and surrounded by a low wall topped with decorative spears. If the fall didn't kill her it would certainly break the bones in her legs, or worse, her back. Then she would no longer be able to walk.

She tried to remember how many days someone could survive without water. Possibly three to five, and as far as she could work out this was her third day. If it rained she'd be able to hang the jug out of the window and collect some water, but the clouds had been stubborn in their dryness. Her small supply of water was exhausted. At least she'd stopped feeling hungry. Fatigue overcame her as she despaired and whimpered his name.

'Dominic!'

She imagined him sitting at the table with his family, his smile lighting up with the pleasure of being there with them. It must be time for dinner.

He might have forgotten she was here . . . or even her existence. When he remembered he would come, and he'd find her all shrivelled up from lack of water. He might even find her dead!

A hysterical giggle left her. 'Then you'll be sorry, Dominic LéSayres.'

Her stomach had given up protesting and was now a cramped, empty void that she hugged against herself.

She made another mark on the wall and cried when the pencil lead hit a rough patch and it snapped.

There was a creak on the stair and she rushed to place her ear against the door panel, her voice cracking. 'Who is it . . . who's there . . .?'

A meow was followed by a throaty purr. It couldn't be her cat because she didn't have one. Lady Florence used to have a tabby cat once but she couldn't remember what had happened to it. Perhaps it was her ghost.

Grabbing up a scrap of torn paper from a small pile in a bowl on the table, she folded it and then knelt and pushed the paper under the door crack. She wiggled it and slid it along the crack under the door. 'Here, puss.'

A tabby paw swiped back and forth along after the paper. The cat was willing to play while the game held its interest. She wished it were her side of the wall. Still, it was someone to talk to.

'How did you get in?'

The cat mewed.

'Through the kitchen window, you say . . . it was left open? They must have known you intended to visit. By any chance, do you think you could open this door, tabby cat?'

There was no answer.

Even a cat was better company than none. 'Please come back to visit any time you wish,' she called out.

As she stood the paper fell to the floor. She gazed at it with some curiosity. It had her name on it and she remembered the letter from Lady Florence that she'd ripped up in a fit of temper. Somebody had picked the pieces up . . . Dominic she imagined. He hadn't been too pleased by her behaviour then, and neither was she now she'd thought about it. She'd been childish.

Carefully, she began to piece the torn pieces together.

> To my dear little companion, Grace Ellis,
>
> By now you might be wondering why I have not treated you as one of the servants. It may not have occurred to you that you were not part of my house staff, but rather a protégé, paid from the purse of Mr John Howard. In exchange I promised him I'd look for a suitable spouse for you.
>
> Men suitable for that purpose lost interest when they realized you had no dowry except for a pathetically small annuity that your mother left you, one that wouldn't keep most of us supplied with hosiery. As to what's left of that you must enquire of your mentor.
>
> My dear, I grew used to your kindness, your competence as well as your honesty. Selfishly, I couldn't bear to part with you so allowed my task to lapse.
>
> Now the problem needs to be addressed, and urgently. I know you will be angered by my interference, but please do set aside the inclination to act rashly.
>
> My nephew, Maximilian Crouch, is a rogue who is disinclined to wed. Like most men I'm sure a little stimulation will overcome his reluctance regarding the marriage bed, allowing him to perform his marital duty when required.

Grace blushed, even though there was nobody to observe it. Heavens! She knew Lady Florence could be outspoken, but not this blunt. What next?

To that end I have left you a rare book, a gift from a
maharajah to my late husband, who carried it back from
India. Both he and my gentlemen acquaintances who came
after him, enjoyed perusing it when the flesh was unwilling.
It's called *Kama Sutra* and is kept in the locked cabinet in
my room. You will recall, no doubt, that I caught you
looking at the illustrations once. How sweet and innocent
the blush you gave!

You have an inclination to be outspoken when your
anger is roused, Grace, but I beg you to think carefully,
and bear in mind that Max is no longer a young man, and
will need encouragement. Remember – men and women
are created to enjoy each other, why else would we feel as
we do?

I cannot think of a better match for you, and at least you
will have a home where you can look after my treasures.

Best wishes for your future.

Florence, Lady Digby.

Had Dominic read this letter? Grace felt sick with shock at
the thought. Then she giggled as she remembered some of the
illustrations, and then she began to laugh. One would need to
be a contortionist.

Lady Florence had been true to herself right up to the end,
she thought.

Another day passed, her only company the cat, a creature that
must feel as lonely as she, for he visited at regular intervals to air
his complaints at the lack of service under the door. She slept
fitfully, but often and was fatigued when she was awake. Grace
found a fan in the dresser drawer and plucked a feather from it
to tease the cat with.

She began to hate the fall of darkness. Gazing over the landscape she watched the houses in the village gradually light their
candles and felt lonely.

The occupants would be sitting down to dinner. She groaned
and pressed her hands against her hollow stomach. If the rooster
came in now she would fall upon him, tear him apart with her
teeth and consume him, feathers as well.

Across the fields the faint outline of the gravestones glowed as the moon rose high followed by clouds. The light wove in and out like a needle pulling thread through embroidery.

The windows iced over and her tongue stuck to the glass as she tried to lick the moisture. It was painful to remove.

Footsteps creaked on the stairs.

She shuddered and placed an ear against the door panel. It was her imagination. It had to be, since it always was.

All the same, she whispered, 'Help me . . . please help me.'

The footsteps stopped and the house went eerily quiet, as though it was listening with her. Her heart beat loudly in the void outside her room.

A sudden creak made her jump. 'Who is it? I'm locked in. Find a key . . . let me out.'

There was a whispered conversation, barely discernable and the cat answered with a mew. The footsteps retreated stealthily.

'No . . . don't leave,' she shouted and banged her fists against the door. 'Help me.'

Grace staggered to the window when she heard the front door close. A man stood there, looking at the house, a dark menacing figure. She shivered when he shrugged and turned, walking down the driveway towards the gate.

Hope left her. She was beginning to feel ill. Her stomach and back ached, her skin felt hot and dry and her thoughts were in chaos.

She gave a small cry, for her voice didn't have the strength to scream at the retreating figure. And then she shrank back and crept under the blankets, too tired to cry out, her heart pounding from the effort.

The donkey began to hee-haw.

She pulled the cover over her head . . . she must be hearing things. All she wanted to do now was to sleep and never wake up.

Noise prevented it. The stealthy footsteps came from different places and then she heard a squeak of the back door opening. A man called out, but cautiously, 'Is someone in there?'

Her voice croaked in reply, her mouth too dry to answer clearly. She managed to scrape out, '. . . Grace Ellis . . . I'm locked in . . . please help me.'

'Is there anyone else in the house?'

'No.'

Someone mounted the stairs taking solid steps now the need for caution was no longer valid. 'Stand away from the doorway, miss, I'm going to try and heel the door open.'

Something crashed heavily against the lock and the man swore as the hatpin fell to the floor.

'I'll have to shoot out the lock. Get under the bed covers in case some splinters go astray.' A short time later he said, 'Ready?'

Another loud crack was followed by the crash of a shoulder against the door.

The window shattered as a bullet ricocheted off the iron fire grate and went through the glass. A stream of cold air filled the room and allowed the moonlight to illuminate their faces.

He smiled at her. 'It looks as though you've been having a hard time of it, missy.'

Grace dragged her legs out of bed, holding the bedpost for support as she coughed on the smoke left behind from the pistol shot. She gazed at the man who gazed back at her, grinning. Surely she was seeing things?

'It's you, Rafferty Jones,' she whispered.

'So it is, and here was me thinking I was King of England hisself.'

The relief she experienced made her weak. Three steps forward and her legs folded under her.

The smuggler caught her before she hit the floor.

Ten

Dominic's business with John Howard was over for the moment. Dressing for dinner, he wondered what he'd done to be the recipient of such largesse. As a courtesy he intended to run the business wisely, and keep John informed.

He had liked Philip Dupain too, finding him to be a man of good sense, who was quick-minded and had confidence in himself despite his humble beginning as the son of a brick maker. They had got on well.

Downstairs, the ladies were dressed in their best. Vivienne wore a dark blue gown with a little velvet jacket. His stepmother, Eugenie, was gowned in pale grey, a colour that on anyone else would appear drab. She was of average height and elegant, with a face much younger than her age implied. Her hair shone with copper lights with a touch of silver at the temples.

Dominic gave her a hug. 'John told me you and he plan to wed in the spring. Congratulations, my dear.'

'You don't mind?'

'Of course I don't mind. We love you and will miss you, that goes without saying, but Alex and I are adults now, and I hope we'll always prove to be a credit to you.'

'I can safely say your mother would be as proud of you both as your father was.'

Dominic was preoccupied during dinner, and that drew notice from his brother who cornered him afterwards.

'What's bothering you, Dom? Is it John Howard's generosity, or Eugenie's engagement? I must admit, they both took me by surprise. No wonder he kept finding excuses to visit. As for Eugenie, I never knew she had it in her to keep that sort of news a secret.'

'Eugenie deserves some happiness after all those years of being our stepmother. John Howard has been extremely generous towards me, and after thinking about it I've come to the conclusion I was the obvious choice to inherit his estate. However, that doesn't mean I have to accept it. Rather, I'll observe his wishes until the day comes when I can find a better way to distribute his wealth.'

'Ah . . . I can see you're going to remain independent, and earn your own fortune.'

'One of the joys of my profession is the money I earn, and my freedom to spend it. I'm comfortably off in my own right now. When John's time comes I'll expect you to head a committee for the disposal of some of his cash since I'm well situated to earn my own.'

'So what has put that frown on your face?'

'It's Grace I'm worried about. I've got one of those uneasy feelings that I shouldn't have left her alone with the Curtis couple.'

'You always were sensitive to the needs of those closest to you.'

'And that ability proved to be right as often it proved wrong.'

Dominic still felt guilty. He thought to himself, It is possible she might be overcome by pique and decide to go to Australia, after all. No . . . surely Grace had more sense than that. Rather, she would choose to wed Maximilian Crouch. The soldier might find enough manliness in him to father a child on her, and do the right thing according to the terms of the will. Then again, he might use a proxy to carry out the act of procreation for him, a not unusual event when a man such as Maximilian Crouch was expected to provide an heir, even when disinclined. If Grace married the man he might insist that she accompanied him to Australia?

There was a tidy amount of wealth involved in Lady Florence's estate, enough to sway Grace in that direction perhaps, he reasoned. Not that he would blame her, since she had nothing much to call her own or support her through life except for a small legacy from her mother.

Lady Florence had been misguided in her conceit to assume that either party would agree to such an arrangement though. Grace didn't strike him as being a woman who suffered from avarice. How could it be when she gave chickens names and mourned them when they were served for dinner? That didn't stop her enjoyment of eating it.

He'd tried to take his mind off Grace during the meal of roasted chicken with all the trimmings. He'd eaten enough chicken of late and longed for a thick, juicy beefsteak slathered in gravy. He doubted if Grace had been shopping, especially since he'd seen the housekeeper and her husband in Poole just the day before. They'd had the donkey cart with them. He hoped the rig had been returned to Oakford House because it had been purchased by Rafferty Jones.

He rubbed his fingers against the frown that occupied his forehead. 'Something odd is going on, Alex. The couple were sailing out of Southampton, not Poole, yet I could swear I saw them in the crowd at Poole. At least, I think I did.'

Eugenie joined them with a smile. 'I couldn't help overhearing. You've always been prone to a vivid imagination, Dominic. Put an idea into your head and you don't let it go until it's proved, one way or another. But you forget that less intellectual mortals cannot read what's going on inside your head?'

Which was just as well on occasion, he thought, and he brought them up to date. 'Gracie is in trouble; I fear. I can feel it. I'm going to cut my visit short.'

Eugenie protested. 'It's gone nine and it's dark.'

'It can't be helped. If I ignore this feeling and something untoward happens to her I'll never forgive myself. Instruct the staff accordingly while I change into my travelling clothes, would you please, Alex.'

Vivienne said, 'I'll do that. A traveller alone on the road invites trouble and I think it behoves you to go with your brother.'

Eugenie gazed from one to the other. 'I'll pack some food for the journey, since you'll be riding for most of the night.'

Alex smiled at her. 'It's only takes four hours at the most.'

'Then you'll need breakfast.'

He gave in. 'Thank you, Eugenie, that's something I was about to suggest.'

Heaving a sigh of relief, for Dominic had not been looking forward to the ride alone, he said, 'Your company will be more than welcomed, Alex, but don't do this out of some misguided sense of loyalty.'

'What's misguided about it? Rest assured, brother, I will always be there if you need me, misguided or not, and on this occasion you do. Besides, no self-respecting felon will be abroad on such a night.'

'As long as nobody mistakes us for villains and shoots us.'

The two men exchanged a wry smile.

Shortly, and buoyed up by a sense of adventure, they rode into the raw night, garbed in the warmest of clothes, greatcoats with double capes over the shoulders and floppy hats that could be worn under a hood and tied under the chin.

Vivienne had filled their satchels to the brim with food, boiled eggs, cheese, ham, and crusty slices of buttered bread, as well as ginger ale in stone bottles. There was also a thick slice of roasted beef, the thought of which made Dominic's mouth water, even though he'd eaten a hearty dinner. At least they wouldn't go hungry for such a short journey.

'Will that be enough?' Vivienne asked, and Alex laughed and kissed her. 'It's enough to feed an army for a week, but you've forgotten to tie a cow to my saddlebag.'

Argus and the chestnut gelding Alex rode grumbled at each other at being dug out of their warm stalls, but they settled when they got used to the darkness and the steady pace Dominic set for them. It was cold, and as they entered a wooded area the rain began to pelt down on them. Alex came up beside him, barely able to see, 'Slow down, Dom, else the horses will run out of energy. Besides, I need to relieve myself.'

'So do I, just be careful of your aim in the dark.'

Argus showed no sign of fatigue. For the sake of convenience they'd stuck to a popular and well-travelled route and had now left the populated areas behind. Since they'd first entered the forested area Dominic's horse had begun to give little snickers and pull against the reins that would hold him back. Now, halfway to Ringwood he stamped his hooves, tossed his head and side-stepped. Dominic kept a tight hold on his bridle, which proved to be awkward when he tried to remount. 'You would choose now to kick up a fuss.'

'Here, let me help.' Alex made a stirrup with his hands and Dominic used it to spring into the saddle.

'He's frothing a bit and has probably got the scent of a mare in his nostrils. You should get him gelded.'

'If that's done, it will still take a year or so to eliminate the wildness from him, if ever. I've considered it, of course, but I'm working on an alternative plan.'

'You've allowed yourself to become too fond of the animal.'

'I admire his independent spirit and I don't want to change it.'

'Don't leave it much longer, Dom. He has magnificent equipment, and nowhere to expend the energy it produces. If it will help to settle him I'll have a couple of brood mares ready to be covered in the spring. He's a strong, handsome horse, and between them they should produce worthy offspring. Does he have papers?'

'His dam was a carriage horse called Nelly; his sire is recorded as an Exmoor Black. He's passed through several hands.'

'Hmmm . . . that doesn't bode well for his future. Very few people would consider buying a practicably unmanageable horse without a decent pedigree. If you sell him, or if he damages someone, he'll end up in the knackery.'

'Sam can manage him.'

'Sam's a whisperer. He has a large dollop of gypsy blood in him and he understands horses.'

Dominic threw his brother a grin. 'Who's being romantic now? I didn't think you were a believer in folklore.'

'Don't you ever wonder why fate put us all in the same place at the same time, and what life would be like, should you not exist?'

'Not strongly enough for me to crouch under my horse's backside and carve his bollocks up . . . I'm not that foolhardy.'

Alex roared with laughter when Argus bared his teeth and grunted.

'Come on, Alex, let's get on the road again. I want to be there by dawn.'

The two men tied their hoods over their hats and started off through the rain.

An hour later and the rain ceased. Everything smelled fresh. A white moon rode high in the sky, chasing the ragged clouds. The weather had decided to give them a premature reminder of how cold winter could be. It was cold, too cold for comfort, but pretty. Raindrops turned into glittering icicles and the ground frosted over.

Dominic thought of Grace, lying asleep, her breath gently lifting her breasts to tease the nipples against the lace of her chemise.

She was innocent and lovely and it would be his joy to expose to her what she was made of. Or perhaps the other way round.

Alex cut into Dominic's dreams of Grace as a faint trace of silvery grey light was painted along the horizon. 'First light.'

'It won't be long now . . . an hour at the most.'

The horses were breathing heavily now and they moved through the continuous cloud of vapour being expelled from their nostrils.

Mist rose from the ground and thickened, so they could hardly see where they were going.

'Stay close to me, Alex. There's a fence to the left.'

There was a forlorn bray from the donkey, and the noise guided them into the garden. Before long the house front came into view.

As far as they could see there was no smoke coming from the chimneys or light shining in the windows.

Dominic led the donkey back to his stable and released him from his rig. He took a moment to comfort the beast and the animal's whiskery nose nuzzled into his palm. Dominic pitched the animals some hay and oats, while Alex manned the pump and filled the water trough. When freed, the donkey skittered for the safety of his stall, where he buried his nose in the feeding trough, his recent woes beginning to fade in the comfort of food.

They found a blanket apiece for the horses and strapped them on, so they'd cool down gradually after their journey.

Fighting his growing unease, for he couldn't imagine Grace leaving without making sure the donkey had access to feed and water, Dominic gave an extra tug to the blanket straps. 'I'm going to bang on the door. If nobody answers I'll enter the house.'

'The occupants might still be asleep.'

'And they might not be . . . they might be waiting for us.'

After five minutes of pounding, and with Alex at his heels they tried the front door, but to no avail. The kitchen door was unlocked, however, allowing them access. The kitchen was cold, the ashes dead in the firebox. Plates, pans and dishes were smeared with leftover food that had dried hard.

'Gracie,' he shouted and his voice bounced eerily off the walls.

'You search upstairs and I'll have a look down here, but wait till I find the tinderbox and get a fire going in the kitchen stove. Then we can boil some water and light some candles. It won't be long before there's enough daylight to see. The girl might be ill, or perhaps she has fallen. Don't worry, Dom, if she's anywhere in this house we'll find her.'

'And if she isn't?'

Surely, if Gracie had wanted him she would have waited for him. The house breathed emptiness. Out in the hall the clock had ceased its tick. The air itself was stale, as if it contained the dying breaths of previous occupants, now worn out and useless, and hanging in the corners like dusty ghosts.

Dominic shook himself. He was not looking forward to his interview with the soldier. What on earth had Florence Digby been thinking of with her attempt to manipulate two people? It was natural that both of them would like to inherit the money, but marriage as a clause was unfair, impractical, and probably illegal. It was a folly to expect Gracie to change the nature of a man like Crouch. He was set in his ways, and those ways were decadent from what he'd heard. Grace hadn't lived long enough to experience love yet, and she would live a lonely life if she wed the man.

Alex sighed with satisfaction when the fire caught. He picked up a jug from the table, recoiling when he sniffed the contents. 'Three days old, at least.'

Had the soldiers already been here – taken Gracie away as if it was the brigadier's right? Panic filled him at the thought. Common sense replaced the panic. His appointment with the brigadier was not for a few days.

He went into the hall with Alex in tow and gazed up the length of staircase into the blackness. Something moved.

He could almost feel her presence, her breath a cool fan against his cheek, her voice a whisper of sound, like a faraway cry. The house seemed to pull him into its wretched depths, so he wished he'd never heard of Oakford House, or indeed, had never met the charming Miss Grace Ellis, who had begun to occupy his every damned thought in any way she could.

'*Dominic.*'

'Did you hear that? I should never have left her here alone.'

'It sounded like a cat to me, or the wind in the chimney.' To prove his brother's point a tabby cat came down the stairs and weaved around Dominic's ankles before heading for the kitchen.

'I must be hearing things. What if—'

'You're not thinking with your usual logic, stop anticipating the worse. What's really bothering you, Dom? Do you doubt that her affection towards you is not strong enough to endure? Or do you doubt your own feelings, perhaps.'

Dominic thought about it. Were he to be honest, all the girl had done was indulge in spontaneous flirtation. He had no reason to imagine her affections went deeper than that except . . . his intuition regarding her was too strong to doubt.

'Your first thought sums up the situation. She may have been persuaded to go to the Antipodes with the house servants. Then again, I arranged to meet the brigadier here with James Archibald. If she refuses him he might try and persuade her to take part in a proxy marriage for a small recompense. She's such a delightful scrap of a woman, and I would hate for her to be forced into an unsuitable alliance. She grew up without a mother to advise her.'

Alex chuckled. 'Surely you don't picture yourself in the role of parent.'

'Definitely not. My regard for Gracie is much more worldly . . . husband, companion and . . . playmate.'

'Then the sooner we find her and get her back to King's Acres the better. She'll have two females there to advise her. Let's start at the top of the house and work our way down.'

Dominic's frown deepened with each step. Somebody had ransacked the house, but as far as he could see, very little was missing. Was it a ploy to suggest the perpetrators were strangers, perhaps? A mirror had been smashed and he would need to go through the inventory to see what had been stolen. His room was a jumbled mess with blankets and the mattress turned over and slashed, so the stuffing was revealed.

'I imagine the housekeeper and her husband would have done this, probably out of spite. They would have been looking for cash, which is well hidden.'

He hesitated at the door of the room she'd occupied on the opposite side of the corridor. The lock was splintered. 'Gracie,' he said against the door panel.

'Allow me.' Alex turned the handle and pushed the door open.

The first thing he saw was a pillow smeared with dried blood.

'Easy, Dom, it's not much blood, and there's very little on the floor, just a few drops.'

Dominic's breath came in a relieved rush; he was thankful for his brother's caution. The scent of her was all around him, rose-water and the lavender sprigs she placed in her wardrobe and dressing table drawers to keep the moths at bay. 'She isn't in here.'

'Did you expect her to be?'

Dominic shrugged. 'I was hoping.'

'Did you imagine you might stumble over her lifeless body?'

'It crossed my mind.'

'Poor Dom, you are in a pother.' Alex took a step closer to the bed, 'What's that scribble on the wall?'

'Numbers. She's counted numbers in increments of hundreds. She would have done that trying to keep her mind active. See how they tail off and become muddled when she tired.' Dominic moved closer and gazed at it, his mind ticking over, and then he took a closer look and smiled.

'That's a smug smile you're wearing, brother.'

'Damn me, if it isn't an attempt to calculate the conversion of a troy ounce into avoirdupois.'

Alex raised an eyebrow. 'It would be easier to climb a greasy pole at the local fair.'

'Hmmm . . . yes, I suppose it would be for a clod like you.'

'What's that loop bit in the middle?'

Dominic ran his finger around the symbol ∞. It's the sign for infinity. Two circles joined, whichever way you looked at it is the number eight. Not only was she telling him she had been there but that she cared for him.

There was a shoe on the bed, impossibly small and dainty. Dominic picked it up and brushed his fingertip over it before setting it back on the bed. He gazed around for its partner as he pushed Grace's belongings into a travel bag thinking how sad it was that she had so little. A skirt, a straw bonnet and shawl. Her Sunday gown was of sensible dark blue and worn with a white apron to protect the skirt. For the sake of modesty, and perhaps warmth, she otherwise wore a fichu. He recalled a sensible skirt of brown checks she wore with a honey-coloured velvet bodice that matched her eyes. She must be wearing that now.

'Come on, this isn't finding the lady. What are you looking for, Dom?'

'Her other shoe.'

'I imagine she must be wearing it.'

He placed the travel bag in the wardrobe. He could collect it tomorrow.

It was light enough to see everything clearly now, including the muddied patch in the hall where the scuffed footsteps indicated a struggle had taken place. Alex bent, and picking up a silver spoon he set it on the hallstand. 'There were at least two people, possibly three. Two women and one man,' he said.

An empty wine bottle lay on its side with two glasses. A closer look of the drawing room revealed a patch of dried blood. It had soaked into the rug.

'It looks as though she fell here and hit her head. Look, there's blood on the piano stool. Your thoughts?'

Fearing the worst, Dominic followed the dried droplets across the hall to the bottom of the stair. 'Somebody's taken her.'

'It certainly looks like it. She was subjected to some rough handling, then dragged across the hall and up the stairs into her room.'

'Where she was locked in and left to die.'

'Forget the melodrama, Dom. You need to keep a clear head. I doubt if the person who carried this out intended to kill her, since they had no reason to. They did it to create enough time to ransack the house without her interference. I think she probably broke that hatpin in the lock, trying to get out.'

'I suspect it was the Curtis couple. Perhaps Jessie Curtis came back and released her. But what happened then? The door to her room was unlocked, and besides, she wouldn't have left this mess. Even if she had, she wouldn't have allowed the fire in the kitchen to go out . . . and those ashes didn't have a spark of warmth in them.'

'Which brings me to my next theory. There was a third person involved. Perhaps someone with legitimate business at the house heard her cry for help, and freed her. Can you think of anyone she may have gone to for assistance?'

'James Archibald perhaps, though she dislikes him. He'll be here tomorrow, so we can question him then if we need to . . . or Reverend Hallam . . . though unlikely. Another point. Had Gracie been able she would have used the donkey cart rather than walk away, leaving the creature in its straps to fend for itself.'

'We haven't looked in the cellar yet.'

'There's no key.'

The door swung open when Alex turned the handle. 'Nevertheless, the door is open.'

'I can hear the kettle rattling on the stove. We'll have some tea and then search the cellar and the outbuildings.'

The kitchen was now nicely warmed and more welcoming as a result. The tabby cat came out of the larder, legs astride a smoked kipper it was dragging by its tail. The tabby's ears were flattened and his eyes slitted with the pleasure of his kill, and though it came from the larder shelf the smelly aroma of smoked fish acted as an incentive, like a donkey following a carrot dangled under his nose.

Alex remarked, latching the larder door as the cat disappeared under the table with its prey, 'He's an enterprising creature, I hope he hasn't eaten our dinner, as well.'

So Grace had managed to attract a tabby cat. Dominic gazed at the creature's tail. 'How long is that cat's tail, would you say?'

He became the recipient of a pitying look. 'About ten inches, why the devil would you want to know that, are you growing one for yourself?'

Dominic shrugged.

The cellar was empty except for a few bottles of wine and a couple more of brandy. A strong, fruity smell permeated the air and there was a crunch of broken glass underfoot. A window, too small to admit the passage of an adult, allowed a little light in.

Dominic's unease increased. Someone had robbed the cellar, most likely the Curtis couple. But they'd need to have someone to buy it – an accomplice. The previously employed, Pawley, perhaps? Then there was the attorney, James Archibald. Dominic had formed an impression he would accept a payment to turn his cheek the other way, and to enhance his retirement pension. There would have been a middleman – an agent – someone who knew the old lady well enough to be trusted. The others would have hung from Lady Florence like leeches, sucking her dry. No wonder she'd taken a liking to Gracie.

He'd listed the most obvious when another name presented itself. A name crawled into his head, one immediately discarded. But he rarely ignored intuition and when the name returned he thought, albeit cautiously – surely not!

He'd be stupid to ignore any connections hereabouts, however slight. Confidence grew in him and the smile he gave was more of a grimace. He didn't like dealing with the unknown, preferring solid facts. Then he remembered that he and Alex had been good trackers when they'd been children, and there was no reason why they shouldn't still be.

Yes . . . he wouldn't be hard to find.

Eleven

Grace opened her eyes to discover she was lying on an unfamiliar bed, in a dimly lit room. There was a man in a chair, shirt-sleeved and waistcoated, a lantern burning on the table beside him.

'Dominic,' she said, her voice husky from lack of water.

When he rose she saw she was mistaken. Where Dominic's face was finely boned and his eyes grey and astute, this man's face was rounded and his eyes were pools of darkness. He was large too, bulkier than Dominic whose elegant stance and graceful walk reminded her of a cat.

When the man cleared his throat she jumped.

Her glance fixed on the jug and cup on the table next to him and she began to tremble with the terrible thirst raging inside her.

Yet she shrank against the wall when he approached with the cup, dragging behind her a feather soft tangle of quilt. She used it to cover her chest, for all she wore was her chemise.

'You needn't be afrighted girl, I won't hurt you,' he said and he held out the cup.

In her eagerness to relieve her thirst she almost snatched it from his hands, and she gulped it down so fast that half the liquid spilled down her front and the rest attacked her windpipe. When she began to choke he handed her a cloth, and taking the cup from her hands he refilled it.

'This time sip it nice and slow, lest you be sick all over me. You've got to get some liquid into that body of yours. It's not much use going to the effort of pouring it in if you're going to cough it all up again. If you can't do it by yourself I'll help you, it's a while since I had a pretty young wench in my arms.'

His voice was a gruff rumble. The chuckle he gave reassured her, but she shrank away from him again and the fog in her brain slowly cleared. 'You're Rafferty Jones.'

'Could be I am, at that.'

'You were a friend of Lady Florence. I don't think I've heard you speak before.'

'I'm not much of a talking man. Speech be a waste of air lessen you've got something to say, like a parson spouting the Lord's will on Sunday.'

'What were you doing at Oakford House?'

'Passing by. I was singing a song to the lord after a jug or two of wholesome scrumpy when I heard a heavenly voice and I thought it was the ghost of Lady Florence herself. Best to leave her wailing in her grave, I thought to mesself. Then I remembered you were there alone, and the front door was hanging open on its hinges, and Daisy was kicking up a ruckus, inviting all and sundry to go in and out, and the house was dark. Happen you might have fallen down the stairs, or been murdered in your bed, or maybe a felon passing by had found you so tasty he carried you off.'

Her face heated. 'A smuggler like you, Rafferty Jones.'

He shrugged. 'That's a fact, and though everybody knows it, nobody says it and I ain't inclined towards beating up young ladies for my pleasure. And neither do I cast my business abroad for all and sundry to know.' Deftly he changed the subject. 'You look as though a flock of sheep have trampled all over you.'

She touched her bruised face. It was tender and she couldn't stop herself from voicing a little vanity. 'Do I look terrible?'

'Reckon you do look frightening, at that, Missy Ellis, and I wouldn't want to run into you on a dark night. 'Sides, I'm going to be wed in a week or so, all legal in the church with a reverend and all. My woman has inherited an inn over Mudeford way. I'll be a respectable businessman then and will have a best hat to wear to church on Sunday.' His face fell. 'She'll give me a right earful when she hears about this. By thunder she can be sour if she don't get her own way. Still, my last wife was a nag, so I'll soon get used to it.'

Grace smiled at the thought of him being respectable. Mudeford was well named, and was used as a drop-off point for smugglers, and was once the domain of overseas traders. She took a couple of sips of water and gazed at him over the cup. Every sip trickled through her body like a stream of rain on a dry riverbed. She felt stronger, and her fear abated. 'You have no intention of hurting me, do you?'

'It sounds as though Lady Florence filled your head with her tales. What she didn't tell you was the truth.'

'Which is?'

'She were in the thick of it, as were several people of her acquaintance in these parts, including the Curtis couple. We used her cellar as a clearing house.'

Grace gasped. 'That's nonsense. I would have known if she'd been smuggling. Besides, she couldn't walk unaided.'

'She didn't have to walk. All she had to do was turn a blind eye to it and keep her mouth closed. The money she earned helped support the orphanage.'

Still Grace felt she should defend her late employer. 'She wouldn't have been dishonest without a good cause. The orphanage was her favourite charity.'

Remembering the condition in Lady Florence's will, with regard to her own future she shrugged. 'I admit she had some peculiar notions sometimes.'

A grin spread across Rafferty's face. 'That she did . . . and she got her peculiar notions free of charge from the bottom of a brandy bottle.'

Aware of the direction his eyes had taken she realized her covering had slipped. She dragged it up and folded her arms over her chest. 'What do you intend to do with me?'

'That depends how well you behave. A sweet little lady like you would bring a small fortune if sold into slavery.'

Her heart began to beat against her ribs. 'Mr LéSayres might have something to say to that.'

'Reckon it wouldn't do him any good. It strikes me he should have taken better care of you in the first place.'

The door opened and a woman entered, tying a spotless white apron round her waist. Her presence eased the tension in the room. 'I heard voices. Has the girl regained her senses, Raff? I told you to let me know when she did.'

'What there is of them, and she's being too pert by far, especially for one who is enjoying the hospitality and protection of my home. I'm getting some water into her.'

The woman snorted. 'Hospitality, is it? It looks as though you're trying to drown her since more has gone down her front than down her throat.' The woman moved closer and gazed at her face. Her voice softened. 'There's a mess you're in, young lady. I'm Jancy, Raff's sister for my sins. Not that he's anything to brag about. In fact he's more brag than bite.'

Raff grinned. 'I've never heard no complaints before.'

'Who did this to you? No, don't tell me . . . it was that Curtis creature I'll be bound. He can be a vicious sod when he doesn't get his own way.'

The smuggler nodded. 'They were after the girl's legacy, no doubt, and anything else they could lay hands. Once they'd used up the cash, you wouldn't have seen their backsides for dust. Then there's the question of the strongbox, and its whereabouts. It's obvious the Curtis couple turned the place upside-down looking for it.'

Rafferty Jones had a lazy way with him, and he turned, casual and friendly, though his eyes were as sharp as flint. 'You don't happen to know where Mr LéSayres hid it, I suppose?'

It was a straightforward question that deserved a truthful answer. 'No, and if I did know I wouldn't tell you. It's not your business.'

When he took a step towards her, Grace grabbed up the jug and lifted it over her head. It was heavier than she'd expected and she couldn't support it. It tipped, and the remaining water poured down her back. Its coldness made her gasp, yet soothed the fiery pain burning in her back. 'I'll thump you over the head with this if you come any closer.'

Raff gave a booming laughed as he plucked the jug from her hands. 'I was just going to refill your cup. It looks like you're making a good job of braining yourself. You're a fierce little minx when your temper rises, like a cornered stoat. Your man will need a strong hand to deal with you.'

The only man she could think of in that way came wrapped in the skin of Dominic LéSayres and her gaze became fierce. 'He'd better not place a hand in anger on me else he'll get a smack around the ear for his trouble . . . besides, I haven't got a man.'

Jancy stepped in. 'Rafferty Jones, stop your teasing. Now, we need some privacy so I can give the girl a wash, dress her and make her more comfortable. After that, if nobody has come for her we're going to take her back to Oakford House until, mayhap, her imaginary gentleman awaits.'

An almost irresistible urge to giggle raced through Grace as she pictured herself posed in a red silk gown on a staircase. *Everyone rise to your feet for Mr LéSayres and Miss Nobody.* Did she know anybody called *nobody*?

Her gentleman? It had a nice sound to it. What if Dominic never came back to Oakford House? Perhaps he'd simply abandoned her. Grace shuddered, for the last thing she wanted was to be in that house alone. 'No! I don't want to stay at Oakford House by myself. Please don't send me back there.'

When her voice caught in her throat she was drawn into the woman's arms. 'There there, I'll keep you company until someone comes. You're safe now, and soon you'll feel much better. There's not much I can do about the bruises and swelling but you know better than I that they'll fade in time . . . some witch hazel to sooth the pain a little perhaps. Raff, you fetch me a bowl of warm water, and a jug beside, and quick smart.'

Sponges, soap – the lavender-scented one that Grace had made for Lady Florence – and towels, were quickly assembled. She pondered on the soap. It was an odd object for Rafferty to steal on his infrequent visits to Oakford House.

Raff's body filled the door frame. 'What shall I do now, Jancy?'

'You wouldn't do it if I told you! To start with you can stop flapping in the doorway like a moth in a spider's web. You can fetch that bodice and gown hanging on the drying rack. It belongs to the young lady and it should be warm and dry by now. Then you can make yourself useful by finding something better to do than hang around us. Go and chop some logs for the fire.'

Remembering her manners, and to give Rafferty Jones his due, Grace said, 'Thank you for your help, Mr Jones.'

His grin spread from one ear to the next and he disappeared.

A few minutes later an arm came through the door with clothing dangling from a hooked finger.

Grace winced as Jancy gently washed her hair and body and she shivered when the woman applied the soothing witch hazel. She put out a small feeler. 'The soap has a lovely fragrance.'

'Lady Florence sent it back with Raff. He said it was a gift for my birthday. I only use it on special occasions.'

'Is this a special occasion then? I was paid to be a companion to Lady Florence, you know. I wasn't a guest.'

'It's said you're a proper lady down on her luck. Besides, it's a pleasure to have another woman to talk to. It was a shame you were left destitute. People speak highly of you. Just the other day I overheard a woman in the marketplace say, "Miss Ellis is an angel".'

When the weight of an imaginary halo landed on her head Grace shucked it off. Goodness . . . she hadn't realized Lady Florence had such a careless tongue. It seemed as though everybody knew her business, and more beside. An angel, was she? Grace grinned.

Jancy sounded angry when next she spoke. 'My brother wouldn't have done this to you, though people will blame him when the dandy folk find out. Them in charge can get mighty puffed up with their own importance sometimes, and won't listen to nobody excepting themselves. That's why Raff brought you to me, so your reputation doesn't suffer.'

A noble cause indeed, Grace thought with a painful grin. 'That was kind of him. They'll listen to me when I tell them it was Brian Curtis who injured me.' She imagined Dominic's expression when he set eyes on her damaged face. Horrified because he'd left her alone, he would feel responsible. But he couldn't have predicted that Brian Curtis would have done this to her. She was sure that by now there would be no evidence of smuggled brandy around. Kegs would have been bottled, labelled and receipted, and safely stored in the cellars of the wine merchant, Jones and Son, plus other outlets.

'I was locked in my room and had nothing to eat or drink. Now I've regained my senses I can remember a few things, like Mr Jones carrying me back here to get some help from you. I'll tell them your brother saved my life.'

'It would be no lie, would it? The colour of the bruises will be witness to it. They be at least three days old.'

When Grace was dressed, Jancy sat her in front of the fire and gently began to brush the damp tangles from her hair. There was a muffled, regular thudding sound.

Thud! Thud! Thud! A pause. *Thud! Thud!*

It was the axe splitting logs. She began to count each blow and the pattern emerged in its own rhythm. It amused Grace that a big, bluff man like Rafferty Jones would meekly take orders from his sister.

Jancy hummed to herself as she tidied up the toiletries. The fire cracked and snapped and the walls gradually receded into a mist. For the first time in a while Grace felt safe as she drifted peacefully amongst her thoughts.

Jancy intruded. 'Let me get you to bed so you can rest properly, I don't want you to slide from the chair.'

Clinging to Jancy she travelled a short distance on wobbling legs and sank on to the warm feather bed. The quilt was laid over her.

'That's pretty.'

'I helped my mother make it,' Jancy said, but from a distance. The woman began to sing in a low melodious voice.

'You have a deft touch with a hairbrush, and a soothing voice.'

'Thank you, miss. I used to work as a lady's maid once, and when Raff weds next month I'll take to the road and I'll put myself up at one of them hiring fares. Raff's woman has already said she doesn't want me living with them.'

'Why not?'

'We dislike each other and every time we meet we spit at each other, like a couple of cats.'

Grace hid a wide yawn inside her palm. 'I'm so tired.'

'Then sleep, my dear, and worry no more. Jancy will look after you. Best you doze a while, Miss Ellis, because it's going to be a busy day with lots of umming-and-arring going on while the men get their deliberations sorted into proper order. I'm going to cook breakfast now and I'll keep it warm until you're ready to eat it.'

'Thank you.'

'I reckon we've figured out the best plan. Raff will tell the truth of what happened, and I will give my account. I may embroider it a little, but from what I hear, LéSayres is a thinking man and a fair one in his dealings. Happen he will recognize the truth in what we say, and believe it.'

'I think very highly of him,' Grace murmured, wondering how high she should go. Very highly was not as highly as extremely highly but it sounded more approachable. Her feelings towards him were warmer than admiration; more like lust. It was all of them rolled into one. It was blissful . . . like love. A heartfelt sigh escaped her. It was love.

'From what Raff tells me Mr LéSayres seems to feel the same towards you.'

'Has Raff been watching us then?'

'Nay, Miss, 'tis gossip that was told to him by Jessie Curtis, the sly minx that she is. Her face says one thing and her tongue turns it into lies.'

'Mr LéSayres is not in the position to offer me anything except . . .' Grace shrugged. 'Perhaps he will hate me now my face is ruined, and not pursue me with such ardour. He makes me feel as though I should respond and I think of him constantly . . . crave his attention.'

'Aye . . . love is a powerful feeling indeed.'

'I didn't say I loved him but he unearths such cravings in me that some must surely be indecent.' A couple of those impure cravings escaped from her mind and strummed her body like fingers playing a melody on the strings of a harp. She squeezed her thighs together and tried not to squirm.

Jancy grinned. 'The lord created man and he created woman . . . and he created them different so they fit together cosy and loving, like. There's no shame in that need for closeness with each other.'

'What if the man already has a family?'

'Then the touch of a lover can create a memory to keep you warm on a cold winter's night. Go to sleep now lest you start to think unpleasant thoughts and wake yourself up.'

An unpleasant thought immediately insinuated into her mind – Brigadier Maximilian Crouch! Would he want her if her virtue was no longer intact?

Yes, for the legacy if nothing else . . . but how would he know she wasn't tidy?

She could tell him on their wedding night, though he would probably notice for himself. It would be a delicious revenge on Lady Florence.

He's a soldier. He has a bad reputation and . . . he might hurt you!

All the kings horses and all the king's men, couldn't put Gracie Ellis together again. Chop! Chop! Chop! she thought, and fear crept into her heart again. She hoped Dominic would come for her soon.

The room darkened when the woman pulled a curtain over a grey dawn intruding through the window.

'Try and sleep, but call me if you need anything, it will be no trouble,' Jancy said, before leaving Grace with her own thoughts.

Despite the regular thudding and the domestic noises going on around her, Grace drifted off into sleep.

Twelve

Rafferty Jones was made aware he had company when Dominic touched the barrel of his pistol against the man's temple and suggested, 'It would be in your best interest to drop that axe, Mr Jones.'

'Reckon it might be, at that.'

The man's muscles twitched with the effort of not making a sudden or rash move and he slowly lowered the axe to the chopping block and took a couple of steps back. Dominic picked it up and threw it into the undergrowth.

'Now you may speak,' Dominic said.

'I'm full of admiration for a man who can creep up on me unobserved. What took you so long, Mr LéSayres?'

The man's jibe was ignored. 'Where is Miss Ellis?'

Rafferty jerked his thumb towards a window in the cottage. 'In there, resting. She'll be asleep by now. The lass has had a hard time of it.'

'Take me to her.'

'As to that you'll have to ask my sister, Jancy. Right now she's cooking breakfast. Happen she might invite you to stay if she's in the right mood and you mind your manners. Then again, she might chase you round the kitchen table with a carving knife.' Rafferty Jones was completely relaxed now. 'If you're not going to use that gun I would suggest you kindly point the damned thing elsewhere.'

'I haven't decided that yet, it depends on the answers I get.'

'If you'd intended to shoot me you would have done it first up. In answer to your unspoken question, the young lady you're seeking had been locked in her room at Oakford House for three days and four nights, and without sustenance of any kind . . . not even water. I found her early this morning and brought her here to my sister, to be cared for.'

Dominic engaged the man's eyes. They were black and unreadable. 'Is Miss Ellis injured?'

'Some. Her face is badly bruised, and she was rambling a little the last time I set eyes on her. As to the rest of her you will have to ask my sister, who soothed her mind and bathed her body and got some water inside her before she lost her wits altogether . . . and damned ungrateful the girl was for my help. You've got a handful there.'

There was something Dominic liked about this man, even though his honesty was highly questionable. 'What were you doing at Oakford House?'

'Passing by . . . and I noticed the door was open.'

'You must have extremely good eyesight since you can only see the roof from the road.'

'Fancy that. I'll have to remember it the next time I go there. My sight is keener than most and I must have mistaken the attic window for the front door. Luckily for the young lady, I'd say.'

'Is there anything else I should know?'

'Nothing that would be of great interest, I reckon. The place was in a frantic mess as if a great wind had made its way inside and whirled it all about. Some bits and pieces might have strayed.'

'But not into your pockets.'

'I'm as honest as the next man in these parts, but no . . . not into my pockets. I wanted to pay for the donkey and cart. Lady Florence was a friend of mine and she doted on that young woman. I was sorely troubled by the state she was in.'

'Would you say the Curtis couple were involved in this crime of violence against Miss Ellis?'

'I can't rightly say, not for love nor money, since I never witnessed the deed being done. The girl will be able to tell you more. Or you could track the couple down, it shouldn't be too hard for I've heard that the *Bonnie Kathleen*, has sprung a leak and it's moored at one of the Poole shipyards.'

Dominic raised an eyebrow. '*Bonnie Kathleen*?'

'The ship the Curtis couple are to sail on?'

'And Brigadier Crouch's regiment, I believe.'

'Where did you get that information from?'

'It's common knowledge, since the soldiers are creating a ruckus all over the place.

So fortune had intervened with an opportunity to have the villains sequestered for a short time. Dominic smiled. 'Thank you for that small piece of information, it will give me time in which to breathe.'

'I reckon the Curtis couple will be running out of money soon and looking for an easy way to earn enough to buy more provisions for the journey.

Dominic had already considered that. The voyage to Australia took several weeks, and reprovisioning didn't come cheaply.

The man had stated his position loud and clear and Dominic's memory was jogged. 'We met at Lady Florence's funeral, did we not?'

'Reckon we might of, at that. You couldn't take your eyes off Miss Ellis for most of the time.'

'Neither could most of the men there. Can you blame me when she's such a nesh little piece.' Trying not to laugh Dominic held out his hand. After a moment Rafferty took it. 'You can tell yon lanky fellow hidden behind the tree to come out now. As silent as sewer rats, the pair of you.'

'The lanky fellow is my brother, Earl LéSayres. Should we take the latter part of your sentence as a compliment or an insult?'

'As you wish.'

There was a click and Alex stepped out from behind the tree, a wry smile on his face. One strike buried the axe blade in the chopping block with the ease of a knife through butter.

His gun joined Dominic's. 'Do take it as a compliment, Dom, and then we won't have to go through all this taradiddle again.' He took in a deep breath and then cast around like a hunting dog. 'Is that breakfast I smell?'

A woman's face appeared at the partially open window. 'Who wants to know?'

Dominic introduced them. 'This is my brother, Lord LéSayres.'

'Welcome to my home, my Lord, a welcome is also extended to yourself, Mr LéSayres. Do come in. I'll find you a place at my table.'

'Thank you, Miss Jones. Regarding Miss Ellis . . . how is she?' Dominic asked, worry uppermost in his voice. 'May I see her?'

'Would you deprive an invalid of a healing sleep, sir? Curb your impatience and allow her to wake naturally, it will be soon enough.'

'Will she recover?'

'Yes . . . given time, if she is looked after and her remaining strength doesn't abandon her. When she wakes I'm going to feed her a small bowl of chicken broth. It will be the first food inside her since four days hence, and it should warm her insides and stimulate her appetite. Take my word, Mr LéSayres, Miss Ellis is in no danger now but she will feel all the better for a little tender care.'

And Dominic was prepared to ensure she was cosseted to within an inch of her life. Already he had an ear cocked for the faintest of human sounds coming from behind the door to the adjoining room.

They feasted on thick slices of fried bread, eggs, pork sausages and rashers of crispy fried bacon dipped in hot tomato chutney.

Replete, Dominic leaned back in his chair. 'That's the best breakfast I've ever had.'

'Likewise, but it's a shame to waste that,' and Alex expertly speared a stray sausage left on Dominic's plate.

A mug of tea washed it down.

Then a tired, scared little voice hesitantly called out Jancy's name and Dominic shot to his feet. The woman was quicker and headed for the room Grace occupied, a bowl of broth in her hands.

Dominic half-stood to catch a glimpse of her and Grace smiled at him through the open door. She looked as though she'd been used as a punching bag!

Jancy came between them. 'Give us a few moments, I want to get some of this broth into her, and she will want to tidy her hair before she receives visitors. I'll call you. Mind you don't bang your head on the beam when you come inside.'

When Dominic finally gained admittance Alex dogged his heels. They found Jancy seated on a chair near the window and Grace propped up against the pillows. The broth was on the table, untouched.

Up close, Grace's face was in a pitiful state and the men gazed at each other, appalled that a woman so young could absorb such punishment.

Lifting her hands to her face she covered the bruises with her palms. 'Dominic, you've come, but don't look at me,' she mumbled through swollen lips.

'Did you think I wouldn't look for you?' He took her hands in his and drew them to his mouth, kissing each one. 'This is my elder brother, Lord Alexander, Earl LéSayres.'

The similarity between the brothers was marked, except the earl had blue eyes. The presence of one LéSayres man was powerful, two, rather intimidating.

For once she forgot to complain about Dominic's kisses, just said, 'I don't want anyone to see me like this.'

'My brother is here to be introduced. When you've recovered enough to travel he will escort you to his home, where you can be properly cared for.'

Grace gazed at the familiar-looking stranger. How very like Dominic he was. 'You are very kind, my Lord, but I don't want to be a problem to anyone. Won't your wife object?'

'The countess suggested the arrangement in the first place. We've discussed the situation of your employment and accommodation with my brother a few days ago, and have already made plans that should carry you over until you can be settled in your own accommodation. Vivienne is quite looking forward to your visit . . . though we didn't expect someone quite so sorely battered when we formulated our plans. Rest assured, you'll be welcomed in my home.'

Dominic scolded, 'Why haven't you eaten that broth?'

'My face hurts and I can't chew it.'

'Jancy made broth so you don't have to chew anything, but just swallow it. Let's see what we can do if I help you.'

'I don't want to eat.'

'Of course you do. Look how thin you're becoming. You will disappear altogether if we're not careful, and then what will I do without a clerk?'

The earl's smile was one of great charm. 'You'd better do as you're told because my brother is as stubborn as they come.'

Dominic tucked a napkin under her chin, scooped out a

spoonful of broth from the bowl and held it to her mouth, saying with great menace that drew a painful laugh from her, '*Eat it.*' When she swallowed he offered her another spoonful.

He melted her mutinous look with a smile. 'There, that wasn't too bad. Jancy's gone to the trouble to make this and the least you can do is eat it. Another one . . . come on, Gracie girl, you know I'm going to win.' Another spoonful followed another, then another. Somewhere along the way her appetite returned.

'Sorry to be such . . . trouble.'

He sighed. 'There, the bowl is nearly empty now . . . just a spoonful or two left. There's no need to apologize to me. I said I'd come back, but I was late and it was unforgiveable of me.' A lump gathered in his throat. 'Look at the state you've managed to get yourself into without me here to look after you. Did Brian Curtis do this to you?'

The shine disappeared from her eyes and she nodded. 'He wanted to know where the strongbox was and wouldn't believe I didn't know.' As she gazed at him through wounded amber eyes, anger burned in him. She should be blaming him not regarding him with such affection.

She opened her mouth for the remaining spoonful.

Afterwards he took the bowl to Jancy. 'I'd appreciate a few moments alone with Miss Ellis. I'll only keep you a moment or two. Alex, you can stay.'

When the woman had left the room he sat on the edge of the bed and gently took Gracie into his arms.

Alex turned his back and wandered to the window, there to gaze through the ivy. It allowed Dominic a thin veneer of privacy.

Grace rested in Dominic's arms, her head against his shoulder. Her hair smelled deliciously of lavender. It was in its natural state, except it was gathered into a green ribbon tied in a bow, to stop it falling into her eyes. Yet it tumbled over her shoulders and was tossed through with fiery glints.

'Tell me what happened, Gracie.'

Her tale matched that of Rafferty Jones. 'Mr Jones frightened me at first with his banter, and I fainted. He must have realized I was ill and wrapped me in a blanket and brought me here to his sister. I would have died without his intervention.'

'That's all we need to know,' he said when she began to tremble, and he nodded to Alex.

The earl excused himself, cursing when he banged his head on the beam. Gracie gave a quiet chuckle wrapped in a sob and said, 'Mind the beam.'

Neither spoke or moved, they just held each other. After a while she relaxed against his shoulder and her breathing became even and regular. She'd fallen asleep again . . . more of an escape after the horror she'd endured than of tiredness, Dominic thought. He lowered her carefully back on to the pillows and pulled the quilt up to her chin.

There was a knock at the door and Jancy returned. Obviously she wasn't going to allow her charge to be left in the company of two men for long. He placed a kiss on the very tip of Gracie's nose, which seemed to be the only part of her that remained undamaged.

Jancy regarded him with approval and whispered, 'It wouldn't be wise to move her yet. The attack would have shocked her and she'll have periods of melancholy when she will sleep, or weep. She has extensive bruising on her body.'

Fury flashed through him. How could any man treat a woman so badly? 'I'll kill him when I catch up with him.'

'Killing him will make things harder, for Miss Ellis would have that on her conscience as well. She would also lose the respect she feels towards you. She has a good heart and appears to be the type of woman who would rather forgive and forget.'

The woman was right. Gracie might display flashes of temper but she wasn't vindictive. 'I promised her a maid and you seem to me to be a sensible woman. Would you be interested in taking on the position in a temporary capacity? Then I will leave it to Miss Ellis to decide if it is to become permanent. I paid scant attention to her reputation when I made arrangements for the Oakford House staff, and I need a woman who can look after her.'

Jancy didn't even stop to consider it, just nodded. 'I've been looking for a position. Your lady won't be well enough to move for a day or two. Raff shouldn't have brought her here . . . he should have taken me to her.'

'Your brother did his best, considering.'

'Considering what?'

'That he didn't want to be caught inside Oakford House in case he was accused of ransacking it, or worse, was accused of being the perpetrator of injury to Miss Ellis. He said he'd heard there were soldiers passing through the district, creating trouble at some of the inns. He thought it would be wise for both him and Miss Ellis to avoid them.'

'Some would call it a likely tale, sir.'

'It's exactly that, since I'm expecting Brigadier Crouch in a few days. It would have been easy to come to the wrong conclusion under such circumstances. My brother would have soon smoked out a lie, though. So yes, we do believe Mr Jones' tale to be the truth. I'm grateful for his intervention and for yours. Your brother will be properly compensated, and so will you.'

Relief filled the woman's face. 'Thank you, sir.'

'Miss Ellis is sleeping now. I've been considering a plan for her welfare and will need any power of persuasion you can put to good use. I will put my plan before you all in case you have any valid suggestions.'

'Miss Ellis seems to be strong willed.'

Dominic grinned and held up a hand. 'No doubt Miss Ellis will see the benefit in my plan and will do as she's told.'

'Yes sir, there's no doubt at all that she'll appreciate your plan,' she said, and Dominic didn't miss the irony in her voice.

Thirteen

Grace woke from sleep with her stomach aching from hunger, her mouth dry and her lips cracked through lack of moisture. Although clear of mind, her body felt stale. She groaned when she moved, testing each aching muscle before she put it to use. Crawling out of a cosily quilted nest she stepped carefully to the washstand, there to scoop water from the washing bowl and splash it over her face. She shivered as the sudden change in temperature brought her to life.

The room she was in was familiar. It resembled every cottage she'd ever been in, with its low beams and its blackened stains over the mantelpiece. In the corner a screen offered privacy for the comfort of the occupant.

Her clothing hung over the chair, washed and ironed, the hose displaying several darns where once there had been holes. One of Lady Florence's discarded winter shawls was folded on the seat. There was only one shoe.

She remembered a woman called Jancy and called out her name.

The woman bustled in, wreathed in smiles. 'You look much improved, Miss Ellis. Your young man has appointed me to the position of lady's maid for the time being. Mr LéSayres says the final decision will be yours. Would you like to dress?'

Grace didn't bother to correct her. If Dominic had hired Jancy to look after her and the woman didn't mind moving to Poole, Grace was not going to throw his generosity in his face, nor question his judgement. 'Where are we, Jancy . . . do you know?'

'In my brother's cottage.'

She remembered Rafferty Jones. 'Ah yes. He gave me a fright.'

'The fool didn't realize how ill you were. When you passed out, he ran all the way here, carrying you in his arms. Fair worn out with running, he was, when he could have used the donkey cart. Now he's explained his actions to Mr LéSayres who says there's no fault in either his intentions or his actions, and Raff feels like a right lump for acting so daft.'

'I'm happy that he did and must thank him for saving my life . . . for there's no doubt that he did. I thought I saw Mr LéSayres earlier. Is he still here?'

Jancy said, 'He was here early this morning. He came to check on your condition and see how you fared. Now he's gone back to Oakford House to clean up the mess and collect your belongings.'

Disappointment filled her at missing him.

'He shouldn't be too long. In the meantime I'm going to give you a nice relaxing bath and see to those bruises.'

'I seem to have lost a shoe.'

'Aye, you have, but no doubt Mr LéSayres will find it. He seems to have a keen eye for detail.'

Ten minutes later Grace folded herself into a metal tub, her

chin almost resting on her knees. Jancy wedged a chair under the
door handle and set to work. Soon Grace's skin began to tingle
under the gentle massage of a fragrant soapy sponge, while Jancy
provided her with a detailed description of the injuries she couldn't
see with some relish. 'That scar on your shoulder is the worse
one. I reckon he used a poker. Luckily, he missed your noggin.'

Grace wasn't sure he *had* missed her head, for it was beginning
to ache, probably due to Jancy's chatter.

Jancy ended with, ''Tis only a little tub and you're only a small
young lady, but I reckon you'll have to stand while we rinse you
off, miss.' You can hold on to the back of the chair for support
while I do that . . . lest you feel dizzy.'

A small torrent of warm water from a jug disposed of the
foam, and a towel was wrapped snugly round her body. Her hair
was subjected to a vigorous rubbing with another towel.

Grace's childhood nanny had used the same method, and Grace
made a sound in her throat. Jancy rubbed harder and the sound
turned into a rather unmusical warble as she went up and down
the scale.

They both laughed when she finished, and then Jancy reached
for a hairbrush and applied it gently to the tangles. 'There's a
lovely mane of hair you've got. I'm sorry the tub is so small. I
expect you're used to a bigger one.'

Not for the last year or so, though, Grace thought. Her father
had believed in hygiene, and crude bathing facilities were
installed in the laundry room of their home. Even the servants
were obligated to soap themselves down and rinse themselves
off with a dowse of cold water once a week – to fortify the
blood, he'd said. That cold drench was to be feared, for
the shock of it drove the breath from Grace's body in one
shivering gasp. Afterwards she felt quite lively, so there had been
some truth in her father's words.

Jancy was still making her wishes known to fate. 'One day I'd
like to take a proper bath, one I could lay down in with my head
sticking out at one end and my feet at the other. In fact, I'd like
a proper bathing room where the water came out of a spout into
the bath. Raff reckons the water could be piped to the bathing
room. I met a woman who worked over Wiltshire way. She said,
not only did they have a bathing room upstairs but two water

closets as well. It was all on the first floor in a tiled room where guests could take their ease and bathe in comfort, and done all private like, hidden behind a curtain.'

'How could they get the water to flow upstairs in the first place?' Grace asked.

Jancy shrugged and looked doubtful. 'I couldn't quite grasp that bit. The pipes were connected to a stream running under the house, I believe.'

Grace wouldn't mind a similar arrangement, a proper tub – one with a pillow to lay her head on. She would close her eyes and float in the warm water, her body relaxed while she daydreamed.

Grace borrowed one of her father's wisdoms. 'We must just be thankful to be alive. The human body has been provided with a wonderful capacity to heal itself, given time.'

'That it has, but we rarely have the time to practise the healing bit since life as a servant is all get up and go.'

'It is that.'

Grace was beset by guilt. 'I'm sorry I'm being such a nuisance.'

'You're not a nuisance, Miss Ellis. It's lovely having another woman to talk to. Once I've emptied the tub I'll cook you something to eat. A bowl of oats with some stewed apple perhaps, and a glass of milk with a spoonful of honey in to strengthen you. There's nothing better than milk to build up your strength and I'll put a little brandy in it.'

Grace's newly found energy quickly faded after she'd made the effort to bathe and eat. She sat on a chair at the window, comfortably drowsing, while Jancy bustled around her, emptying the bathwater and doing chores. She gazed at the view outside, at the dark green cascade of ivy almost obliterating the small cottage window and began to feel weepy. Damn it, she'd wanted to stay awake, she thought, when her eyelids began to droop. She forced them to stay open while she took in what she could see of her surrounds, in case she needed to run away.

Run away from what? More importantly, to where? Certainly not to Oakford House. She'd never go there again, not by choice and not by herself. It felt as though the house had turned on her.

Rafferty's cottage was on a slope at the edge of a forest. It was small, and of the type of dwelling used by a gamekeeper or woodsman.

A flash of red and a robin alighted on the ivy. Holding her breath she watched it dart amongst the leaves searching for insects. Then she blinked and he saw her and fled, leaving a trill of warning behind him.

The bed beckoned, the quilt caught in a thin beam of pale sunlight that turned it into jewel colours. 'A pretty quilt . . . did you make it?' she asked Jancy and the woman smiled.

'I helped my mother make it, she work for a dressmaker and was allowed to take the scraps home. She taught me how to sew while we worked together making the quilt and I'm taking it with me when we leave. She called it our winter quilt. Raff's woman has got her eye on it. I told her if she wants a quilt she can make her own.'

Yawning, Grace rested her eyes for a moment. The lids felt heavy, as though she had no control over them. She struggled to keep them open.

'Would you help me back to bed please, Jancy? I'm exhausted?' Tears squeezed from under her lids and trickled down her cheeks.

'There, there, I've been talking too much and I've worn you out.'

Grace heard her father's voice. 'Shock affects people in different ways, my dear . . . Listen to your body. Sleep if you need to and I'll look after you.'

'Just a short nap then, Papa,' she murmured, and thus comforted her thoughts drifted into a soothing twilight. Though drifting, she felt her body begin to heal. Like a clock it was one tick at a time. She was aware of things going on around her. Once she thought she saw Dominic's face, and felt his kiss against her cheek, as soft and dreamy as thistledown, and she knew he was watching over her too.

Sometimes the room was light and sometimes gloomy as though clouds sailed over the sun. A horse neighed and her eyes flew open. 'Argus!'

A voice said against her ear, 'No, it's me, Dominic.'

'But I heard you neigh.'

He chuckled. 'That was Argus singing you a song. You're regaining your wit so you must be improving. I thought you'd never wake. How do you feel?'

Her gaze tangled with his, slightly befuddled. His eyes were full of concern. She hated him seeing her so dishevelled. 'I feel wobbly and would probably fall on my face if I tried to stand, but I do feel stronger. I didn't hear you come in, I'm so happy to see you.'

'Then why the tears?'

'I don't know. I think I may be feeling sorry for myself.'

He chuckled as he gently dabbed at the tears with a handkerchief. 'You have reason to. You were asleep when I arrived, and that was half an hour ago. 'You've been asleep on and off for a few days, and I've been worried.'

The thought was almost unbearable. 'You needn't have worried, my papa watched over me and my head feels clearer now.'

A dimple appeared at the corner of his mouth when he smiled, and his voice filled with laughter. 'Your papa, did you say? I didn't see him when I came in. You should ask him to call on mine when he's got the time. Perhaps they could share a jug of ale.'

'Please stop being a tease, I miss him and I thought I heard him whisper just as I went to sleep. He said I needed plenty of sleep to heal, and he'd watch over me. The thought comforted me. It's no different from your mother shooting across the sky on a star.'

Reaching out she touched his face in case he thought she was out to destroy his boyhood dreams.

Her hand was cupped in his and he bore it to his mouth and placed a kiss in her palm before folding her fingers over it. 'Forgive me for being insensitive.'

How could she do otherwise when he was looking into her eyes with such a soft, tender expression? 'You're forgiven.'

'Do you think our parents would approve of us?' he asked.

She chose not to interpret that as a reference to them as a couple. Of course her father wouldn't approve of her embarking on a love affair with Dominic. However, had she been born a son, the result of her journey through the tender years into manhood would have been quite a different affair than her journey into womanhood.

Even though he'd been a doctor, her father had been embarrassed as he'd tackled the subject of her impending womanhood.

He'd warned her of several traps lying in wait for the unattached female, of disease stemming from loose living the most unspeakable, and leading to death. Not that it had stopped him in practice, she'd learned much later. Further enquiries brought an irritable, 'Men are weak, and women are stoic. That's all you need to know.'

He'd suggested she should wed as soon as possible and bear her husband some children because that was why she'd been a born a female . . . besides, that's what her mother would have wanted for her, he'd added as an afterthought, and that had been that.

Dominic cleared his throat to capture her attention, his head slanted to one side as he waited patiently for her answer.

She skirted around his question as best as she was able. 'My father was imprudent in his ways, but I loved him nevertheless. He would have downed several glasses of brandy while deliberating on the subject, and then examined you for disease. After that he'd shoot you for trifling with my affections, I imagine.'

Though looking slightly shocked, Dominic managed a chuckle. 'Examine me for disease? Shoot me! It doesn't sound as though he'd be able to stand up straight enough to take aim.'

'They left us, not the other way around, which is not to say we shouldn't act on the wisdom of the guidance they offered us while they lived. I miss my mother all the more because I never knew her, and because of that I sometimes feel betrayed by her, though I know it wasn't her fault that she died. My father did his best. Tell me about your mother, Dominic?'

He thought for a moment, a slightly guarded look on his face. 'I have always held my mother in the greatest respect. I admit though, that I built her up in my mind. Eugenie became a mother to us and we love her dearly. My mother was a magical figure that occupied my mind. She would have liked you, I think, as will Eugenie. As for my father, he was similar to yours, except he had sons of whom he was proud. Now we have their approval do you feel strong enough to make the journey to Dorset?'

'Will you be travelling with me?'

'I have to finish my business here first. It's taken longer than I expected. My brother will look after you, and Rafferty Jones will accompany you as far as Poole.'

'Do you trust him, Dominic?'

'Not entirely, but my brother will run him through if the need arises.'

The thought startled her. 'Good gracious . . . does your brother often do that to people? He appears to be so pleasant and relaxed.'

A grin slowly traversed his face. 'Don't let his lazy manner fool you. Alex is a crack shot, and good with a sword . . . though I've never known him to use his skills in anger, there is always a first time, especially if those he loves are threatened. As for Raff, he's wary of entering the territory of his rivals. All the same, I'd rather have him for friend than foe, and money will secure his friendship. After all, he does regard himself as a businessman rather than a felon.'

'Dominic, I suspect you don't want me to meet the soldier. Why is that?'

'You suspect right. Brigadier Crouch has a bad reputation and has been described as a rogue. I believe he's fought, and won, several duels.'

'Lady Florence told me he's been mentioned in despatches on several occasions, so he must be brave.'

'Or foolhardy.'

A knock came at the door and Alex said, 'The carriage is here, Dom.'

'We won't be long.'

Grace couldn't help but tease him a little. 'Are you afraid he'll be dashing and handsome and I might fall in love with him?'

Dominic's brow wrinkled. 'From my enquiries I believe the man to be unattractive. It's said his lifestyle is written on his face. Though the fortune eventuating from such a union would tempt some women, I don't believe you're one of them, so no, I don't think you'll succumb to any temptation he might offer.'

'Do you think I'm too scatterbrained to handle a fortune – that I'll go out and spend a legacy on diamonds, rubies, and fans decorated with rare peacock feathers?'

'You're not the type of female who'd squander money on fripperies or to pluck a peacock and cause it to suffer nakedness for the sake of your vanity. You're a sensible young woman, Gracie, but you wouldn't have much say in the matter. Once the brigadier gets his hands on the estate he will likely gamble the fortune away, and in a very short time. You would be left with nothing but debtors queuing up outside the door. We both know what that's like.'

Several moments of contemplative silence ensued while they gazed at each other. The connection between them was broken with a slightly ironic smile from Dominic. 'I think I'd enjoy seeing you dressed in peacock feathers.'

'First you must capture your bird and pluck it.'

'Precisely . . . am I succeeding in that particular endeavour?'

More than he knew. She was reluctant to admit it though, for to do so would be to commit to a course of action she wasn't quite ready to take yet. Love without honour . . . her mind elbowed the notion away. 'I'm very much afraid you might try but I'm reluctant to encourage you to take the first step.'

Dominic placed himself in her shoes. Grace was young, innocent yet surprisingly strong-minded and even worldly at times, and she'd been subjected to a severe beating. According to Jancy, Grace had survived that by a whisker. She had nobody to turn to or confide in.

'You needn't be afraid of me, Gracie, I'll not push you into anything you don't want, though I might try and persuade you to stray from the straight and narrow from time to time.'

While her blush fired up again another line of poetry came to him. He placed it at the back of his mind.

But who would be revealed to whom when the moment of truth arrived?

'The time will come when everything will be just right between us, and we'll know it,' he said, and was gone.

Fourteen

The plan was for the small group to travel during the busiest time of day. Grace and Jancy would occupy the inside of the carriage. The earl and Rafferty Jones would act as outriders, and they, as well as the coachman, would be armed.

The carriage was waiting for them on the road beyond the copse. The vehicle was well maintained, though a little scruffy on the outside. The interior was redolent of polished leather. Dark red curtains deflected the gaze of the curious but created a slightly suffocating effect.

Matching dark bay geldings completed the rig, well schooled and strong looking. They waited patiently, flicking their tails while the coachman began to secure the small amount of luggage on the rack. They turned and nodded their heads when the coachman patted their muscular rumps. 'We'll soon be off, my lovelies.'

The coachman was another member of the Jones' family and a man of enterprise. He proved to be chatty. He'd purchased the carriage and pair at a bankrupt sale, he said, and had tidied them up and put them to work immediately.

Dominic ignored the fact that the man was a third cousin to Rafferty Jones, and, by association, was probably dishonest. The act of rescuing Grace had brought the Jones family together with his for the time being, but it wouldn't take much for them to close ranks if needed.

The rig smelled a little of brandy, as though a keg had dripped some of its contents onto the floor. Dominic knew his assumption was unfair. It was obvious these people didn't earn much, and were he in the same position he'd probably bend the law to his own advantage too.

Raff's woman turned up. Betty Bunce was about thirty and carried the signs of a hard life on her face. Arms akimbo, mouth as pursed as a withered apple, she watched the luggage being loaded, saying nothing, but throwing the occasional harmful look at Jancy, who returned it with equal venom.

The sudden shriek that erupted from Betty made them all jump. 'That bed quilt stays with the cottage, Jancy Jones.'

'Who says?'

'I do say.'

'Well, you can unsay it. I helped my mother make that quilt and it was a labour of love because she placed the last stitch the day before she died. I'm not handing it over to the likes of you.'

Betty turned to Raff. 'You said I could have everything in the cottage.'

'I didn't know about it then, did I? Some things belong to Jancy, including half the cottage. If you don't like it you can bloody well lump it.'

'You must have seen them working on it.'

'Mebbe I did and mebbe I didn't, but I reckon this. You've got a needle and thread and you can get some cloth, so you can make your own damned quilt. That's my last word on the subject.'

'But you said I could have it. You should keep your word lessen it get out in the district that yours 'ain't worth a tuppeny turd.'

'Well it 'ain't mine to give.' Raff gave her a hard stare and dug his heels in. 'I can't give you something that isn't mine.'

'Perhaps and I'll tell the revenue men.'

Raff cracked his muscles and the woman fell silent. Grace tried not to smile when the LéSayres men exchanged a grin and Dominic spun a coin. Alex snatched it from the air and slipped into his waistcoat pocket.

'Get away home, Betty, who invited you here anyway?'

'Nobody, but I heard something was going on and it involved a woman who'd been kept captive. I thought I'd come and see it with my own eyes.'

'Well, have a good look because that's the only one you're getting. I hope you're all the wiser for it.'

Grace was now being helped across the path towards the carriage, a veil covering her face.

'I heard she was to be sold to a harem belonging to a camel seller. Make sure you get a good price for her.'

'Her weight in peacock feathers,' Dominic whispered and a snort came from under the veil.

Betty's hands covered her stomach. 'I came to make sure we got our fair share of the ransom. Don't forget I'm carrying your brat.'

Jancy butted in, 'Are you sure it's an infant? It looks like you've got a suet pudding tucked away in there.'

Betty's shriek doubled in sound and fury. 'Did you hear that, Raff?'

'Everybody in the county heard it, I reckon. Get yourself back to the inn and stop sticking your nose into my business . . . and don't tell anyone about what you've seen, especially to any soldiers who might visit the inn. This has nothing to do with you, or with them, and there's no ransom involved.'

Dominic had heard enough squabbling. Time was passing; they were already an hour late, which meant it would be nearly dark by the time they reached Poole. He wanted Grace out of the district before Maximilian Crouch and his cronies made their presence known. Placing his arm around Gracie's waist and enjoying the way her body leaned into his, he helped her into the carriage and settled her inside. He stood on the step and smiled at her, then lifted her veil. Unobserved, he managed to slide a kiss across her cheek to linger a while on her mouth. 'Try and keep out of trouble from now on, and promise me you won't wed a sheik while we're apart.'

This time her snort was soft, and her smile tenuous. There was a tremor in it that warned she was close to tears. She kissed her finger and placed it across his lips, then jerked her hand away as if she had admitted too much with the tender contact. 'You'll take care, won't you, Dominic?'

The tentative caress warmed him. 'This is strictly business and shouldn't take too long once Crouch turns up.'

'I keep thinking I've forgotten something important. Did you pack my medicine chest?'

'Yes. It's under your seat.'

Turning to Jancy he put some snap into his voice. 'It's time to go.'

Betty had followed after them and she stretched her neck this way and that, trying to see inside the carriage. Raff tried to block her view with his body, but seeing an opening Betty lunged at the quilt.

Jancy was quick, and had been expecting it. She jerked the quilt out of Betty's hands, hurled it through the open door of the carriage and gave the woman a slap that sent her reeling backwards. 'That's all you're getting of mine except my brother, and he's too good for the likes of a thieving magpie like you.'

Betty would have fallen if Raff hadn't caught her. 'That witch hit me!' she squawked and stooped to pick up a stone.

'She should have made a better job of it.' Dominic stepped in and took the stone from her, frowning. 'Get yourself off home, woman, else I'll bring a complaint against you. Jancy, get in the carriage and see to your mistress. Any more of this aggravation and I'll leave you behind. Do you understand?'

'Yes, sir.'

Raff said, 'Apologize to Mr LéSayres, Betty, and get along home like I told you to.'

'Sorry, but it weren't my fault,' the truculent Betty mumbled, and offered Jancy a baleful glare.

When Jancy laughed, Betty slunk off.

Jancy stuck her tongue out at Betty's retreating back, muttering darkly to Raff, 'You bloody lunatic, you'll rue the day you met that little madam, mark my words.'

'Enough now. Like it or lump it, I'm going to do the right thing for the infant. You know where I am if you need me, Jancy. And remember, half the cottage is yours.'

Dominic could imagine the cat fight if she ever tried to claim it.

Jancy had tears in her eyes as she hugged her brother.

Grace only just managed to swallow her giggle, but the earl caught her eye and chuckled.

Ten minutes later they were off. It was much later than Dominic had planned, and the lowering winter sun pointed long shadows towards Dorset. Soon dusk fell below the horizon and the moon illuminated the landscape with a soft incandescence.

Grace fell asleep, her head cradled in a cushion. She woke when the rolling motion came to a halt, and stretched.

The sound of voices filled her ears.

'Why have we stopped?' she called, her heart thumping as she hoped it wasn't a highwayman.

The earl appeared. Opening the door he held out his hand to help her down. Jancy scrambled down after her. 'We've reached Poole,' he said. 'Here, we'll change carriages and Raff will return to Ringwood with his cousin. I thought you might like some refreshment while they transfer the luggage to the LéSayres carriage. There is a private room for your use with comfortable chairs, so your appearance won't invite comment. I can recommend their pies and the landlady will make us some tea, unless you'd prefer ale, or cider.'

Grace guessed the cider would be the rough variety of scrumpy, which was highly intoxicating. She had tried it when she was fourteen, a tumbler full of the liquid that she'd mistaken for an oddly flavoured ginger ale. The result had been dire. She'd staggered all over the place and the guests had laughed and made fun of her. Eventually her father's amusement had become irritation and a servant had been despatched to take her to her bed. She'd awoken the next morning with a ferocious headache and a lecture from her father on the proper behaviour expected from a lady.

Hastily, she told the earl, 'We'll have some ale, it will take less time and quench the thirst better. Would you thank Raff and the coachman for their kindness and their help on my behalf, please.'

'I will, but please stay in the room until I come for you. The innkeeper's wife will see to your needs if you have any.'

The refreshment was carried in and the landlady bobbed a curtsy. 'Is there anything else you'd like, my Lord?'

Alex shook his head. 'Thank you, but we'll be on our way as soon as possible.'

Grace suddenly remembered what she'd forgotten, and delayed Alex with a hand on his arm and a tragic, 'My cat . . . we've left him behind.'

The earl's smile reminded her strongly of Dominic. What was he doing at that very moment, she wondered.

'Don't sound so tragic. We can soon find you another.'

'Tabby helped save my life; can we go back for him?'

Alex looked askance at her, unbelieving. 'Certainly not . . . it's the middle of the night.'

'You don't understand, I promised Tabby he could come with me, and Raff promised to find a cage for him to travel in.'

'Good lord . . . you mean it. The animal is a stray. Cats are resourceful and he'll be adept at fending for himself.'

'Because he had no choice; and of course I mean it. He might get himself shut in the house and starve to death. Or he might die in the snow.'

'Hmmm . . . I don't know if you've noticed it, my dear, but there isn't any snow to die in.'

'There could be some before too long, after all, it's winter. Besides the soldiers might mistake him as vermin and shoot him.'

'Dominic has told me your logic was dubious at times, and

your imagination, vivid. It proves to be true and I'd be grateful if you'd control your wilder flights of fancy. However, perhaps you can describe your feline saviour.'

Head to one side Grace regarded him. She'd built up a picture of her cat in her imagination. He'd been handsome, with an abundance of striped fur, yellow eyes, a bushy tail and a loud purr. She related that description to the earl, then added, 'Of course, I didn't actually see him properly; I just saw his paw under the door and teased him a little.'

'I see. There *was* a cat in the house; it stole a kipper from the larder. It was short-haired, had the end of his tail missing and its ears were tattered from fighting with other cats. Dominic suggested we made a stew out of it, but we couldn't catch it. Besides, the meat would have been stringy.'

Despite his affability and the amusement in his eyes Grace knew she wouldn't get around the head of the LéSayres household easily.

'Come now . . . I was teasing you, my dear. All the same, I will not risk returning for the cat. You must see that.'

'Yes . . . I was silly. It's just . . . the presence of the cat provided me with hope and comfort when I despaired.'

Jancy soothed, 'Don't you fret, miss, I'll send a message back with Raff to give to Mr LéSayres. If all else fails I'm sure Raff will give the creature a home.'

'What about Betty?'

Jancy snorted. 'Happen the fleas might do something useful, like jump off the cat and infest her instead. If they do they'll drop dead from the poison in her blood.'

Alex sighed, obviously bored with the subject. 'Cats are territorial, and I have a sufficiency of them in my barn. You can have one or two of the kittens and train them to be indoor cats once you're settled in your own premises. We also have two Irish wolfhounds, and neither animal would welcome a strange cat let loose into our home.'

Gently, but firmly, the earl had just reminded her she was his guest. He would expect her to be mannerly, and observe the customs of his household. And, of course, he was right.

She hid her disappointment. 'Yes, I'm sorry, my Lord. I wasn't thinking, and you've been so helpful and kind. So has Mr LéSayres.'

'Ah yes . . . my brother . . . Dominic seems taken with you. I must admit I was surprised when I learned that he'd hired a woman to be his clerk, especially one of your tender years. People will talk, I imagine.'

'I expect they will for a while, but surely the interest will only last while the concept of a female clerk remains a novelty. I will try not to cause too much of a sensation. Would I be wrong in concluding from this conversation that you disapprove of me and would prefer the position was offered to another – a man perhaps?'

'You do me an injustice if you think that's the case, but there is more to your relationship with my brother, is there not?'

'If more exists, it concerns nobody but us. I hope you will believe me when I say that nothing untoward has happened. Dominic has been quite charming, if dishonest in his approaches. If anyone needs guarding against being hurt, it's me.'

'Dishonest! My brother is the most honest person I've ever known and as far as I can see he treats you with the utmost respect.'

'His interest is sometimes a little overwhelming. I've never had much to do with men, except older gentlemen of the medical profession . . . men of science.'

'They are men, nevertheless. Are your feelings towards my brother based on indifference when my eyes seem to tell me otherwise?'

'Far from it, I should charge you with lack of perception, my Lord.'

'Why were you engaged in a servant's position when you are so obviously intelligent?'

'You think servants are unintelligent? Who would clean your home and cook your meals? Who would saddle your horses—'

'Yes, yes . . . I get the point, Miss Ellis, and no, I do not think that. It was just badly worded. In fact, I will give them all a Christmas bonus for their trouble. Would you care to answer my question without descending into debate?'

'It was a case of circumstance. I learned to run my father's household from an early age. As I grew older he taught me some apothecary skills, plus some simple medical and diagnostic skills.'

'Ah yes . . . your father's skill as a doctor was well known.'

'When he died I found myself penniless. I understand that Mr John Howard arranged the position I held, and I believe he provided my salary too. I hope to thank him personally before too long. As for my feelings towards Dominic, they are certainly not indifferent. But if anything comes of it other than shreds, remains to be seen.'

'So there is a problem?'

'I'm confused, since I'm constantly drawn to a path that will lead me astray – and I cannot believe I'm seriously considering taking that path. Furthermore, if Dominic feels the attraction for me, as he indicates, then he would not encourage my growing affection towards him.'

The earl cleared his throat, clearly nonplussed. 'I see . . . at least, I think I do, and the conversation is not one I'd prefer to continue with. I shall converse with Dom about your future position within my household.'

'I beg your pardon, my Lord. Dominic is your brother and he cares deeply for you . . . for all his family. I have no wish to be the cause of any friction.'

Firmly, he told her, 'No doubt my wife will be happy to offer you counsel if you feel you need it. Now, I must go down and supervise the changeover.'

'You did ask me, my Lord, so you must take some of the blame for my answer.'

Alex smiled to himself as he bowed his head. He supposed he had. Miss Grace Ellis was a dainty little maid. He liked her. His brother had certainly got this young woman on the run – or was it the other way round?

Dom's way of thinking had always intrigued Alex and Grace Ellis was a bright and tender flower, but strong when she needed to be. No wonder his brother was enamoured by her.

Yet . . . he puzzled, what possible reservation could she have concerning Dom? His brother was intelligent, handsome, clean in his habits and honest. He also came from a good family. Did she need anything more in a man?

He reminded himself to ask Vivienne to put out some feelers. She'd soon ferret the truth out of Grace Ellis.

'Dishonest . . . not my brother Dom,' he said out loud.

Fifteen

They'd said goodbye to Raff ten minutes previously and were now on the road, heading for King's Acres. They travelled in a well-upholstered vehicle with a crest on the door. The cushioning saved them from the heaviest assaults from the ruts – assaults that teased out every existing bruise in Grace's body and tortured it to its limit.

The road was iron hard. Jancy didn't seem to mind being tossed around. She'd found a position amongst the hand baggage on the opposite seat and was sleeping, her mouth open a little. Wrapped tightly in her quilt, her hands clutched it to her, as though determined to never let it go. A full moon sent bands of white light across Jancy's face. It seemed like a lifetime to Grace since she'd almost been in the same position.

Grace left the maid to her dreams and hoped they were good ones. Her own dreams were intense, and mostly related to Dominic. She was enveloped in a blanket of soft cream wool and now, as her body was beginning to heal, her thoughts became increasingly intense, as if Dominic was a magnet drawing her to him. Little scenes played out in her mind, illustrations from the Indian book that her imagination reacted to.

She'd hidden the book, buried it at the back of the cupboard in the room Lady Florence had vacated. She wondered what people would say if they knew she harboured such thoughts. But did that matter, when she had no relatives to condemn her for her behaviour? She'd often dreamed of being claimed by a man of some note, who was caring and tender, one she could share her life, her interests, and her dreams with. Not one of the ilk of the sheik Betty Bunce had in store for her. She had found the man, but he had a serious flaw. According to Jessie, he was already married.

A niggle of doubt gnawed at her. Why hadn't he mentioned it? Most men she'd been acquainted with usually spoke of their wives or their children with fondness, if only in passing.

She wrestled with the notion for a few moments, and then tried to drag her mind away from the temptation that was Dominic. Perspiring a little she pushed the blanket to one side.

Apart from the coachman, she recalled there were two armed outriders now, including Alex. Having tired of the cold, Sam had joined them inside the carriage, the lights of which were on but they threw only a small glow into the darkness surrounding them. They were there for the carriage to be seen, rather than provide light, though some did illuminate the interior. Sometimes the carriage slowed to a crawl, collecting tension to it, but nobody challenged them and as the road began to wind through the gentle curves of hill and dale the sense of danger eased.

Finally they came to a halt. The bark of dogs became louder and when the earl dismounted he was whipped by wagging tails. Wet noses thrust into his hands and the dogs turned themselves inside out vying for his attention, and then thoroughly sniffed Grace, the stranger amongst them.

For a short time she was surrounded by doggy breath. The earl had a few quiet words with the coachman. The horses whinnied as they were led towards the stable block, their flanks steaming. Jancy went with them.

The quiet of night gathered around them. Obviously she wasn't going to be afforded the same relaxed familiarity that she'd had at the cottage, Grace thought.

'Miss Ellis?'

The earl took her arm and led her up several steps into the candlelit hall. Two women stood there. Giving them a wide smile, the earl kissed the younger on the cheek, and the elder on the hand. 'May I present Miss Grace Ellis to you both. My wife, Lady LéSayres, and my stepmother, Lady Eugenie.'

Grace bobbed a couple of curtseys and her muscles cramped. She staggered upright.

Lady LéSayres stepped forward and took her by the arm. 'Steady, dear.'

'My Lady,' Grace said, and then turned to the older woman. 'Lady Eugenie.' To round her clumsy entrance off she remembered her veil and pulled it from her face.

The eyes of both women widened and Lady LéSayres gasped

while Lady Eugenie whispered, 'Good gracious, what on earth have you done to the poor girl, Alex?'

'You know me better than that, Eugenie. As you can see, the young lady has been in the wars. Perhaps you'd be kind enough to take her under your wing.'

Eugenie stepped closer to examine her bruises more clearly. 'What has happened to her?'

'No doubt she will tell you herself, since her voice is still intact.'

'Please do not blame the earl, my Lady,' Grace begged. 'It's not his fault. I was set upon by a servant and locked in a room with no sustenance . . . not even water. A smuggler called Rafferty Jones rescued me.'

'Goodness, what a terrible time you've had.' Eugenie slid her arm around her waist and walked her towards the stairs. 'You must tell me all about it.'

'Mr LéSayres and the earl arrived to rescue me.' Grace fell silent, though she was jittery, as though all her nerve ends were tied together in a great twitching knot that she couldn't unravel.

Although Grace tried to prevent it a shuddering sob burst from her. 'I'm so sorry . . . so sorry. I seem to cry for no reason at all and I didn't intend to unburden my troubles onto your shoulders.' Grace cupped her hands over her eyes but the tears still kept seeping through her fingers. 'Oh dear, I didn't mean to upset you. Please forgive me.'

Eugenie gathered her into her arms. 'Hush, my dear, there is no need to apologize when you have every reason to cry. You are safe here and the journey has tired you.'

Through her tears Grace looked around her. 'Where's Jancy? Dominic appointed her to look after me.'

'Your maid will be familiarizing herself with your chamber, I imagine. Come now, you and I will talk over some refreshment while you gather yourself together.'

The younger lady of the house smiled at her. She was not conventionally pretty, but tall and elegant. She was lovely in her own way with a perfect oval face. Her smile was both warm and welcoming. 'Welcome to our home, we will talk in a little while.' She turned to her husband, an edge of panic in her voice. 'Where is Dominic, why isn't he with you, Alex. He's not injured, is he?'

Alex shrugged, and then he took his wife's face between his hands and kissed her, bringing a tint of colour to suffuse her cheeks. 'Dom hasn't finished his business yet. I'll be rejoining him as soon as I've eaten. A fresh horse is being saddled and I'll take as many of the Dorset Yeomanry who will join us. There were one or two at the inn who seemed eager to defend the honour of their regiment for the sport of hunting the brigadier down. Once captured, he and his men are to be confined to the barracks until his ship sails.'

'Then you are expecting trouble?'

'It's just a precaution, my love, a minor matter. The brigadier and his men are fast becoming the cause of embarrassment to the army. It has happened before and will happen again, no doubt. Unfortunately, this time one of them is Dominic's client. They are Australia bound, so will not remain in the district for much longer.' He touched his wife's face, a tender caress with the back of his finger. 'You know how efficient Dominic can be. He'll just need a signature or two on some papers, then the estate will be placed in the hands of the lawyers and the courts, and he'll be free of it.'

Lord LéSayres was the master of understatement. His voice was soft and untroubled as though such events were commonplace. Grace recognized the same trait in Dominic.

How grand LéSayres Hall was. It overwhelmed her, made her feel small and insignificant. Grace hoped Alex was right and it was as easy for Dominic as he'd described. She went up the stairs with Eugenie, the fragrance from the cassoulet drifting up after them.

Her chamber was large, but made cosy by the fire burning in the grate. Shadows leapt and danced. Grace removed the all-enveloping travelling cloak and laid it across the sofa. Her shoulders drooped. The bed issued an invitation but she must not sleep yet, she must eat her host's food – food made especially for her, to help her heal.

She wanted to cry again, for they'd been so good to her, a stranger.

Jancy came in with a tray, which she placed on a table. She looked tired.

'You may leave the tray,' Lady Eugenie said.

'Beggin' your pardon, my Lady, but my mistress looks fit to drop, and may need coaxing, for her appetite is not what it should be.'

'And you are?'

'Jancy, my Lady. I'm Miss Ellis's maid. Mr LéSayres himself appointed me and he ordered me to look after her.'

That last sentence, stated with some authority, brought a smile to Lady Eugenie's lips. 'And I have given you another order. You may safely leave your mistress in my hands tonight, Jancy. Off you go now.'

She hesitated. 'I haven't had time to unpack Miss Ellis's night attire.'

'There's some in the chest. Just place what's required on the bed, and then you may leave. You can join the rest of the staff in the sitting room, or you can go to bed yourself. You know where your bed is . . . just above this room, and there is a staircase to it behind those hangings in the corner. The door can be locked on this side if there is a need for privacy.'

'Yes, my Lady.'

'Anything else can wait until morning. Did you have something to eat, Jancy?'

'Yes, my Lady. I had some broth and some bread in the kitchen, and the cook gave me some biscuits and some milk to take to bed, in case I get hungry in the night.' Jancy sighed with satisfaction. 'I have a bedroom all to myself.'

'No doubt the housekeeper will want to familiarize you with the household practices. She can do that in the morning.'

But Jancy hadn't finished establishing the importance of her relationship to Grace. 'Is there anything I can do before I go, Miss Ellis?'

'Thank you, but no, Jancy. I'll see you in the morning. Goodnight.'

After Jancy left they seated themselves at a low table in front of the fire.

Lady Eugenie laughed. 'Your maid is determined.'

'Jancy is trying to make a good impression on everyone because she needs this position. She was good to me when I needed it, and Dominic trusts her with my welfare.'

Lady Eugenie uncovered the broth, saying, 'Then I would rely on his judgement, which is usually sound. Do you love him very much?'

Grace didn't pretend it was other than Dominic the woman referred to. Eugenie was too astute to be fooled. 'Yes, I'm afraid I do.'

'Afraid?'

'It's hard to love somebody when on their part it can only be superficial. That it might cause scandal . . . especially since he's employed me as a clerk.'

'I was once the nursemaid here. At first I stayed for the sake of the boys, who were still babies. Then I fell in love with their father and we became a family. I said I wouldn't wed him until he gave up drinking. He tried many times, only to fail. He didn't fail as a father though. He loved his sons and they were aware of it . . . and he loved me. At the end he was in terrible pain. He told me he wouldn't die until I became his wife and I'd have to put up with his bellowing.'

Grace placed a comforting hand over Eugenie's. 'I'm so sorry.'

Eugenie's manner became brisk and she removed her hand. 'One must get over these things unless you want to live your life in misery. I had the boys to keep me busy. Now . . . eat your broth else I'll get into trouble with the cook.'

Grace swallowed a spoonful of her soup. It wasn't as tasty as Jancy's had been. 'Yours is a sad story. Did the late earl's pain ease after you were wed?'

'He had no strength and I saw no reason to try and do otherwise than lessen his pain, and allow him the comfort of as much brandy as he needed.'

'How did his sons take their father's death?'

'Luckily, they had each other. My stepsons have always been a support for me. Growing up they collected a variety of bruises and bloodied noses from both children and adults, who made hurtful comments. The LéSayres family attracts scandal and a little bit more won't hurt it.'

Grace giggled and Eugenie smiled. 'That's better. Dinner is over now but I daresay we can serve up something more substantial than the broth if that doesn't curb your appetite.'

'I'm sure it will. I haven't been hungry these past few days.'

'Then we shall find a way to tempt you. Now, you'd better
get on and eat that before it cools, young lady, while I sort some
night attire for you. I will expect you to eat it all.'

Grace had barely finished it when there was the sound of
activity outside. Eugenie crossed to the window. 'The earl is
leaving. God go with you, Alex.'

There was a noisy clatter of a horse that faded into the distance.
Immediately, fear attacked Grace again. 'He must think Dominic
is in danger.'

'They are brothers who are used to looking after each other.
Alex is just taking precautions. Look, the moon has risen to light
his way.'

Indeed it had. Its light frosted the needles on the pines creating
a little miracle of sparkling luminescence. Grace was awed by it.
'It's so pretty here.'

Eugenie drew the hangings across the windows.

'It's a shame to close out the stars.'

'The curtains help to keep the warmth inside during the winter
nights.'

'Dominic told me he used to watch his mother fly across
the sky on a star when he was young. He said he'd show me
which one some day.'

'Dom was a sensitive child who needed to be loved and the
tale of the star comforted him when he was small. I had thought
he'd put it behind him. You are honoured Grace, for it's not a
memory a man would usually share.'

'There is a ring about the moon. A good omen, I think.'

'As well as a sign of frost . . . we will ready you for bed, then
I can examine your bruises with more ease.'

'They no longer hurt and they are beginning to fade. Given
time they will heal themselves.'

Eugenie's tone of voice invited no argument. 'Nevertheless, I
will examine them.'

She was thorough. Fetching a medicine chest she bathed the
bruises in witch hazel. A drizzle of the liquid created shivers to
course down Grace's spine, like the touch of Dominic's cold
winter fingers drifting across her neck.

Soon, Grace was enveloped in a large flannel nightgown and
she and Lady Eugenie sat before the fire, a lap rug apiece to keep

the draughts at bay. Grace tucked her feet under the nightdress. 'This gown belonged to a very large maid, I think.'

Eugenie laughed. 'It certainly isn't designed to entice a lover to your side.'

'As if I would be so forward.'

'Making love is a delightful way to wile away the time.'

'So I have been informed by my former mistress. Lady Florence gave me a book . . . on the subject. It makes me blush to just think of it so I left it in Oakford House.'

'Such a pity. I have heard of such books, but I have never seen one. I'd certainly like to.'

Grace blushed.

Eugenie's smile gently teased her. You're such an innocent. 'If I have shocked you, I'm sorry.' Picking up a brush Eugenie began to draw it through her hair, unravelling the knots. She had a gentle touch and it was relaxing.

'I am not shocked. It's just that I have not experienced . . . I have never known a man.'

'Of course, I should have thought. You are young yet and had no mother to teach you how to become a woman.'

'Oh, it's only partly that. My father taught me to prepare medicines and under his instruction I have also birthed an infant. And I have seen pictures, of course. However, I was unprepared for the strength of the emotional pull of being in love. It seems to rob me of the ability to think straight. I don't know how to act, or what to do.'

'Do nothing, since I expect you will respond to Dominic when the time is right.'

'He said that one day soon that time will be right, and we won't even consider if it's right or wrong. But there are some obstacles in my way. His family . . .'

Grace had warmed towards Eugenie and found her so easy to talk to that she was almost tempted to tell her all her troubles and her guilt over Dominic's family. Eugenie was a beloved member of Dominic's family, she remembered.

'Is what right or wrong?' Lady LéSayres suddenly came into the room, picking up on Grace's words.

Grace didn't know whether to leap to her feet and curtsey or not. To be on the safe side she stood and bobbed. 'My Lady.'

'Let's not be stiff with manners and titles, my dear. Call me Vivienne when we are in an informal situation, and if you will allow, then I shall address you as Grace . . . such a pretty name.'

'Won't the earl mind?'

'I shouldn't think so. My husband regards himself as a farmer, and while he is proud of his title and estate, and he loves to entertain, he does not behave in a superior manner or pretend to be anything more than he appears to be on the surface. In fact, he calls his favourite cow Duchess.'

Grace smiled at that. 'He is certainly well mannered . . . as is Dominic.'

Eugenie nodded in agreement and a motherly smile appeared on her face. 'They were good boys, a credit to their parents.'

'Dominic respects you as he would his birth mother.'

'Thank you . . .' Eugenie turned to the elegant Vivienne. 'I was about to go to bed. Will you stay a while?'

'Not tonight. Grace looks tired, and we can talk tomorrow. I've come to tell you both that my husband has departed with two robust men as companions. This is so he can be of support to his brother, should the need arise.'

'Is that likely?'

'Alex feels there is a slight possibility. If nothing else his appearance should act as a deterrent. Apparently Dominic has an appointment with an attorney at Oakford House tomorrow afternoon. He hopes to get the matter sorted out as soon as possible.'

Grace stifled a yawn.

'Our guest is done in,' Vivienne said. 'We'll put her to bed and then have an early night.'

Soon, Grace was tucked under the blankets, relaxed and as warm as a rabbit in its burrow. A kiss brushed her cheek. 'Goodnight my dear, I will see you at breakfast. Sweet dreams.'

The light from the candle retreated and the door closed quietly behind them, leaving just the red glow of the fire.

Grace imagined Dominic alone in Oakford House, the draughts stealthily opening and closing the doors. She reached out to him. 'Sleep well, my Dominic,' she whispered, though he wouldn't be hers for much longer. She snuggled into the comforting arms of the waiting bed with tears in her eyes. He was well loved by the occupants of this great house, for they all spoke fondly of him.

So where was his wife?

But Grace couldn't sleep; her mind tumbled with fear. Madcap plans presented themselves one after another, disguised in a cloak of what seemed to be good sense. She would go to the meeting at Oakford House and put forward a plan to suit the situation. After all, it did concern her.

Came the scoffing reply: *And what plan might that be?*

She sat up in bed, saying quietly, 'I will think of one on the way back to Ringwood.'

Uneasiness churned through her stomach again. The earl must have believed Dominic to be in deadly peril to consider mustering some soldiers to the cause . . . and all over a signature. She pictured an army of military gentlemen, uniforms a blazing red, feathers decorating their shakoes, and carrying lances as they trotted along the road, great guns on wheeled carriages pulled behind them.

Not that they'd actually have a gun carriage for one old soldier they were putting out to grass. She hoped they didn't shoot him.

She could do something to help. She could agree to marry the brigadier after all? Perhaps he wasn't as bad as everyone imagined.

Goodness, you are in a sacrificial mood, my dear.

'Dominic will be furious if I return to Ringwood,' she said out loud.

The earl will be furious too, and Vivienne and Eugenie will offer you no sympathy at all, no matter how much you grovel.

Stop being so sarcastic. The only alternative is to marry the brigadier and become Dominic's lover. Perhaps I shall be like Lady Florence and have several lovers.

Then you will have to send Dominic LéSayres back to his family, and serve him right. You were raised to be something better than a slut and Dominic has been deceitful in his dealings with both you and his wife.

'He doesn't deserve me.'

Shored up by that thought and now full of resolve, Grace threw off the bedclothes and picked up a nightlight. She headed up the servant's stair, her eyes adjusting to the dim light the lantern offered.

Jancy was asleep under her precious quilt, her past, present and future wrapped securely around her. Her clothing was laid neatly on a chair.

Grace didn't rouse her maid. She didn't want to suffer through her advice or risk being overheard if voices were raised. In fact, the less Jancy knew the least trouble she would attract. She slid the clothing off the chair and carried the garments away. Nobody would recognize her with her battered face, and her appearance, that of an impoverished maid, would surely repulse any man who thought to chance his luck by approaching her.

Nevertheless, to that purpose she carried a makeshift weapon, a ned that Sam Rider had made for her. The foot of some discarded hose was filled with sand and knotted at the top for a good grip.

Sam had shown her how to use it too. 'One good thump in the right place will cripple any man and give you time to get away,' he'd said, and she didn't ask him which was the right place, in case he became embarrassed.

Sixteen

Grace wrote a hasty note of apology to her host, and left it on her pillow for Jancy to find and deliver.

Outside the comfort of her room the layout of the house was unfamiliar to her. The staircase wound down into the darkness and she kept a hand on the banister close to the wall, lest she lose her balance. When the long clock in the hall drew in a whirring breath and started to chime the midnight hour, Grace jumped and nearly fell down the remainder of the stairs.

The dogs gave her a fright, appearing from nowhere to investigate the disturbance. She prayed they wouldn't bark as the pair circled her offering soft huffs and snarls that were a mixture of threat and an entreaty to be petted. They allowed her to pass after she paid the toll of an ear fondle apiece, and without any menace they escorted her to the front door before they retreated back into the darkness. Grace slipped out and gently closed the door behind her.

She stood for a moment, trying to get her bearings. A door

hinge creaked over to her left and there were a number of horse noises before they settled again and fell quiet.

It was cool, but not too cold and the sky was spangled with stars. It would not be clear for much longer for a thin, knee-high mist rose from the land to dampen her boots and the bottom of her travelling cloak. The air was salted with wood smoke from the chimney pots and it scratched at her throat as she strode off, full of resolve.

Behind her a twig snapped.

She stopped breathing and stood still. All she could hear was the urgent beat of blood against her eardrums. Then an owl hooted and a fox barked in the distance as it went about its bloody business. The silence of the night suddenly came alive. Something squealed and there was a scuffle in the undergrowth. There was no danger in the dark night, for those creatures which she could neither see nor hear would mostly be scared by her approach, and run from her.

Grace had been on the road for about an hour when she began to tire. The mist had crept higher and her pace decreased. She began to wish she'd stayed in bed as she entered the wooded area. When she emerged on the other side and her feet found the depression of many carriages in the earth, she sighed with relief. Her feet had carried her to the main highway. Up ahead, floating in the mist like a ship on an unearthly sea, were the lights of a distant inn – one she remembered as occupying a prominent position on Bourne Heath.

'Thank goodness,' she whispered and seated herself on a grey stone marker while she debated whether to return to King's Acres or go on. The marker had an arrow pointing back towards the house. She traced her finger over the indentations in the stone between her calves and ankles. *LéSayres Hall. Three leagues.* A rapid calculation gave her a conversion to one mile. She seemed to have been walking forever without covering much ground.

There was the pad of a footfall and a pebble rolled to give a muffled clink against another. The moon disappeared and the mist thickened around her. A shiver crawled up her spine. She had the feeling she would touch somebody if she held out her hand.

'Is anyone there?'

Silence greeted her enquiry, except a hedgehog ambled across her path with a rolling motion. She smiled as she nudged it with her toe. 'It's you giving me a fright, is it?'

The creature curled into a ball. Not surprising, since, though it was a peaceable creature it carried formidable armour in its prickly jacket to call on if needed. After a safe time passed it found its feet again and ambled off along its way.

So did Grace, though she was beginning to be scared by the enormity of the step she'd taken. There could be a murderer hiding behind every bush just waiting for a fool like her to rob. Not that she had anything worth robbing. She did have her ned inside her pocket though, and the weight of that was reassuring as her hand closed round it for a few seconds.

As she neared the inn noise came to her, an ebb and flow of raucous laughter, a foul expletive and something being smashed. Horses fretted.

Perhaps she should go back. But whatever she decided, she must rest for a short time. Wrapped in her cloak she found a stunted tree and sat in its dark shadow, with her back against the trunk and the cowl covering her face. The mist enveloped her and although it was cold she felt safer now she couldn't easily be seen. After a while she grew warmer, and, turning on her side, she rested to regain some of her energy.

She became alert some time later, reminding herself not to fall asleep, in case the cold carried her off. Her body ached, but her energy had returned thanks to Eugenie's chicken broth. The hairs on her neck prickled when she heard breathing. Obviously they didn't mean her any harm, else they would have taken advantage while she was resting. Perhaps it was a fox. The breathing stopped when she hissed, 'Who are you?'

'Sam Rider. I'm sorry, Miss Ellis, I mean you no harm so don't you be afeared.'

'Have you been following me?'

'The earl thought you might do something like this and he told me not to allow you to take any of the horses, but to stay with you and keep you out of harm's way. I promised I would. I slept outside your door, and you almost tripped over me when you left.'

'I thought I'd tripped on the rug. Why didn't you make yourself known earlier?'

'I didn't want to raise the household and I didn't think you'd get this far. I thought you'd return to the house and raise a rumpus trying to get back in. It's a cold night.' Removing his heavy coat he placed it back around her shoulders. 'It will give you more protection from the cold than your own cloak and I have my leather jerkin on.'

Grace wasn't sure if she liked Lord LéSayres being able to read her so well.

'I'm sure the earl didn't intend for you to follow me all the way to Oakford House on foot. You frightened the life out of me.'

'Sorry, miss, I didn't mean to give you a fright. I had a look at the inn while you were resting. There are Dorset Yeomen volunteers in there, three of them, and they're as tight as ticks. We need to avoid them.'

'Is it the brigadier and his companions?'

'I don't think so, miss. They're not proper soldiers, and are wearing blue jackets with black trim. They don't appear to be the soldiers Mr LéSayres is expecting, just locals looking to make a name for themselves. There is a price on the brigadier's head.'

Any thoughts Grace might have harboured about returning to the safe haven that was King's Acres were forgotten. 'They might be the renegades. It matters not, since we must try to warn the earl and Mr LéSayres of their position. We have no horses so must hurry.'

'Leave it to me, miss. I'll borrow one of their horses, and scatter the rest of them. That will give us a clear start while they round them up.'

'I thought you were told not to touch the horses.'

'His lordship meant the estate horses, not those belonging to the Yeomen.'

A convenient display of male reasoning, she thought.

'Will you wait for me here and look after my coat? It will hamper me if I have to run.'

She placed a hand on his arm. 'What if you're caught? Be careful, now, Sam they'll probably shoot you if they catch you.'

He grinned. 'Don't you fret, Miss Ellis. They won't even know I'm there.'

'They'll hear the horses.'

'There are ways and means, miss, and I always carry sugar

lumps in my pocket. Horses will do summersaults for a piece of sugar.'

Grace gave a muted giggle at the thought of such an unlikely and comical act.

There was a shout from the inn, 'Put your hat on the bar and sing us a song, Hal.'

'Diddle dum dee,' someone else called out.

Hal didn't need much prompting. A fiddle began to play, feet stamped time on the floor and his raucous voice sang out:

> An 'andsome young maiden named Dora,
> diddle diddle, dum
> raised her skirt higher than she oughter
> diddle diddle dum
> For the fiddler to cheer and admire
> diddle diddle dum
> The parson did troth them, but true
> diddle, diddle, doo

'Louder gentlemen . . . let's wake the dead in the cemetery.'

The singing took on a new tone with different voices competing. It was out of key for a few verses except for the chorus, which collected the loudest cheer no matter how many times it was repeated. And no wonder, Gracie thought, grinning at the gusto with which the last rollicking few lines attracted:

> And now to his light-of-love the fiddler sings,
> come straddle my saddle and fiddle with me
> and I'll dance with you darling on diddle dum dee.

The place erupted into whistles, diddles, dums and daddles, and tankards were thumped on the table with bucolic gusto. There was a swell of noise when they shouted with one voice, 'More . . . more!'

Sam said, 'Good, they've only just started to get warmed up. There's a splintered tree up the road a ways. I'll meet you there . . . lessen you want to return to King's Acres. Reckon I could get you into your room without too much trouble, and nobody any the wiser. You know, the earl will ring a peal over you, and

I expect Mr LéSayres himself will give you a tongue-lashing after he went to all that trouble to keep you out of harm's way. As for me, I daresay I'll get a clout or two . . . or worse. The soldiers might hang me for stealing a horse. They might hang us both.'

Shame filled her.

Grace couldn't imagine Dominic being angry enough to take her to task, but then, she'd never so blatantly ignored his instructions before. A mountain of guilt tightened her stomach into a knot. Dominic's feelings would be hurt, but surely he wouldn't allow the soldiers to hang them.

'We will only borrow one horse. By the time it's missed nobody will hang us since we'll just say we found the horse wandering and we was bringing it back to the inn. The earl might dismiss me though.'

Gracie was tempted to abandon her plan for a moment. Then her resolve strengthened. She would be earning enough money as a clerk for both of them. 'If he does I'll employ you.'

Gracie's nap had replenished her energy and she stepped out purposefully, leaving the noise of the inn behind. Sam went in the opposite direction.

As promised, Sam was waiting along the way for her, and astride a stout farm horse. He didn't give her time to feel nervous, for she'd never ridden on such a large animal before, except for Argus of course, and Dominic was a more solid figure to cling to than the flimsy Sam, who seemed to be perched on the horse like a flea on a dog's back.

'Come on up then.' He reached down, and, grasping his wrist, she was swung up behind him. He waited until she adjusted the cloak so it covered her legs and tied the ends together to keep it snug.

'Keep a tight hold of me,' Sam said, 'and tell me if you feel you're slipping.'

'Where are the other horses?'

'I removed their saddles and left them and the horses in a field not far from the inn. I've scattered them a bit and one or two might make their way to the forest. They'll be safe there, but easily found when daylight comes. The saddles are easy to find. We'll be safely at Oakford House by then. This one will find its own way back to its companions. Horses like company.'

The horse had a good turn of speed, in a lumbering sort of way and was an easy ride. Sam kept it at a comfortable canter so as not to unseat them, or tire the beast. They covered the ground quickly, with Grace clinging to Sam's slight figure, which she found to be surprisingly sinewy and strong. In his turn he used the animal's flowing mane as a rein. The raw night stung their cheeks as the hooves of the horse thudded on the hard-packed ground beneath them.

Eventually Sam brought the animal to a halt, slid down from its back and helped her down. He gave her some sugar to reward the horse with and its tongue rasped over her palm, all gritty and moist. The animal rumbled with pleasure and took a last lick.

'We walk from here,' Sam said. 'It's only a mile or so to Oakford House. Give me five minutes to take the horse to the highway and point him in the right direction, then I'll come back for you. Just sit on this stone and don't move.'

It was a cold seat, and one she couldn't recall as seeing before. There was a moment of hesitation in Sam. 'If I don't come back you must make your own way, but wait until it's light.'

'Don't come back . . . why shouldn't you come back? Sam, don't you do anything that's likely to harm you.'

But Sam was gone.

After a good ten minutes, Grace began to fidget. *Only a mile or so,* he'd said. *How long was the 'or so' part?* She gave a wry smile. Her behind would have blisters upon the blisters after that ride. Gazing around her in the rustling darkness she fancied there were some lighter patches, and tried to get her bearings. He'd gone off to their left . . . to Oakford House.

It was the longest few minutes Grace had ever experienced as she sat in the darkness. A fitful breeze sprang up, the noisy squabbles and sudden rattles of brittle winter foliage made her jump. It brought with it the faint, piquant odour of the mud flats when the tide was out and the market vendors calling loudly, 'Cockles and mussels alive, alive oh! Fresh oysters, crabs and eels.'

She became uneasy as the minutes ticked by, and something disagreeable clawed at the back of her mind. What landmarks were there within a mile or so of Oakford House?

She could be anywhere in this rising mist. Near to Mudeford perhaps. It was a well-named spit of muddy land that supported the inn of Betty Bunce, and it was just the place for someone like her. Or was she in Lymington? Everything looked different at night. If Rafferty Jones married Betty to claim the inn it would be out of greed, for she was the most unlikeable woman Grace had ever met. Though, like the cat, she had never really met her. Raff didn't display any strong feelings towards her, and certainly he didn't seem to love her. Still, Betty carried Raff's infant inside her, and who was she to pass judgement on others, especially people she hardly knew. Many people made a marriage of convenience.

Haven't you decided to do the same thing, you hypocrite?

That's different.

How?

I don't know. It just is. To start with, Dominic is a married man with a family. If I stay with him someone will tell his wife so she is bound to find out. That would bring shame down on her.

Dominic's stepmother was in the same position, and she wasn't regarded as shameful.

Will you please stop mixing me up . . . go away.

You will need to eat, and Lady Florence has been kind to you. She wants her nephew to be settled and she wants you to be settled. Marriage is the only way to get out of this predicament and still have sufficient means left over to support yourself.

I'll tell Dominic the next time I see him. He'll understand.

She was beginning to shiver and was wondering what had happened to Sam when she sensed rather than heard another person. She stopped breathing and her fingers closed around the ned in her pocket. 'Is that you, Sam?'

A tantalizing smell of lime soap teased her nostrils and her sense of unease crumbled as she whispered, 'Dominic, thank goodness it's you,' and her eyes teared up. 'Where's Sam?'

'I made him a bed on the chaise longue in the housekeeper's sitting room. It's next to the kitchen so if he leaves the door open he will be warm. The other bed chambers are locked, except for the one I'm using.'

She forgot her resolve. 'It wasn't Sam's fault. Your brother told him to look after me . . . are you very angry?'

'I'm absolutely seething, my dear.'

He didn't sound it.

'I told Sam to keep an eye on you, not clatter around the country-side with a herd of stolen horses in the dark, waking everyone up. First it was my brother with the local Dorset Yeoman volunteers in tow – a villainous-looking bunch of weasels who headed for the nearest inn at my brother's expense and who are still there, I imagine. Alex and his man are sequestered at Rafferty Jones' cottage. Now I'm dragged from my bed to rescue you again.'

'You don't sound as though you're seething,' she said practicably. 'Where's Rafferty Jones?'

'Fishing . . . or so I'm told.'

'For fish or for brandy?' she asked.

Laughter huffed from him. 'I wouldn't hazard a bet on that one. But I haven't finished complaining yet.'

'Then please do and forgive me for interrupting.'

'I'd just got back to sleep when Sam came rattling at the door. He told me he'd left you sitting on the lid of Lady Florence's resting place. And here you are, enthroned. All this for a signature on a paper.'

He made it all sound so trite. Her blood ran cold as she imag-ined the grisly scene under her. No wonder she'd felt so uneasy. 'I'm on Lady Florence's grave? I'm sorry to put you to so much trouble, Dominic, truly I am.'

The sigh he offered sounded heartfelt. 'Woman, you are begin-ning to be a damn nuisance.'

His answer brought a nervous scrape of laughter from her and she reached out an arm. 'Where are you?'

There was a change in the atmosphere, a disturbance, and the impression of a warm breath against her cheek. He was close . . . too close for comfort but not close enough. Her fingers touched against his skin, found his mouth and followed the curve. 'I need to tell you something.'

He kissed her palm. His thumb anchored her chin while his fingertip was a whispery stroke along the parting of her lips. 'So tell me, my precious.'

Inner sense told her this wasn't the time to remind him he had family commitments, after all, he only had a limited supply of good will, and she had the feeling she'd used most of it up.

The warmth of his body began to draw her cold one towards him. It didn't surprise her that they fitted together so well. His arms supported her and his thighs snugged hard against her core and captured him in a shockingly intimate embrace she couldn't have escaped from, even if she wanted to.

She didn't want to. The embrace they were in was tender. His arms were strong, and warm and her face rested comfortably on his shoulder. There was just a heartbeat between them, a steady, warm pulse that beat in tandem with hers. She couldn't resist taking a small lick with the tip of her tongue. A faint fragrance of limes drifted about him, and she sucked in a deep breath, which was noisier than she meant it to be, so she followed it up with a sigh and, 'I like your smell.'

Her behind, which was almost attached to the stone edifice was decidedly cold, and getting colder by the second.

Laughter huffed from him. 'Are you going to eat me or inhale me?'

She would like to do both.

'Am I rewarded with a kiss for the rescue? I'll be gentle.' His breath stirred through her hair and he didn't wait for an answer. He tipped up her chin and took possession of her mouth. There was more than one method of kissing, she learned over the next two or three minutes, and all of them were delightfully tender – and deadly.

There was a sense of something begun but not finished when Dominic released her, and this wasn't the place to remind him of it. 'Now . . . what was it you wanted to tell me?'

Tell him you are going to marry the brigadier to save your reputation . . . go on, you know you want to.

What shall I say?

Give him the truth straight from your heart. Take courage from me. Don't think and on the count of three: one, two, three . . .

She blurted out the first thing that came into her head.

'I love you.'

He took her by the hand, laughing. 'Tell me something I don't know. Come on, Gracie girl, you're cold and have barely recovered from that beating. We both need some sleep, and without Lady Florence looking over us . . . or should that be, under us?'

Grace shivered at the thought. Although she had seen a cadaver on occasion, never one in the process of decomposition. Her father had drawn the line at that.

Her nearest experience had been a dead cat in the laneway that she'd poked with a stick. Its appearance was quite gruesome and its smell so offensive that she'd been sick in the hedge. 'Perhaps Lady Florence just wants to know the outcome of her mischief.'

'I could inform her of that now.'

That sounds definite. He's made his plans and he's not going to tell you what they are.

She could but ask . . . and perhaps flatter him a little. Lady Florence had told her that men enjoyed compliments, and they didn't like women who were shrill. She could compliment him on his ruby waistcoat. He always looked so clean and elegant, in a subtle kind of way, with only a dash of the dandy in him displayed in his choice of waistcoat. His clothes were expertly tailored.

Perhaps commenting on his toilette was being a bit too personal, though she could always polish his buttons and make them shine. But he would have a servant to do that, she supposed.

Or his wife.

Softly, she cajoled, 'Dominic . . .?'

'No . . . certainly not!'

'But I haven't said anything yet.'

'Say it then.'

'Much as I like you hugging me, my rear end is so cold it's almost frozen to the stone.'

The chuckle he gave curled softly into his ear and he closed his arms around her and slid his hands down over her waist and under the rise of her seat before lifting her down. 'You have such a pretty little rump. Let's get on our way, else I'll leave you behind with Lady Florence for company.'

'Hah! There's nothing subtle about you, is there?' she said.

'No, I don't suppose there is. I seem to have run out of subtle.'

She leaned in to kiss his cheek, found his mouth instead. She kissed him anyway.

'My thanks for the rescue, Dominic.'

'My pleasure entirely, since I enjoyed it too; you were worth returning for.'

He kissed her again, and she hugged the warm glow she felt inside her.

Seventeen

Dominic seemed to have been awake forever.

They'd spent what was left of the night together in the only bedchamber habitable, and with a fire burning in the grate. They had remained fully dressed except for their footwear. A feather bolster had created a barrier between them and he'd left two candles burning on the chest of drawers.

He'd woken from sleep when her stockinged foot, such a sweet little creature, had crept under the bolster and curled comfortably around his ankle, as if looking for its mate.

The bolster had been Dominic's idea, and was better than the original arrangement of him being ensconced in a chair that had seen better days. There he tossed and turned, trying to get comfortable, his grunts and sighs growing louder and louder until Grace took the hint and called out with some exasperation, 'For goodness' sake, Dominic, you haven't got to be such a martyr. There's plenty of room for the two of us to sleep on this bed.'

And there had been, for Gracie with her angel breaths was oblivious to his manly discomfort. He gazed down at her feet, the soles exposed when she'd drawn up her knees, and then turned over and taken the bedcover with her.

She was as innocent now as she had been when he'd tucked the cover over her, despite the enticement of just being near her. How easy it would have been to throw the bolster aside and then slide in beside her and love her just a little.

It still would be.

His body stirred and he gently kissed the arch of her foot. Her toes curled. She sighed, and then turned over. The foot escaped along with the rest of her into the protective mound of bedding.

He could love her now, snuggle into her warmth and bring her softly from sleep into a live and vibrant existence. He doubted if she would object if her air of disappointment to the presence of the bolster had been any indication.

Another sigh and she turned again, exposing a bruised cheek, which he gently kissed. He wasn't a violent man but Dominic would like to kill the nasty little swine who'd inflicted this injury on his love.

'Mmmmmm . . .' she murmured and stretched. Her hands raked the air like a cat sharpening its claws while her body slowly moved in a sinuous stretch.

Oh, God . . . there was no resistance in him now. Beyond the candles the shadows danced. Reflecting on the window glass the panes flared like a woman dancing in a rainbow-coloured skirt.

Her eyelids fluttered, and then opened, the lovely golden orbs were warm, still somnolent with sleep and shining like those of a doe. They gazed at each other in the flickering light, their mouths saying nothing, their eyes exposing everything. She was irresistible and he had no resistance.

She blinked and her eyes widened as they absorbed the light from the guttering candle. Love had changed her, yet there was no outward sign until she reached out to touch his face.

The cover slipped, exposing shapely breasts thrusting against the fabric of her bodice. Dark eyelashes quivered and she whispered his name – the sleepy mispronunciation of which tickled him. 'Demonic, did you sleep well?'

'I didn't sleep at all,' he grumbled.

When she giggled it was clear she'd realized her mistake in pronunciation.

'How demonic are you?'

Surrounded by her laughter he dragged the bolster from the middle of the bed and threw it aside. 'That you have yet to find out.'

'When will that be?'

There could never be an invitation quite as blatant. 'My sweet angel, what are you suggesting?' he whispered, and then he grinned. *An angel?* Not his Gracie, and Dominic was in the mood to prove it.

He crossed to the door, turned the key in the lock and then returned to her and held out his hands. He'd half expected that she'd protest and push him away. Instead she whispered, 'I need you to kiss me.'

'You know how it will end up? But you don't, my love.' He doubted he would get another opportunity as easy as this one.

'Then show me.' She pulled him down into the space the bolster had occupied and he slid under the bedcover with her. He inclined his head and tasted her mouth, sipping it like wine warmed by the sun. It was poetry.

A lover's kiss into musk, he thought.

His palms brushed across the nubs of her breasts as they nestled in his palm. His fingers stroked with the opening of each tie of her bodice. 'I'll help you to remove your gown,' he said, his voice husky with the need growing in him, and he stopped thinking.

When his mouth joined with hers again Grace knew she was about to cross the line. She didn't have the will to stop herself – she didn't want to.

The expressing of love was quite exquisite, Grace thought. The skin covering his shaft was silky and alive, responsive to her touch. He guided her hands on his body and while doing so, brought her to a peak in an unimaginable frenzy of shared and mindless lust.

Aroused, he had been bigger than she'd been led to believe men were, but she was accepting of him, her body eager to accept each thrust and kiss. They melded together perfectly, as though they'd been designed that way, and indeed, nature seemed to have designed them too with every twist of her body accommodating of him easily.

His mouth explored her body gently, mindful of her bruises, no doubt. His fingers skimmed lightly across her breasts, his tongue circled the rosy nubs and explored the secrets of her body. Grace welcomed every touch with a gasp of delight.

She wasn't ashamed by her behaviour, but she felt like a wanton, desirable creature lying naked beneath the bedcover, which was embroidered all over with flowers. It seemed as if she was lying in a spring flowering meadow, the air alive with the hum of bees and kisses that became jewelled butterflies flavoured with delicate spring fragrances.

Hugged into his body she smoothed the hair back from his forehead and kissed his eyelids. She sighed, for already her naked flesh was telling her she wanted more of him. If they were going to have a permanent relationship, and she admitted to herself that she didn't have the willpower to resist him, it would be best to sort out the terms now.

A trifle tentatively, she said, 'Dominic, there's something I need talk to you about.'

'Must it be now?' he murmured, his fingers sliding over the curve of her behind in a most distracting manner.

'Especially now,' and she dragged in a ragged breath. 'It's about time we discussed . . . well, your wife, I suppose.'

Dominic sat up in such a hurry he nearly fell off the bed. 'My what?'

'Your wife.'

A bucket of icy water couldn't have been more effective as a passion killer. Propping himself on one elbow he gazed at her. Did she really think he was a married man? Her expression was questioning rather than condemning yet even while she was thinking him wed, she'd also been willing to participate in some loving exercise.

He found his voice. 'You think I'm a married man? Yes, you must do else you wouldn't have raised the subject.'

'I don't mind . . . well, I do a little bit . . . more than a little bit really. I just wished you'd told me.'

All this time she'd thought him to be married. Amusement cut in. 'Who told you I was married?'

'The servants at Oakford saw you kissing a woman and she had an infant in her arms. And every time I asked questions about your family . . . well, you didn't seem surprised, and you diverted me and I never really got a straight answer.'

'Perhaps you never really asked a direct question on the matter before.'

'As well, I was looking in the church register not long ago. There is a record of a marriage in the church. Dominic LéSayres and Charlotte Carter. I just had time to read it before . . .'

He placed a finger over her lips. 'That would be Dominic Christopher LéSayres. He was my great-grandfather's brother. While you were *researching* me in the parish records didn't you check the date?'

'Oh . . . I never thought . . . I wasn't prying, honestly. I was helping to clean the pew Lady Florence used in the church. It was one of my tasks every week.' She shrugged. 'I wasn't looking for you in there . . . I sometimes did some clerical work for Reverend Hallam, and I remembered the name and I was just curious. Then when Jessie told me she saw you kissing a woman and you had a child in your arms . . .' She shrugged. 'I put two and two together and came up with five.'

He couldn't help but murmur, 'But the plot thickens. Now it seems I have a child, as well, and no doubt will find a record of his christening in the local church register. You might just remember I have a young nephew and I'm named as his god-father.' He paused before saying, 'One thing we should discuss. You thought I was a married man with a child yet you decided to overlook that small legality and offer me the ease of your body. Personally, I don't feel the slightest remorse at what took place between us.'

She turned away from his condemnation. 'Neither do I because, although I tried hard not to, I fell in love with you, I couldn't stop myself. And if you think I'm going to apologize for that, well, I'm not. Not for anything, and that includes my bad behaviour. Oh yes . . . and perhaps we should mention your bad behaviour, as well, Dominic LéSayres. You took advantage of both me and the situation.'

'That's what men do.' Softness crept into his voice. 'And I fell in love with you the moment I saw you.'

Her heart gave a giant leap when he turned her towards him and drew her into his arms. Inclining his head he placed his forehead against hers and fisting one of his hands under her chin brought her mouth level with his. His eyes were as fierce as those of an eagle but his mouth was like a touch of fire. 'Do you believe me when I say I have neither wife nor child?'

After a slight pause, she said, 'I think so.'

'Don't you trust me, my Gracie?'

'I want to . . . yes . . . I think so.'

He chuckled. 'That will suffice for now. Now we must rise and get dressed.' He slid out of bed and strode naked to pick up his clothes. She closed her eyes, and then opened them again, just as his trousers slid up over his buttocks. His body was lithe, the muscles of his back lean and taut.

Dominic was aware of Grace's glance on him, sizing him up.

He wasn't vain about his looks or his body. Everything was in proportion and worked as it should, when it should.

'Must we?' she said.

He stopped in his stride and turned. Her bare foot emerged from under the cover and her big toe wriggled, beckoning to him like a lure at the end of a fishing line.

The trousers took a downward dive and he stepped out of them. Three strides took him back to her and he leaned over the bed and planted a kiss on her mouth.

That wicked little foot of hers tickled his dangling appendage. Immediately, it sprang to attention.

'I guess it can wait a little longer,' he said.

Eighteen

Downstairs, Dominic discovered that Sam had stoked up the kitchen stove and the kettle had begun to sing.

He investigated the larder and found some cheese and bread. As well, there was a thin slice of smoked ham, not really enough for three. Two jars of preserved apples and some oats looked edible, and emerging from the depths a glass jar contained festering pickled pilchards. When he removed the lid the stink nearly choked him.

He hadn't bothered getting provisions in since he hadn't thought to cater for visitors, especially the unwanted kind. Hopefully, this should be his last day in Oakford House. He hadn't expected to have guests. There were many things he hadn't expected, and he smiled, grateful that his life had taken a step in the right direction.

His liaison with the ever-delightful Gracie Ellis had started the day off well with some unexpected physical exertion. Afterwards, Grace had fallen asleep her head snuggled against his chest, the exposed skin between the bruises as softly glowing as the skin. A glance at her back had revealed the extent of her injuries, and although the bruises were beginning to fade he could only imagine what she'd been through, and marvelled that her small body had supported his without complaint.

He closed his mind on the vision and centred on the oats. 'I could cook some oats and we can finish off the fruit.'

Sam gazed with hungry eyes at their meagre supply.

'You may share the ham with Miss Ellis,' Dominic said.

'Then there won't be any for you, sir.'

'It wouldn't be the first time I've gone hungry, but I've finished growing, so it doesn't matter. You still have a way to go, Sam Rider.'

'One of the hens is still running loose and I might be able to find us an egg or two.'

Sam went outside and after a while came back with three eggs, and a beaming smile on his face. 'Edith laid some eggs.'

'Good for Edith, and well done to you for finding them, Sam.'

'Hens be creatures of habit and use the same nesting place if they can.'

'All the same, you have sharp eyes. I think what we have will stretch to three now. Drop the eggs in a pan of boiling water and cook them for eight minutes . . . and make the tea if you would.'

'Tea is for posh folks and Lady Florence wouldn't let me have any, not even the leftovers. She said one drop would give me a taste for it and I'd get ideas above my station.'

'Lady Florence won't know. Do you think nurturing ideas above your position in life is wrong, when you've hardly lived?'

Sam scratched his head. 'Reckon I haven't thought about it much, though be blowed if I know what nurturing means.'

'It means you care for someone and you do your best to look after them. It's like a duck with her ducklings. Or perhaps it's a baby, who cannot fend for itself. His parents love and teach him until he grows into a man and can then look after himself. That's what nurturing means, especially when applied to those we love.'

'Nobody wanted to nurture me. I was left on Lady Florence's doorstep like a bag of old rubbish. They said I was a gypsy.'

Dominic didn't know quite what to say. 'That was unfortunate. I expect your parents were poor and tried to give you a better life. You have made some good friends, have you not? And you have received an education of sorts, I believe.'

'From Miss Ellis?'

Yes . . . just like his Gracie to do that, Dominic thought. 'It was good of her to spare the time, and you can improve if you work at it.'

'That's what Miss Ellis said when she was learning me to read. When I said it was too hard, she took me by the ear and said, "Do you want your head to stay empty, so questions rattle around inside it without you being able to provide answers? If you do then I'll not waste any more of my time on you. Never ever tell me you can't do anything again." Fierce, she was, and as hissy as a polecat with its tail caught in a trap.'

Dominic told himself he needed to discourage Sam from discussing Gracie in such a casual manner. He understood that Sam was accustomed to addressing her thus when she'd been Lady Florence's companion, but he needed to learn not to be so familiar. Dominic was formulating a reply when Sam blurted out, 'Miss Ellis is a good girl, and she needs to be wed.'

Tempted to tell the lad to mind his own business, it occurred to Dominic that Sam might be in the throes of first love.

Dominic's first love had been a rather thin woman with pale blue eyes who sang louder than any other female in church. When she sang a high note her voice warbled. She usually wore a cream coloured gown with little blue birds embroidered on the bodice and every time she hit that warbling high note the birds seemed to come alive and quiver on the swell of her bosom. Dominic had thought her to be a bird angel.

He dragged his thoughts away. 'Are you suggesting I should propose to Miss Ellis?' He wondered if Sam had overheard something he shouldn't have. Marriage wasn't a bad idea though, one he'd been toying with ever since he'd first met Grace. It had been wrong of him to take advantage of her, but the opportunity had been there and he was just a man. It occurred to him he was using the excuse to justify the action, as many man did.

Sam hung his head. 'I'm sorry, Mr LéSayres. I didn't mean—'

'I know you didn't.' Dominic took Sam by the shoulder. 'There's something I need to say to you, Sam. Miss Ellis is not a subject suitable for discussion between us, but I will overlook it on this occasion because of your regard for her. Do you understand what I'm saying?'

'Yes, sir, I'm sorry sir,' he mumbled, and he flushed.

Dominic poured some warm water into a jug decorated with pink cherubs joined together by a ribbon. 'I'll take this up to Miss Ellis so she can tidy herself.' Then, so the lad could regain some of his pride, he placed his pocket watch on the table. 'Can you read the time?'

'Yes, sir.'

'Good, then you'll know when the eggs are cooked. I advise you not to eat any of those pilchards, they stink to high heaven.'

Upstairs, Grace was an untidy mound under the bedcover. He placed the jug of water on the washstand and gave her a gentle shake.

One eye opened to gaze warily at him . . . then the other. Awareness followed. She gave him a small, shy grin, and then she scrambled upright, her hair flying, saying with some alarm, 'Is it time? Are they here?'

'It's time to rise. I thought you might like to wash and tidy yourself up. You can use my soap and hairbrush.'

'I'm all crumpled.'

'I'm not surprised.' He grinned, his glance going from her feet to her head, absorbing her. 'You're not as crumpled as I'd like you to be but that gown is shabby. I'll see if I can find something suitable in Lady Florence's wardrobe. She wanted you to have the contents, anyway.'

It wouldn't hurt her to unbend a little, Grace thought. If she refused to take the gown somebody else would, for Raff wouldn't hesitate to rob the place, and as for Betty Bunce, her eyes had been darting everywhere in Raff's cottage, so any goods she could get her hands on in Oakford House would soon end up on a market stall.

'A taffeta gown was delivered a week before she died. She never wore it and it's still in its box. She bought quite a few garments in the weeks leading up to her death, told me to leave them packed in case she went dancing. As if she could, she just liked pretty things.'

'I'll fetch them.'

He returned within five minutes and placed the box on the bed. 'Don't take too long if you want some breakfast. It's not much but it's all we've got.'

There were several garments in the box. The gown she chose

was a fall of cream petticoats. It had pretty puff sleeves, embroidered with yellow roses that matched those on the bodice. There was an overdress and pelisse of pale gold silk with a feathered bonnet to match. He had also brought with him a cashmere shawl for warmth.

'I'll wait outside in case you require anything further.'

She'd barely dressed when he knocked at the door again and said against the panel, 'Are you ready?'

'No, not quite, I need to tidy my hair.'

The door opened and Dominic's head appeared as he offered, 'I can fashion a braid. I used to practise on my pony's tail when I was a child.'

Stepping into the room he picked up the hairbrush and ran it gently through her hair, an action so intimate and relaxing that Grace envied the pony he'd practised his braiding skill on, and nearly fell asleep on the spot. 'You have a gentle touch, would you consider becoming my maid?' she murmured as he deftly braided it and tied the end with a green ribbon.

He kissed the pulse just under her ear, and then laughed when a shiver ran down her spine. 'I'm glad you appreciate my skills. Were I your maid I doubt if we'd get much work done, and what an eager little lady you turned out to be.'

'I didn't mean . . . you know I didn't mean that . . .'

'Didn't mean what?'

He nibbled her neck where it joined her shoulder and whispered in her ear, 'It was about time you were bedded, Gracie Ellis; did you enjoy the experience?'

She turned, certain she was blushing like a beetroot. 'You promised to behave like a gentleman . . . now you're being totally outrageous.'

'I am behaving like any gentleman would. You'll know it when I'm not. Stand up now, my sweet – allow me to take a good look at you.'

She promised herself not to engage his wintery eyes but couldn't resist the pull of them when he said, 'Do you remember what you said to me when you arrived yesterday?'

Only too well, and the shrug she gave was almost a squirm as she lied. 'No . . . I just said what came into my head . . . I was tired and I cannot remember.'

'I love you.'

Was he reminding her of what she'd said to him, or telling her that her feelings towards him were reciprocated?

He kissed her. 'So, my love, if you didn't follow me to Ringwood because you were smitten by me, why did you follow me?'

'I don't know . . . I had a plan, I think, and yes, I did enjoy your attention but I wouldn't dream of telling you that.'

His voice plucked a silky soft warning along her spine. 'A plan . . . pray tell me of it.'

'Alas, because you are trying to intimidate me, the plan has fled from my head as if it decided it was no longer of importance to such a learned gentleman as yourself.' She grabbed a plausible excuse from the air. 'No doubt I thought you needed the services of a clerk to record your meeting with the brigadier.'

He began to laugh. 'How convenient a memory you have. I got exactly what I needed, and don't you dare make a record of that. How can you look so innocent and cast a lie so convincingly at the same time?'

'It's not easy. Can you forgive me?'

'You're quite exquisite, my Gracie, so how could I not forgive you.'

'I doubt if Vivienne will, after this. Besides, people will talk.'

'Nonsense, my sister-in-law has a wonderful sense of adventure and I expect the pair of you will get on famously once you've offered her an apology. As for people gossiping . . . nothing will change that. I expect many of the gossipmongers knew your father.'

'Which is no commendation since they encouraged him in his foolishness.'

He brushed a kiss over her forehead, left another on her nose and her mouth found her own response. He held out his arm for her to take and they went down for breakfast, exchanging a kiss on every step they took.

Having eaten his portion, Sam went out to give Argus a feed.

When the lad returned, Dominic cautioned, 'Report back if you notice anything out of the ordinary. Try not to be seen or heard. We will be in the morning room.' He wished, though, it was still the cosy bed they had so recently vacated. He hoped the sun would appear to warm the room. He didn't think it was worth lighting another fire, since he hoped the affair would be over and done with and they'd be on their way home well before dark.

'Yes, sir, I promise nobody will see me.'

'Sam tracked me from King's Acres, and I didn't even notice,' Grace said.

It wasn't long before Sam returned again, his eyes shining with youthful excitement over his part in the adventure. 'The mist is beginning to thin and I saw two men on foot skirting the boundary around the meadow. They seem to be heading this way. One of them is Lord LéSayres, I think. And Daisy is missing from the stable.'

'The donkey and cart has been sold to Mr Jones. He took possession of her yesterday. Well observed, Sam. I'm also expecting James Archibald's carriage so you can keep a lookout for him if you would. He won't be here until the mist clears, which rather depends how thick it is at the Southampton end.'

Grace gave Dominic a sharp glance after Sam had gone. 'It sounds as though you're expecting trouble.'

'The trouble I'd anticipated did eventuate, but not in the way I expected. It had honey-coloured eyes and was hidden inside an ugly brown cloak, but she still kept me awake half the night, especially when she used my legs to warm her cold feet on.'

Grace opened her mouth, and then closed it again and smiled, blushing a little at the compliment. 'How unfortunate.'

'Oh, I don't know, it was quite pleasant imagining how you would feel without the bolster. Your toes are flirtatious, and when I kissed your foot good morning, your toes wriggled at me and invited me in.'

She laughed. 'I have very ticklish feet and would have known if you'd taken any liberties with them.' She closed her eyes for a moment, imagining a repeat of the same act and her toes responded, then she said, because she didn't want to be a distraction to him, 'You should have kept your mind on your job, Dominic LéSayres. Tell me what you are expecting, without the personal trimmings.'

'What I'm expecting is to get the brigadier's signature on a paper, a properly witnessed legal agreement to place Lady Florence's worldly goods in the hands of the court. When you sign a similar deposition I will present my account to the court for payment at the same time. That should be the last I hear of the affair.'

She couldn't quite meet his eyes. 'You know the brigadier will not be reasonable.'

'He might be if he doesn't set eyes on you. Yes . . . I've figured out why you're here. You have some idiotic and entirely romantic scheme fermenting inside your head about the brigadier. How did you get to be such a bird wit?'

'Not so, Dominic, have you considered that my idiotic and romantic schemes might embrace . . . another man. My mind is in turmoil, knowing my life can never be as I would want.'

His eyes lightened. 'Goodness Gracie, such drama. Did you come all this way to tell me what I already know? What is it you want? The same as me, I suspect – someone to love you, a home to live in and children. You can have all those things as soon as this mess is sorted out. Did you intend to offer yourself up as a sacrifice on my behalf? Do you think I'd allow it? I'd die rather than let that man harm you.'

'A sacrifice, how conceited you are. It just happens that I don't want you to die, and not for any reason except . . . just except,' she flung darkly at him. 'And you have no right to run my life to please your way of thinking.'

'I know. Now tell me, why did you come back to Ringwood when I told you to stay at King's Acres? I arranged it for your own safety, you know, not to get rid of you . . . but just at this moment I'm inclined to put you over my knee and smack your pert little arse before throwing you in the stream to cool off.'

'How did I get to be such a bird wit?' She gave a careless snort, and then she grinned when he glowered at her. She couldn't help it, she loved everything about him, including his frown. 'Did you want the truthful reason, or the version that would feed your vanity and soothe your ruffled feathers?'

'The truth.'

'The truth is . . . I don't really know why.'

'And the other reason?'

'Oh . . . all right, if you insist. I was scared for you and I thought that if I wed the brigadier, as Lady Florence had suggested I should, then he'd leave on the *Bonnie Kathleen* when she sailed and I'd never see him again. At least he would have the fortune he was entitled to as the only living heir. It was mean of Lady Florence to arrange matters this way.'

'And you'd have a sizeable fortune too.'

Colour rose in her face. 'If anything deserves a slap, that remark does. You know I don't want any of it and I don't want him . . . especially now. You know as well as I that any fortune that comes my way will be entirely under his control. The old lady did me no favours, but caused trouble for everyone associated with her. Marriage to the brigadier would bring an end to it.'

'On the contrary, it would simply make matters worse.' The expression in his eyes softened and he pushed a wispy lock of her hair aside. 'You are too intelligent to think matters will be as simple as that. As your husband he would have certain rights.'

Privileges she'd conveniently sent crawling to the back of her mind like an army of slugs. Her lip curled.

'He doesn't have a bad reputation without reason, and you don't have to wed the brigadier, Gracie. You can wed me instead. I'm in need of a wife.'

'Hah!' she exclaimed, then a little less forcefully, 'hah . . . You don't mean it.'

'I rarely say anything I don't mean.'

The idea stole her breath from her body. Mouth open she stared at him, and then gulped in some air before stammering, 'Would . . . wouldn't that rather complicate matters?'

'Delightfully. Sam thinks you should be wed.'

'You've discussed it with Sam?'

'Not in depth, it slipped out in a man-to-man discussion. Had he been older, he'd have proposed to you himself. The lad has reached the age when he needs to start sowing his wild oats.'

'Oh,' she said faintly.

'My pardon, Gracie. He'll get over his disappointment. I'll go and fetch him. He's rounding up our companions and has gone to feed Argus. I imagine he'd enjoy giving the bride away.'

Dominic returned, minus the lad.

'I've sent him to the church, to alert the reverend. Once we have taken our vows and the wedding is over then the court can sort this out. To be fair, I'll recommend that Lady Florence's estate be awarded to the brigadier, on the grounds that you've become my wife and can no longer fulfil the conditions stated in the will . . . therefore rendering the condition null and void.'

'Yes . . . I suppose we could tell him that, but would he believe it?'

'Once our marriage is recorded in the church register across the field and he has checked the records, he will have no other choice.'

'I've been told the brigadier's behaviour is unpredictable. He might try to kill you?'

'If he succeeds you can look forward to becoming a wealthy widow.' He gazed at the clock. 'We have an hour or so in which to hunt down Reverend Hallam and take our vows.'

'He's awfully dour, at times, and will probably refuse.'

He held out a hand to her and smiled, a smile all at once self-deprecating. 'Come on, Gracie girl, where's your sense of adventure? I can guarantee I'll make you a better husband than the brigadier ever would. As for Reverend Hallam, money will talk.'

She entered into the spirit of the game. Dominic would certainly make a better husband. Hadn't she already tasted a delicious sample of what he had to offer?

And he didn't have a wife . . . not yet. She shouldn't have believed the gossip.

Of course he didn't have a wife, whatever put such silly notion in your head? He wouldn't be taking her to the church, if he had.

Dominic wasn't the type of man to treat a wife and child so shabbily. And he hadn't made love to her just to walk away.

Her toes curled at the thought. There was such a relief in her that she could have leaped in the air like a spring lamb.

Dominic closed his hand around hers, keeping her anchored to the earth. An owl hooted, and was answered by another.

'I didn't think owls hooted during the day.'

'Didn't you, my love? Obviously, these are special owls.'

Cupping his hand around his mouth he sent a couple of quiet hoots into the air, then smiled innocently at her and drew her into his arms. He held her close for a brief moment. 'You smell delicious and you look lovely.'

The owl hooted again, but quieter, a rustle of bushes and the earl and his estate manager appeared from behind a tree. The earl gazed at them and shook his head in a way that made her blush.

He aimed a grin at Dominic. 'Well done, brother. It's about time you put in an appearance.'

'I allowed the lady to sleep in.'

'Ah yes . . .'

Grace turned her face against his shoulder when Dominic asked him, 'Were there any objections from the reverend?'

'Reverend Hallam indicated he will allow you to exchange your vows before him in exchange for a donation to the poor. He said he is not usually in favour of hasty marriages, but he can understand why in this case, and how the will could cause problems for certain parties. He agrees with you in thinking the legacy should remain with the brigadier and he has included a handling fee in his calculations. He wants to speak to you both to make sure you are taking your vows for the right reasons.'

'That's only to be expected. I'm sure my bride will be worth every penny.' His smile fell on her like a sunbeam, even though it was grey outside.

The charm of it captivated her, and she was so dazzled that she missed the doubtful glance exchanged between the brothers.

Nineteen

As Dominic had expected, everything could be bought at a price, though it was steep.

After a half-hearted discussion on the purpose of marriage, Reverend Hallam agreed to perform the rites of matrimony.

'Are you sure you know what you're doing, young lady? You've only just met this young man.'

She squeezed Dominic's hand. 'May I remind you that I know the brigadier not at all, but if a comparison is made I'm sure Mr LéSayres would prove to be extremely respectable.'

The vicar chuckled. 'So I'm given to understand. Be that as it may, Lady Florence has provided generously for you. She'd be annoyed if she learned that you had turned her nephew down.'

'Then I won't tell her. I'm well aware it's a generous gesture – and I enjoyed her company when I was in her employ. However

I don't want her fortune, or her wisdom from beyond the grave, and I certainly don't want her nephew. Besides . . . I love another.'

Dominic circled her palm with his forefinger.

'Very well . . . as long as you know the possible consequences.'

He turned to Dominic. 'As for you, young man, I suppose there is no doubting your integrity for you wear it for all to see. Do you love Miss Ellis?'

'Without a doubt, sir . . . and with all my heart.'

He shrugged, and then smiled. 'What better reason can there be to wed? I trust you will have thought it through carefully.'

'Yes, Reverend,' they lied together, for it had been entirely spur of the moment.

'We'd better get on with it then.'

Grace was already acquainted with the reverend and Mrs Hallam since one of her duties had been to accompany Lady Florence to church on Sundays. The couple had been regular visitors to Oakford House when Lady Florence had been alive, and Grace had been kept busy running ran back and forth, sometimes being required to play the piano to entertain them during tea. She enjoyed it, for her own piano had been sold to pay her father's debts.

Often, they'd talked about her, as if she weren't there and it seemed her father's demise had brought out the worse of him in the minds of acquaintances, rather than the best.

'They say bad blood will out and it has. Dear Lady Florence, you are so good to her. A girl without means or relatives can so easily be corrupted and will attract the lowliest of men. We will pray for her soul.'

Grace decided her soul could fend for itself.

Now the same woman offered Grace a simpering smile, for she was about to rise up the social ladder. 'Congratulations, my dear Miss Ellis . . . such a wealthy suitor and a match made in heaven when one considers your present circumstances, something a girl in your position wouldn't have expected.'

'I don't see why not, Mrs Hallam. Being poor is a matter of circumstance. It doesn't change the way you are . . . other people do.'

Taken aback the woman mumbled, 'It would be more ideal if your mama were here to advise you of the duties involved with

marriage and what to expect on your wedding night. She would
be so proud of you.'

Not last night, she hoped, since her groom had already demonstrated the duty involved, and she was happily looking forward
to more of the same instruction.

'I'd be quite happy to act in that role of advisor,' Mrs Hallam
said.

The woman meant it sincerely, and she looked disappointed
when Grace said, for she'd suddenly remembered the *Karma Sutra*,
'Thank you, Mrs Hallam, but I'm well informed. Lady Florence
gave me a book that explained the umm . . . the *duties* of marriage.
As well, my father was a doctor.'

Dominic's lips twitched.

It wasn't long before they were standing in front of the reverend.
The wedding guests were seated in the front pew. Dominic's
brother, Lord LéSayres, his estate manager, and Sam Rider and
another estate employee.

Standing next to the reverend's wife Sam looked solemn. He'd
been trying out his line practising it over and over again, so he
wouldn't forget it. Now the time was close he was nervous.

The reverend's wife had a severe eye on him and affected a
superior manner for the occasion, pulling it on like a Sunday hat.
Mrs Hallam also had a romantic streak, Dominic mused, for
she'd kindly offered them breakfast to celebrate the union – the
cooking of which had been handed over to the maid, for
she determined not to miss one moment of this elopement – or
the glory of having her signature rub shoulders in the parish
register with that of the earl.

> Dearly beloved, we are gathered together here in the sight
> of God, and in the face of this congregation, to join together
> this man and this woman in holy matrimony . . .

Dominic gently squeezed her hand and she gazed up at him. He
was so calm, whilst she trembled like the last leaf on a winter
bough, defying the breeze that would pluck it.

There was something not quite right about this wedding,
she thought. It was too fast. But then, she had never attended a
wedding before.

Wilt thou have this woman to thy wedded wife, to live together after God's ordinance in the holy state of matrimony? Will thou love her, comfort her, honour and keep her in sickness and in health and, forsaking all others, keep thee only unto her, so long as ye both shall live.

'I will,' Dominic said.

'Wilt thee have this man . . .'

'I will.' And the smile Grace sent her beloved was returned.

'Who giveth this woman to be married to this man?'

'I will . . . Mr Sam Rider, groom in Earl LéSayres' establishment.'

The reverend gazed over his glasses at the lad standing proudly with the bride and groom, then at Alex. 'Isn't he rather young for such a responsibility, my Lord?'

'All he needs do is place Miss Ellis's hand in yours and then—'

'Yes, my Lord, I'm aware of how to conduct a wedding ceremony.' The reverend's gaze settled on Dominic.

Dominic said, 'Then, please get on with it, Reverend Hallam. We haven't got all day.'

The reverend shrugged. 'Very well, Mr LéSayres, on your own head be it.'

'Then shall they give their troth to each other in this manner—'

Sam interjected, 'What's a troth?'

The reverend sighed. 'The use of the word troth, means promise.'

'Why don't you say promise, so ordinary folks knows what you're talking about? Ouch!'

The earl had taken Sam by the ear and now manhandled him into the nearest pew, where the reverend's wife was seated. Her gimlet eyes speared him.

'Mind your manners, Sam,' the earl said.

'But Miss Ellis said if I came across words I didn't know, then I should ask what they meant.'

Mrs Hallam raised her lorgnette to examine Sam before condescending an opinion. 'The poor ignorant child, but then, one cannot expect anything more from a lad with gypsy blood in him. Has he been christened? I can see the devil's mark at work on his forehead.'

Sam scrubbed at his forehead, then sounding injured he

answered back, 'I can read and write. Miss Ellis taught me. And
Mr LéSayres told me I rode his horse like a bat in a storm. He
didn't say I belonged to no devil though. As for that mark on
my forehead it were a gnat bite.'

The woman gave a shocked gasp. 'I will ask the reverend to
take a strap to you if you don't behave yourself.'

The reverend sighed. 'And he will refuse, on the grounds that
a wedding, in whatever form, is a happy occasion. We are all
God's creatures, Mrs Hallam. Do try to be charitable.'

'But the boy is not christened.'

Alex patted her on the arm. 'Come, come, Mrs Hallam. Let's
get the wedding out of the way, and then your husband can dunk
the lad's head in some holy water. You can act as his godmother
should you wish.'

Mrs Hallam nodded.

'So will I,' the estate manager said.

Mrs Hallam's nose began to twitch and she cast it about in the
air like a dog trying to fix on a scent. Lifting a handkerchief to
her nose, she uttered majestically, 'Whatever is that disgusting
odour?'

Sam obliged her with an honest answer. 'It's horseshit, madam.'

There was a moment when everything went quiet, and then
laughter tore from Grace. The tension eased and everyone joined
in except Mrs Hallam, who swatted the lad several times with
her parasol and had him jumping into the aisle to escape her.

Breathing heavily the woman dragged him back by his collar
and said sternly, 'If you say another word I'll ask God to cast you
from him, you bad boy.'

Sam's eyes displayed the fright he felt at the thought.

Grace turned and engaged Dominic's eyes, brimming with
laughter. She told him, 'Sam is overexcited, allow me to settle
him down before we continue.'

'I love you,' he whispered, planting a kiss on the lobe of her
ear. 'Remind me to give the lad a bonus.'

She beckoned to the boy, telling him quietly, 'Sam. I'm trying
to be married to Mr LéSayres and it's a solemn occasion. Can
we get through it without any more interruption from you?'

'Will God cast me out?'

'No . . . and he'll be looking in the other direction at the

moment. If you decide to be christened you will receive a certificate with your name written on it.'

Sam smiled.

'I expect the reverend might be more inclined to answer your
questions then.'

'And he might not,' the reverend said, with a remarkable
keenness of hearing, and he chuckled. 'This is the most memor-
able wedding I've ever officiated over. Now I have a christening
to add to the list. Shall we get it over with so we can have some
breakfast.'

They could smell it as it wafted into the church from the
nearby rectory – tantalizing little snatches of cooking on the
breeze – sausages made from the flesh of some unfortunate pig,
eggs, ham from the same pig, but the flesh sultry with apple-
wood smoke. And there would be slices of black pudding spiced
with herbs fresh from the garden, and mushrooms that grew wild
amongst the graves in the cemetery and were plucked from the
soil at the rising of the dew.

Dominic's mouth watered and he eyed the reverend, wishing
he'd hurry up and get it over with. Obviously the man liked the
sound of his own voice with all its cadences. His wife had full
lips, slightly pursed, and a splendid span of breast and hips. He
imagined that she catered for her husband's appetites admirably.

He had no doubt that Gracie would cater to his needs, as
would he to hers and he wondered what she was thinking as they
gazed with a solemn intensity into each other's eyes and vowed
to love, honour and obey each other always. He offered his bride
a smile and she blushed, though her bottom lip trembled with
the emotion of the moment, and there were tears in the corners
of her eyes. He remembered her telling him that when she was
a child she'd wondered what soul was. Now he felt it, pulsating
between them like a pure white light – a faint essence drawing
them together as one in this country church with its smell of
mice and the dust of innumerable weddings floating in the air.
Sound receded and he felt at one with all that had passed and all
that was yet to come.

He gazed up at the painted glass windows. They were probably
a donation from some knight, home from his fruitless search for
the legendary Holy Grail and paying homage to his lord by buying

himself a place in heaven. The colours picked up the winter light as they melted into the frosted glass.

He had an urge to hug Grace close. She deserved a better wedding than this clandestine affair. She deserved flowers in her hair, a ball to introduce her to the society she would live in, and a feast to celebrate his good luck in finding her.

His stomach rumbled and she stifled a giggle.

Dominic took the LéSayres signature ring from his little finger and slid it onto the third finger on her left hand. It would do until he had one made for her − a sign of his possession of her this day.

He smiled, imagining her proclaiming, 'Hah!' to such a notion. Yet, despite her air of bravado she was a tender little creature.

Finally they heard the words.

'I now pronounce you husband and wife together.'

Dominic kissed her, a chaste flutter of butterfly wings on her mouth before he raised her hand to cover his heart. He would plunder her later, when time permitted. 'Your eyes are full of dreams, Mrs LéSayres, and our wedding breakfast is waiting.'

She slid her arm through his and their fingers intertwined. 'I will wear your name with much pride, my Dominic, and when we have children I will wish for a son who resembles his father.'

'And with my pleasure.' Dominic hadn't thought that far ahead, but it provided him with an idea, a line to end his poem with − *a new star shooting across heaven.*

Mrs Hallam took Sam by the ear. 'And now for the christening.'

'Must I?' Sam wailed, appealing to Grace. 'The breakfast will get cold.'

Mrs Hallam smiled. 'There will be no breakfast for you if you don't behave, boy. You came into this church a sinner and you will leave it as a Christian. Is that understood?'

And as if recognizing the woman was a force too big to be reckoned with, Sam seemed to deflate. 'Yes, Mrs Hallam.'

It didn't take long to turn Sam into a Christian, though he shivered a bit as the cold water trickled through his hair and under his collar.

The reverend said to Dominic as they were about to leave the vicarage, 'Miss Ellis is a pleasant young woman and Lady Florence thought highly of her.'

'Mrs LéSayres,' Dominic reminded the reverend when Gracie joined them.

'Ah yes . . . my pardon.' The reverend kissed Grace's hand. 'Be good to one another. I wish you much happiness in your journey through life. Mrs Hallam and I will miss you at the Sunday services.'

When Dominic pressed a gentle kiss against her mouth and the couple smiled at each other the reverend was left with no doubt.

'As for you, young man . . .' A black leather bible decorated with gold lettering was placed in Sam's hands, along with a highly decorated certificate. 'I hope you will read a little of this every day and you will gain comfort and wisdom from its pages when needed. I've recorded your name, the date, and the occasion of the presentation in the flyleaf. Thus you will always stand as the founder member of any family who may follow you.'

It was another hour before they returned to Oakford House, their appetites satisfied, at least, for the present. There was still no sign of James Archibald, the brigadier, or of any soldiers.

Tiredness was fast overtaking Grace now the excitement of her flight and her subsequent marriage was wearing off. The wedding hadn't been very romantic and she spared a moment of regret that they hadn't waited . . . but she couldn't marry the brigadier now, even if she wanted to. She went upstairs to rest for a while, and was joined by the tabby cat. The creature cosied up to the space behind her knees and purred noisily. She hoped he didn't have any fleas.

Downstairs, Dominic joined Alex and the pair took a walk around the garden. There were still patches of frost where the midday sun hadn't reached, and there was something desolate about it.

Dominic said, 'There are too many people here. Many of them earn a living that isn't exactly honest and they can smell trouble. I have other matters to deal with and if the client doesn't put in an appearance by noon tomorrow I'm going to extract my fee, and declare the brigadier *in absentia*. The whole mess will then be in the hands of a magistrate. In the meantime I'm going to send everyone home, since the countryside is awash with rumour and that might be keeping the brigadier at a distance.'

Alex smiled. 'You're not sending me anywhere, Dom. Whether you want me or not I'm staying until those papers are signed, if only to watch your back. Don't worry, I'll stay out of your way.'

'That's what I hoped you'd say.'

'If I may also say, Dom, you're looking incredibly smug. Are you going to send your little lady back to King's Acres?'

'Yes, she's not over that beating she took yet, and is looking fatigued. I'll send for the hack we used before, as far as Poole. Once there, your steward can hire a carriage and escort them to King's Acres.'

'Do you think Grace will stay this time? I fully expect Vivienne to fly into the boughs when she sets eyes on her again.'

Dominic chuckled. 'If Vivienne does she has just cause, and Gracie deserves it.' But Dominic wondered . . . Gracie would be expecting a reaction from Vivienne, and would respond in a manner to create as little discord as possible in the household. She was quick-minded and adroit with her answers to questions.

He made his arrangements and then went upstairs to gaze down at Gracie's sleeping form. A noise came from a small moving mound under the quilt. A rat! Cautiously, he pushed the quilt aside so he could grab it.

It was no rat, it was the cat – it had sought her out. He gazed down at it and then smiled, whispering, 'I'll be damned.'

She woke, observing him through sleepy eyes, and then smiled. 'Dominic.' Spoken like that, his name was so full of husky promise that it sent tremors skittering through him.

'The carriage has arrived to take you and Sam to Poole. From there you can hire a carriage. My brother's estate manager will escort you and see to the details. You needn't stir, I can carry you downstairs.'

Her eyes cleared and her gaze was drawn to the squeaking noise coming from the bedcover and she exclaimed, 'Look Dominic, there are two dear little kittens!'

'Yes . . . I've seen them. Did you hear me say you're leaving?'

'Yes,' and she sucked in a breath, took a stronger stand. 'I'm not leaving without taking my cats. They will starve to death.'

'Are we going to argue about this?'

'Of course we're not. There's a woven basket in Lady Florence's room that the cats can travel in . . . and that old shawl on the chair to keep them warm. It's cold outside.'

'Look at me, Gracie.'

Her eyes were misty with unshed tears and he brushed the hair back from her forehead. 'I don't want to leave you, my love, but you're proving to be a distraction and a bigger responsibility than I need at the moment. You must promise to do as I tell you.'

Her eyes cleared. 'We've hardly said our vows and already you're issuing orders, however, on this occasion I will promise to do as you ask.' Her arms slid round him in a fierce hug. 'You don't really mind about the cats, do you?'

One of the kittens rolled onto its back and squeaked with alarm when it couldn't roll back. It had a fat stomach, white socks and sharp little teeth.

Dominic turned it over again and guided it to its mother's teat, sighing in resignation. He had to admit, they were pretty little scraps of fur, but they would grow into animals that killed for sport as well as food, and reproduced themselves often, and with regularity. 'I'll go and fetch the basket and shawl.'

Grace gave the cat family a thoughtful look. 'I could almost swear the cat I saw last time was a male.'

Dominic could swear to that too, but he wasn't going to. It had been a battle-scarred, smelly old tom and he wasn't about to encourage that notion. A cat was a cat and this tabby little lady and her small family had touched his heart with their beguiling little mews – well almost. His mind scrambled for a plausible reason to help her accept a cat she'd never seen before. 'As I recall you were running a fever at the time.'

'That must account for it.'

As he straightened up to leave, she said, 'You wouldn't lie to me would you, Dom?'

'Never,' and he placed his hand on his heart and planted a kiss on her upturned face. 'You're not being logical, my love. If the cat had been a male it wouldn't have given birth to a litter of kittens, would it now?'

'It had crossed my mind . . . as does the thought that there might be some fine trickery going on.'

'Sleight of hand, do you mean?'

'Are we really married? It happened so fast I can barely believe it.'

He drew her away from the necessity of him providing an answer to that question with: 'Poor Sam gained a godmother.'

'And didn't he splutter when the holy water splashed on his face. Mrs Hallam told him it was his sins being washed away.'

'And he told the reverend he might become a priest now he was sinless.'

'Then God help us,' they both said together, and laughed.

Dominic patted her hand and he grinned as he walked away, but nervously. What would she do when she realized the wedding had been almost entirely illegal, for Dominic didn't live in the parish, the customary banns had not been read, and neither had they obtained a licence from the bishop.

Like the reverend had said to him afterwards.

'You must tell her as soon as the court papers are signed and accepted. No doubt Miss Ellis will understand your motive for the deception.'

Would she, when he already felt guilty for lying to her.

Twenty

Ringwood

After the carriage had carried Grace, Sam, and the basket of cats away, Dominic exchanged a glance with his brother.

'I'm tired of waiting, Alex. I'm giving James Archibald and the brigadier until noon tomorrow when the *Bonnie Kathleen* is due to set sail. After that I'll have Oakford House boarded up. In the meantime I'm going to prepare an account of what's taken place here, to put before a magistrate.'

'You can place the matter before me for a legal ruling.'

Dominic shook his head. 'I've already considered doing that because you're conversant with the whole shabby affair. However, some might think you are biased. People talk, and they twist things, and I don't want Gracie's name dragged through the mud.'

'Have you forgotten that your lady is one of the foremost claimants named in the will?'

Dominic grinned. 'How could I forget it? Gracie has signed a waiver, which was countersigned, first by myself and then by your estate manager. She isn't claiming anything from Lady Florence's estate, least of all the brigadier for a husband.'

'Wedding and bedding the delightful Miss Ellis was a calculated move on your part, Dom, and I've noticed a beauty emerging from under those bruises. Nobody can accuse you of being short on intelligence but sometimes you can be downright manipulative. What plan do you have in mind?'

'It's the plan of having no plan at all. Make no mistake, Alex, I love Grace and I believe it when she says she loves me. If she changes her mind when she discovers she was tricked then I can only persuade her that it was for the best. I'm going to sit here for a while, get on with my work, and wait to see if something eventuates.'

'Be careful, Dom, these are hardened villains you're dealing with.'

'Which is marginally better than freezing one's balls off in the church tower. Though I admit the church is a good vantage point when the weather is clear. Once the mist rises, the view from there no longer exists.' Dominic sighed. 'Alex, all I want is some signatures on a sheet of paper so I can pass the will on to a court official. It's a simple procedure yet the authorities of two counties have become involved and through their interference it's now become a farce. It shouldn't be this hard.

'As for Gracie, I married her because I love her, and because I couldn't bear the thought of her married to an old man. I admit that marriage fit rather neatly into the situation at the time, but it wasn't as calculated as you imagine. It was a declaration of love on my part, and, as such, will be honoured when convenience allows.'

'Reverend Hallam took some convincing, but as usual, money talked.'

'Doesn't it always.'

'The tower doesn't look like an easy place to escape from if a retreat was needed. I'm going over to the farm beyond the church to see if I can purchase some food,' Dominic said.

'I'll do that, in case your clients arrive.'

'Don't be long because I can smell moisture in the air. It mists up early at this time of year, and it's stealthy. It creeps out of the mud flats and fouls the air like stinking breath.'

The truth was, Dominic was looking forward to returning home and getting back into his work routine. To all intents and purposes he now had a wife to care for, or almost. He could soon make it completely legal, something he was looking forward to. He must try to turn her away from becoming his clerk though, for he'd come to the conclusion that it would be too inhibiting for the other clerks. However, an idea was forming in the back of his mind.

Alex returned from his forage looking pleased with himself. Hanging from his saddle to his right was a square canvas bag containing a loaf of bread, a pot of honey, cheese and some potatoes baked in their jackets. There were also lamb pasties, still warm from the oven – all neatly packed for ease of carrying and a minimum of damage to the containers. To distribute the weight on the horse and complete the purchase, the bag on the left contained a flask of brandy, a bottle of wine and a small keg of ale.

Dominic gazed at the initials on the polished silver flask. They belonged to Lady Florence's late husband. Dominic couldn't remember seeing the flask at Oakford House when he and Gracie had carried out the inventory, but perhaps the former master of the house had gifted it to someone.

He decided not to make a fuss about it for he had no wish to put himself to the bad of the people living here – people who had placed their trust in him. Not only for the sake of Lady Florence's memory but now, for his Gracie.

He felt a little niggle of disquiet when he thought of her. He should have kept her with him. If anything untoward happened to her now he'd never forgive himself. She was inclined to be impulsive and he hoped she reached King's Acres without incident, or at the least, she didn't create a situation that caused one, which was the more likely alternative.

He turned to Alex. 'It's going to be cold tonight. You might as well stay in the house. I could certainly do with the company.'

'You're tired, Dom. Take some rest? I'll call you if anything suspicious happens or visitors arrive.'

'Just don't shoot them before they have time to state their business. I don't want a full-scale war on my hands.'

It seemed to Dominic that he'd only just dropped off to sleep when he was woken by a shake to the shoulder.

'The attorney, James Archibald, has arrived,' Alex said.

Dominic groaned and gazed at his watch, surprised to note that he'd been sleeping for an hour and a half. He could have done with more and he ached all over, the result of bending a long man into a short chaise longue he supposed. It was better than nothing though.

He rose, cradled his back in his hands and worked his thumbs up and down his lower back muscles. Then he stretched until his spine clicked into its proper position. Tidying his clothes he made his way to the morning room and pulled a smile to his face. He held out his hand. 'Mr Archibald, at last. I'd almost given up hope . . . welcome.'

Poole

The harbour town was all of a bustle and a stiff breeze coming off the water played havoc with the ladies' skirts and the men's tall hats alike. Grace's escort found her a sitting room to share with another woman. As well as the tavern there was a ladies' parlour that could be serviced by an inner door. Another door opened on to an outside courtyard and offered access from the road.

When Grace offered the woman a smile and bade her good day, she was subjected to a rather disagreeable stare.

Grace supposed she did look untidy and travel worn since her gown was anything but fresh, and Dominic's hastily fashioned horse's tail was becoming unravelled. Her unwanted companion was equally, if not more, dishevelled.

She closed her eyes for a moment or two, thinking of Dominic.

How gentle his hands had been against her neck and scalp. She'd leaned back into his palms and he'd laughed and placed a well-aimed and upside-down kiss on her mouth.

'Not now, Mrs LéSayres. Much to my regret, I have work to do,' he'd said.

Her eyes flew open. She must try and stay awake.

The landlady came bustling in, and her smile encompassed them both. 'I daresay you ladies would like some tea while you're waiting for a cab. Mrs Edwards?'

'Certainly not!' her companion grated out. 'Ladies do not partake of refreshment in public houses, especially with people they are not acquainted with.'

The landlady sniffed at such a notion. 'I daresay you're able to introduce yourselves then. Miss Ellis . . . may I be of service to you?'

'You're busy, and tea is too much trouble. I would appreciate some watered ale though, and I would be grateful if you would make sure the lad travelling with me is suitably refreshed.'

'Yes, Miss Ellis.'

As the landlady began to depart Grace removed the lid from the cat basket and asked her, 'Can you spare a saucer of milk for my cat? She has kittens to feed and must be hungry.'

'Certainly, Miss Ellis.'

Thank goodness word hadn't got out about her marriage into the LéSayres family. Her escort had made sure she was settled before going into the tavern to wash the dust from his throat with a tankard of ale.

Mrs Edwards gave a rather gruff bark of a cough. 'If you'd permit me, Miss Ellis, perhaps you would allow me to join you in the same . . . only I'd prefer the ale full strength. It's much more fortifying. Bring us a jug, woman.'

The landlady was back with the refreshment in a few minutes and Grace's companion indicated the table with a wave of her hand. 'Leave it there on the table and close the door when you leave.'

Gracie received hers with a smile, and then, seemingly in defiance, the landlady banged the jug, and the old woman's tankard on the table, and, her back stiff with affront, bent to make a fuss of the kittens. Her voice softened. 'Dear little things.'

'Vermin, they should have been thrown in the river to drown,' Mrs Edwards barked.

Someone should throw her in the river to drown, see if she'd like it. Grace examined the woman a little more closely. She was of a stocky stature and square of chin. The blue gown she wore under a travelling cloak had seen better days and she still wore the cowl.

Grace found the woman's manner odd. She would have much preferred her own company.

Grace poured some milk into a saucer. There was also some roughly chopped meat. The cat sprang in a graceful arc to land on all fours. Her ears flattened, her eyes slitted and she looked as though she was smiling with the pleasure of her kill, even though it had been provided for her. Her purr increased, like a woodsman with a saw.

When Grace thanked the landlady the woman left with a smile on her face.

'You shouldn't encourage such people to be familiar,' the woman said.

'Mrs Edwards . . . I would prefer not to be told what to do by a complete stranger. Our host is doing her best to accommodate us, so perhaps you should take a leaf from your own book.'

The woman poured the foaming ale into two tankards. 'That's what she's supposed to do.'

'You've left no room for the water.'

'Full strength won't hurt you. It's only a tankard.'

Grace supposed not. She hadn't set eyes on Sam since he'd stepped down from the Jones's carriage and wondered where he was. He was of an impressionable age so he was probably hanging around the soldiers and learning their vulgar songs and curses. She smiled as she remembered his behaviour at her wedding and the antics of Mrs Hallam as she tried to control him. She shouldn't have laughed, but she'd been unable to stop herself.

Her companion's voice intruded into her thoughts again. 'We're not entirely strangers, Miss Ellis. We met when your father was treating me for . . . for an *adult* ailment. You were about as high as my waist. Your father pushed you out of the room, I recall, and you poked your tongue out when he turned away. Over the years I have often wondered what had happened to you.'

Grace thought that was extremely unlikely. 'Well, now you do know.'

'You must tell me all about yourself.'

'Must I? How very tedious. I think not since I'm not very interesting.'

'Nonsense, my dear. I overheard a rumour just an hour ago that you were about to wed?'

So news had begun to leak out. 'Really . . . one shouldn't listen to rumours.'

Grace could hear the mother cat lapping up the milk and the urgent squeaks as the kittens rolled about in the warm dent that their mother had recently vacated trying to find her.

Grace wondered, had she called for her own mother after her death, oblivious to the fact that she would never see her again? Had she laid in her crib in the empty nursery calling for someone to hug her, to soothe her fears when she was scared in the night? There had been a void in her own life until Dominic had come to fill it, strong and dependable.

Sorrow filled her, for a mother she'd never known, for a father whose habits had destroyed him, and had almost destroyed her as well. As for Dominic, his background was similar but he cared, and he showed it. It was not just the physicality of loving but the intimacy when his arms were around her in comfort.

When the cat finished her meal she stood by the door, gazing back at Grace.

Grace let her out and she found a patch of earth to scratch in before licking her paws and washing daintily behind her ears. She returned to the basket to see to her family and Grace left the lid off to give her some air.

'You had a position with Lady Florence Digby after the death of your father, I believe?' the woman said.

She supposed the woman was from the village to know so much of her. 'I acted as her companion and carer and I was sad when she passed away. Did you know her then? I didn't see you at her funeral.'

Mrs Edwards crossed one leg over the other, and then, hampered by the skirt she wore, she cursed it and reversed the action. She had big feet and her riding boots were well worn.

'Lady Florence was my aunt,' Mrs Edwards said.

'I can't recall her ever mentioning she had a niece.' Dominic had never mentioned a niece either.

When the woman leaned forward to pick up her ale, her sleeve slipped up her arm, just enough to expose a small portion of his wrist. Grace had never seen a woman with such hairy, muscular wrists.

There had been something odd about her companion right from the start, now Gracie noticed her peculiarities. Apart from well-developed shoulders, her voice was deeper in tone than that of a female. In fact, Mrs Edwards could easily be passed off as . . . a man.

A man . . . was that it? Was Mrs Edwards a man?

She tried to shake the thought off. She was being stupid, thinking such a thing. Hadn't she paid a penny to see a bearded lady at the county fair last year, and gently pulled her beard to see if it was a real one?

Nevertheless, Grace proceeded with caution. 'We seem to be talking at cross purposes and I think we should put our cards on the table.'

'As you wish. You may take the floor first.'

'Without wishing to cause offence, I am beginning to wonder if you are what you seem to represent.'

'The veritable wolf in sheep's clothing, you mean?' Mrs Edwards gave a high-pitched giggle as she threw the cowl off. 'And you're the adorable blushing lamb I'm about to wed. My soldiers will love you, Miss Ellis.'

Grace brought Dominic into the fray. 'I will never be your bride since I'm wed to another. I feel I must inform you that I'm wife to Mr LéSayres. For that reason alone you cannot pursue that particular clause in the will. Instead, my husband has come up with a plan to put before the courts on your behalf, one of benefit to you.'

'And himself by the sound of it.'

'You misunderstand, sir. My husband is an honest and honourable man. As for myself, I have no wish to inherit anything from the will for if I'd agreed to marry you then my half would go straight into your pocket. I have signed a waiver to that effect.'

The brigadier's gaze sharpened in on her. 'Are you travelling alone?'

'You are too inquisitive.' A quiver of pride leapt into her breast when she gently twisted the ring on her finger. 'I do have escorts and it won't take long for them to appear if I call them.'

His lips pursed. 'It appears that the district is teeming with the

Dorset Yeomanry, and there is quite a kerfuffle going on over which one will shoot me dead.'

'Place me first on the list.'

'It's easy to say and much harder to carry out.'

'I don't think I'd have any difficulty.'

He smiled at that. 'They are saying I came out of the bog and performed some witchery on the horses.'

'And did you?'

'Very droll. It happens that someone is removing saddles and scattering the horses. They are milling all over the countryside and causing chaos. I suspect, it can only be someone from your side.'

'My side? I have no side.'

Grace suspected Sam's hand in that. Well done Sam, she thought, keeping herself from laughing as best she could.

Leaning forward the brigadier giggled again. 'The yeomanry are searching every carriage, including the private ones. The men are sodden with drink and have no respect, especially for women. You're such a pretty little gift for my soldiers . . . it would be a pity if they didn't live long enough to enjoy you.'

Grace's mouth dried.

'How many escorts did you say you had?'

'I didn't say.'

'Your husband isn't one of them. Where is he . . . at Oakford House?'

Grace didn't answer that. 'My husband is merely the executor of the will. He has come up with a plan that will enable you to inherit everything, should the courts agree. The least you can do is display some good sense and give him a hearing.' Grace sucked in an impatient breath. 'You're not as fearsome as you present, brigadier.'

He looked at her and smiled. 'Let's hope you don't goad me into proving you're wrong. Someone has given you a good beating.'

'I wouldn't have described it as good.'

'Allow me to guess who inflicted it? It wouldn't have been LéSayres.'

She smiled at the thought of Dominic hurting her. He was too gentle a man.

'Was it that servant couple who worked for my aunt? I caught them selling part of my legacy in the marketplace, or should it be *our* legacy. They were with a man called Pawley. I recognized him from my infrequent visits to my uncle at Oakford House in the past. My aunt said he used to steal from her. I'm touched that you'd rather take a beating than steal a chunk of my silver metal. As it turned out, I sold it to a silversmith for a rather nice profit.'

'Anything missing will show up in the contents inventory, and my husband can't be held responsible for any losses since you chose to ignore the safeguards that were made.'

'My . . . you have been a busy little snippet.'

'I had no choice, since my husband kept me employed with the inventory. You will find everything in order should you care to look at the papers. What did you do to Jessie and Brian Curtis?'

His gaze snapped to her face and lingered there. 'Why should you care?'

'Because I wouldn't like to have anyone's death on my conscience . . . not in the pursuit of money.'

'Ah yes, the money. It always comes back to the money. The woman didn't appear to be downhearted at being parted from the worm she called her husband. She had a bruised face and a swollen jaw.'

So Brian had beaten Jessie, too. Poor Jessie.

'Curtis was encouraged to join the King's navy.' The brigadier placed his ale on the table and began to remove his woman's garb, emerging from under his drab cloak and gown like a flamboyant poppy in his scarlet soldier's uniform.

'You look more handsome dressed as a man; you remind me of my late father.'

'Thank you m'dear, I'll take that as a compliment.' He held his side and groaned.

'Are you in pain?'

'It's nothing that a dose of laudanum won't cure.' He gave her a sharp look. 'Do you have any in your bag?

'No, but there's some at Oakford House and your aunt always kept some on hand.' And at least she would be taking him in the right direction, even if she was his hostage, and Dominic might shoot her by mistake.

Grace reminded herself that the poppy's heart stored powerful opiates that robbed people of their senses. It was addictive, and could kill if not handled properly. The brigadier's empty eyes reflected an addiction to the narcotic.

She'd be the first to admit her knowledge of medicine was restricted to her father's books, his unconscious teaching of it and her ability to absorb it. Doctoring was a profession closed to women, except for the birthing of children. Therefore she was limited. More likely the brigadier was suffering pain from a war wound. Or he might be constipated, in which case a good dose of liquorice would affect a cure and improve his disposition.

She felt a sudden surge of pity for him. 'I'll mix you a dose when we reach Oakford House.'

'Why are you being nice to me? Dammit girl, I've just nabbed you and I might kill you. Aren't you afraid?'

'Is that what you did to Jessie and Brian . . . kill them?'

'Not at all. The men were given a choice . . . a fight to the death for the woman, or to join the king's navy. There just happened to be a ship in the harbour needing extra crew. As for the woman, I daresay she will manage, since she seemed to be the resourceful type.'

Grace's blood began to run cold and she felt a moment of pity for the Curtis couple, despite the way they'd treated her.

The brigadier seemed tired and swayed on his feet. He'd begun to perspire.

'Are you going to drink your ale?' he said.

'I'm no longer thirsty.'

'As you wish.' He reached for it, downed it in a couple of gulps and belched. He held out a hand. 'Come along, my dear.'

Fear sliced through her calm. 'I'm not your enemy though you have chosen to make me one, and I'm not going anywhere with you willingly. I'll scream for help.' She wondered if she could appeal to his finer feelings, but when he placed his hand over her mouth she doubted if he had any.

'Screaming is a waste of breath since nobody will hear you above the din, but hear this. If you do scream I'll kill the first person who comes to your aide, whether it be man, woman or child.'

The noise from the tavern had increased with two separate authorities trying to out-curse and out-sing two different, bawdy drinking songs.

But it was worth trying and she wasn't going down without a fight. She opened her mouth, and as his hand closed over it she dug her teeth into his fingers. It was the brigadier who screamed.

'That's no way to treat a prospective husband.' He swore, and taking her by the hair he dragged her, bumping painfully, across to the courtyard door. Without ceremony she was pushed through it and dumped in the arms of a soldier. 'Here Willie, you take her.'

Willie tied a kerchief round her face whilst she kicked and struggled. He cuffed his hand around her throat, squeezed her windpipe and said against her ear, 'Don't fight so hard, girl, and then you'll not get hurt.'

The brigadier warned, 'I might need her to bargain with, so keep her in one piece for the time being.'

The third man spoke up. 'We should leave the woman and get out of here.'

Willie leered at her. 'Spoils of war, Oliver, and she's quite a prize.'

'I didn't join the army to fight women. I joined to defend my country from the Frenchies – not that I've seen any yet.'

'You can tell a Frenchie by the colour of his backside as he runs from the British.'

Oliver laughed at the joke. 'I daresay the French make the same remark about the British. Besides, I don't like wenches who are unwilling.'

The brigadier sighed. 'Then I would suggest you rejoin your fellow officers in the barracks if you're afraid of the outcome. Willie and I can manage without you. You don't have to join in, though she's a lively one and we might need you to hold her down.'

Willie squeezed her thigh with bruising fingers. 'She feels like any other light-skirt to me, but smells sweeter.'

'And you smell like a thousand decomposing tomcats,' she yelled at him, which was the worst insult she could think of.

'The lady has a vivid imagination,' Willie said, laughing. 'Here Oliver, you can carry the baggage. I need to relieve myself and I might be a while, since I rather fancy the serving wench. Just follow the brigadier and I'll catch you up.' He picked her up and practically threw her up to the second soldier, the one called Oliver, who jerked her the rest of the way by her arms.

She kicked out at him and missed.

He pulled the kerchief from her face and dashed it to the ground. 'I beg your pardon Mrs LéSayres. My mount is restless and I didn't want you to fall under his hooves. Would you care to repeat what you said?'

Now her voice was no longer muffled she made it quite clear. 'I said . . . you're a stupid idiot.'

'Yes, madam. I quite agree.' He set the horse in motion and they headed for the road.

She carried her tirade further. 'You are also dim-witted and grotesque, and if you lay one finger on me my husband will kill you in the most painful way possible. Do you understand?'

'Your humble servant, Mrs LéSayres.'

'How do you know my name?'

'I must have overheard it at the inn.'

'Please let me go,' Grace whispered. 'My husband will pay any reward you name for my safe return.'

'There are too many men of ill intent abroad, and to let you loose amongst them while their blood is up would invite trouble. Trust me, I'm on your side, and please don't give me any trouble. The sooner I deliver you to your husband the better for all of us.'

Trust him? Grace was halfway to doing that, for he was polite and appeared not to display the aggressive tendencies of his companions. But that could be a trap.

'If you really didn't want trouble you shouldn't have invited it.' Grace elbowed her captor in the ribs. 'I'm not a sack of turnips to be thrown about.'

He swore when the horse began to buck under them. 'Keep still, you devil.'

With a silent apology to the horse Grace dug her heels into his flank. The beast squealed and surged forward. Oliver's foot tangled in one stirrup and he was forced to release her so he could use both hands to secure his seat and take control.

The flailing legs of the horse missed her for the heartbeat or two it took her to roll out of the way, and then she scrambled into the undergrowth, picked herself up and began to run.

She heard a whinny from Argus and headed in his direction. Would this nightmare ever cease? Grace wished she'd never heard of Lady Florence. There was a drumming of hooves and a horse came up beside her. The soldier called Oliver leaped off. Taking her wrist in a firm grip he stayed her flight and talked quietly but with a sense of urgency. 'I'm a friend of the LéSayres family. Now . . . please mount the horse so I can safely take you to your husband, otherwise I shall attach you to a rope and will make you trot the rest of the way. Take your pick.'

No wonder the authorities were eager to see the back of these soldiers. The rough and tumble of the other side of the world seemed the best place for them.

She snorted. It was an expression of disapproval Lady Florence might have made . . . and it sounded satisfyingly scornful. Then she scowled, which felt infinitely better. 'Dominic will kill you.'

'On the contrary, he will be glad to see me, and more than happy to get his wife back in one piece, I should imagine.'

He wouldn't have sent her away if he'd be happy at her re-appearance. She'd be happy to see Dominic again though.

As she mounted the horse she managed to land a kick on Oliver Tuttle's knee.

'How many times do I have to tell you I'm on your side? Woman or not, I'll spank you if you goad me again,' he roared.

Grace closed her mouth.

Twenty-One

Oakford House

James Archibald mopped his face. 'Forgive me for being late, Mr LéSayres. The main road is blocked and I had to prove who I was and state my business before the yeoman would let me through.'

'I admit I'd nearly given up on you, but there should be enough afternoon light left for our purpose.'

'What is going on, and where are your clients?'

'Like you, they must be held up, for they haven't yet arrived. I'm glad you have, though. A situation has arisen that needs attention and I need a credible witness.'

James cleared his throat and took a sip from his brandy flask. 'Do you have any ale at hand, my throat is dry.'

'I have a small amount of ale at hand and will water it down. The labourers will come to board the house up, and I bought it for them.'

'Goodness, I daresay the labouring man can slake his thirst with water. However, I doubt if it will be necessary since a reputable gentleman of my acquaintance has expressed a desire to take up a lease on the place if it becomes available . . . or indeed, purchase the house outright. I would suggest he could act in the capacity of caretaker until the will is proved. I can supply you with references.'

'All the better, Mr Archibald. However, the house must be left in a secured state. Once the matter has gone before the court to decide who owns it you can apply to the owners.'

'Owners? I understood the brigadier and the housekeeper . . . Miss Ellis, wasn't it? I was looking forward to a wedding.'

'The brigadier will not be wed to Miss Ellis.'

'Oh . . . and may one ask why?'

'Because Miss Ellis is married to me.'

James Archibald couldn't disguise the surprise in his eyes. He smiled as the obvious presented to him. 'Well, young sir, may I offer you my congratulations on winning both the hand of the fair lady and her equally fair fortune. A neat move on your part, yes indeed. I'm in awe.'

Dominic, who along with his brother had survived childhood penny-poor for most of the time, found it hard to cast off the contempt he felt towards this man. 'You misunderstand, sir. My wife has no fortune except for a small legacy from her mother, which Mr John Howard has managed for many years.'

The attorney followed after him into the kitchen. 'You offered a penniless servant marriage? Goodness me, Mr LéSayres, what is the world coming to? I do hope she is properly grateful. Even so, society will never accept her.'

'It's me who should be grateful, and to hell with society. May I remind you that Mrs LéSayres comes from a family of good repute and she has no need to prove herself or be grateful to anyone – including you.'

'Of course . . . of course . . . no offence meant, dear sir. I had forgotten her family connection. Her father . . .' He shook his head as if trying to remember, so Dominic helped him.

'Doctor Harold Ellis . . . I will leave you to ponder on that while I fetch your ale.'

'Ah yes . . . and the girl's mother was a cousin to the Landsdown family, many times removed. It was quite a romantic tale, I believe. There was a scandal when the pair eloped. Later, her mother died in tragic circumstances, in childbed. Harold Ellis was inconsolable and he took to the bottle.'

Dominic said quietly, 'There's nothing romantic about that. Be careful, Mr Archibald, this is my wife's family you're discussing. Men have been challenged for less.'

The attorney pressed his kerchief against his brow. 'Quite so. No offence meant, and I do beg your pardon, Mr LéSayres.'

After a short silence Dominic nodded. 'We will adhere to the business at hand. I suggest three options that might act as possible solutions. Firstly, the fortune should be awarded in its entirety to the soldier. After all, Brigadier Crouch is Lady Florence's only legitimate kin and he has a valid claim in his own right. Option 2: The legacy could be awarded to a charitable organization. Option 3: It could be shared equally between them. I will recommend the first option.'

'Your reason?'

'If I hadn't intervened in the matter Grace may have been forced into becoming the brigadier's wife, or just as bad . . . boarding the ship to the Antipodes to search for gold with that Curtis couple who worked here with her.' But wasn't that what he'd done, only more gently? Unknowingly she'd become his co-conspirator in an invalid marriage?

An owl hooted, Alex's signal to warn him that someone was approaching.

'While I fetch your ale perhaps you'd care to read the papers I've prepared.'

'A moment sir, you omitted to mention Mrs LéSayres. What of her claim?'

'Mrs LéSayres demands nothing from the estate and makes no claim. The waiver is there as a safeguard.'

'You put forward an unusual case for the brigadier. I don't know what to say except I believe this is the first time I've met a totally honest man. Some might think you a fool but I admire you.'

'Thank you, Mr Archibald, I'll accept that as a compliment while recognizing I'm not without fault. In actuality very few people I've had dealings with consider me to be a fool.'

Dominic found his brother in the kitchen, along with an agitated estate manager. They were strangely muted for a group of men.

'Something has happened. What is it?'

Fear filled him when the estate manager informed him, 'Mrs LéSayres was captured by the brigadier and another soldier. A third one, William Reeves, known as Willie and supposedly the worst of villains, received a few smacks from a yeoman's truncheon to the head when he took a fancy to the serving wench and dropped his guard, along with his trousers. He came off the worst. He's been delivered to a ship that's waiting to set sail and the ship's surgeon is trying to stitch his split face back together. The brigadier is still at large; he's a wily old sod.'

'And the other man?' Dominic asked.

'Oliver Tuttle is not considered dangerous. He's from these parts so is known to the locals. If Mrs LéSayres is in his charge she will not be physically hurt. He was here to inform the brigadier of his imminent capture. Do you know him?'

Alex nodded. 'I know him from our university days. I recall he was not without courage, but neither was he cruel.'

'I don't feel as though I'm doing enough to be of help to her.'

Dominic gazed doubtfully at Alex, who smiled reassuring him. 'I attended Cambridge with Oliver Tuttle. It's believed he has Grace with him and she's unharmed.'

'Is that fact or supposition?' Alex asked.

'The latter, my Lord.'

Dominic cursed as he engaged the eyes of his brother's agent. 'Tell me what happened?'

'We were at the inn waiting for a cab to take us on to Poole. Mrs LéSayres was in the ladies' parlour taking some refreshment while we changed carriages. There was an elderly woman in there, so I thought she was safe. However, it turned out that she wasn't a woman, but a man dressed in women's clothing. He approached Mrs LéSayres and threw off his cloak to reveal a soldier's uniform. Your lady tried to fight him off but there were three of them. She was dragged through the courtyard door by her hair and pushed on to his companion's horse.'

Dominic winced. Now sick at heart he knew he'd never forgive himself if Grace were injured. 'In which direction did they go?'

'The landlady said the youngest of the soldiers whispered to her that they were going to bring the young woman here, to Oakford House, and he would do his best to keep her from harm. Oliver Tuttle, she said his name was.'

'When everyone realizes the soldiers were those they were seeking they rushed to get their horses, only to find them wandering all over the road with their saddles removed and scattered. Only two of the three soldiers' mounts were ready to be used.'

Dominic reminded himself to give Sam a bonus. 'If the brigadier comes here we should be able to sort this mess using reason. Do not resort to violence unless my wife is in a place of safety, and it's unavoidable. I don't want to start a war. Do any of you have weapons?'

'I have a pistol, but it's not loaded,' the estate manager said.

Alex was already loading his. 'So have I.'

'Don't use them unless they're needed.'

He hoped Gracie kept a cool head. She was intelligent and brave, but everyone had a breaking point. 'Now, I would suggest you find somewhere with a vantage point. You need to secure yourselves until we see what eventuates.'

'The two upstairs windows will do.'

When the attorney sidled towards the door Dominic stopped him with, 'Mr Archibald, you must stay here for I will need you to act as a witness.'

Trembling, the man sank into the nearest chair.

Dominic didn't blame James Archibald for being in a funk, since he was about to retire and the brigadier's reputation had gone before him. 'Take courage, Mr Archibald. If all the tales told of this man were true I would have been dead days ago. We are dealing with a man who has very little self-control, so you will be safer here in the house. The brigadier knows he's in the wrong, for he stands to lose everything. Attacking us will not further his cause, and he surely must know that by now.'

If he didn't then Dominic had sorely misjudged the mettle of Gracie.

Alex shifted to a position by the fireplace and shrugged. 'He will be expecting opposition and will smell a trap if you're the only person in sight. Remember, he has a fully armed soldier with him.'

'Who will be on our side if it's who I think it is. Grace is in good hands.'

There was the drum of horse's hooves and Dominic moved to the window to watch one of the soldiers appear. He was well past middle age . . . and looked tired.

Gracie followed with Oliver Tuttle. She slid down from the horse. Oliver created a barrier between Grace and the brigadier, who staggered a little.

Dominic dashed down the stairs, his heart pounding in his mouth and his skin crawling from the thought of the danger she was in – danger she seemed unaware of.

He threw himself through the front door into the carriageway in time to see Gracie side-sweep Oliver. She held out her hand to the brigadier. 'Give me that pistol too before you shoot yourself, you idiot.'

When he wavered she plucked it from his hand with an exasperated sigh and threw it into the undergrowth, where it exploded.

Grace gave it a surprised look, seemingly uncertain of what to do.

Dominic's mouth dried.

The brigadier rallied a little. 'Now I can't defend myself.'

'You wouldn't have to if you didn't make such a nuisance of yourself to begin with. If you would care to look up at those windows you will see an armed man standing at each. If they'd intended to kill you then you'd be dead by now, which is not to say they won't kill you if the mood takes them.'

Dominic took her in his arms and his eyes sought hers. Her heart was beating like that of a wild creature caught in a snare. 'Did they treat you roughly, my love?'

'Just a little. The brigadier nearly tore my hair from my scalp. The one called Willie insulted me verbally. Oliver nearly jerked my arms from their sockets, but he did it for my own good, lest I ended up under his horse's hooves. At least he was polite.' Her voice began to wobble and tears filled her eyes. 'He roared at me like a wild bull when I kicked him.'

Oliver bowed. 'My pardon, madam, it was the only way I could think of to stop your tirade.'

Dominic wanted to laugh at that. This brave little snippet of a woman had disarmed an experienced soldier and relieved him of his pistol. After her rough handling she was tattered and torn, smeared with mud and her hair tied in knots. Yet a harsh word made her collapse into tears.

She said now, 'I believe the brigadier to be ill, and he's tired, so please so don't treat him harshly.'

'It's not for me to be judge and jury of this man's behaviour. I'm here for one reason, and the sooner we get it done the better so I can take you home.'

Dominic smiled at the other soldier. 'Well met, Oliver. I believe you roared like a wild bull at my wife.'

Tears welled up in her as she realized she was safe. 'Argus is upset. Shouldn't someone go and tell Sam there is no need to stir the horses up any longer.'

Dominic held her against his shoulder. Her hair was a wayward knotted mess, and the urge to kill the brigadier for hurting his lady was strong in him again. But the man was too old.

'Did you want me to swear out a complaint for the way you were treated? Is everything well with you, my love?'

'I guarantee it.' the brigadier said. 'Your woman has told me some tale about the legacy. She said you had a plan.'

'I do, and this could have been settled a week ago. Come into the morning room. James Archibald is waiting to witness the signatures. He also wishes to present you with an offer from a professional couple to buy or lease the house, should it be awarded to you. I'd intended to offer a recommendation for you, but after today's debacle I'm on the verge of changing my mind.'

Her honey eyes came up to his, wary, for she didn't know him well enough yet to read his moods. His present mood was anger, and a manly need to offer some revenge on Gracie's behalf. But the man was too old, no matter how skilled he was. Dominic could hear his breath wheezing in his chest.

Grace pleaded into the silence, 'The brigadier is in pain and

I have promised to mix him some laudanum to ease it, after which he will give your plan for the legacy a hearing.'

'Will he indeed.'

Oliver stepped in. 'Due to your bravery on the field of battle and your many citations, the army intends to retire you with full honours.'

'I can't wait,' the brigadier said, sarcasm uppermost in his voice as he glanced up from his signing. 'Am I under arrest then, Oliver?'

'No sir, but you must regard me as your official escort to London, where you will appear before the generals.'

'Do you have papers stating that?'

'In my lodging.'

'Then I'm in nobody's charge except my own until you get those and show me them.' The brigadier finished his signature with a feathery flourish.

'And what of your behaviour towards my wife, am I to let that go without punishment?'

'We could fight a duel over her, in which case you would lose, since I'm an expert with both sword and pistol. Then your brother would be forced to challenge me. I would also kill him. However, I have no time to exhibit my prowess with weapons, and duelling is a messy business. Perhaps you'd allow me to apologize instead, Mrs LéSayres.'

The brigadier bowed over Grace's hand and said with great charm. 'With the greatest sincerity I offer my deepest apologies, Mrs LéSayres. I have never thought to take a wife, but I'm sorry I missed the opportunity on this occasion. Your husband is a lucky man,' he said and he placed a kiss on her hand.

She snatched her hand away and moved behind Dominic for safety.

'What do you want me to do with this scoundrel, Gracie?' he said.

She clung to his arm. 'Nothing that will bring you harm. I believe the brigadier suffered a severe injury to the head on the field of battle. He told me it requires constant medication, and his heart is erratic.'

'And you believe him?'

'Yes . . . I'm aware of the signs.'

So was Dominic, but only because she was standing so close to him. 'That may be so, my dear, but you can mix the doses of medication while he remains here with me. Then I'd like you to rest for a while.'

Once he was free he would find time to render her hair wayward all over again.

'I beg you to be lenient, Dominic. He has not caused injury to anyone. It was the soldier they called Willie.'

'Who is now badly injured, I believe.'

'I don't wish trouble on anyone, and I don't want to see you dead.'

Dominic grinned, knowing, as did she, that he was susceptible to her pleading. 'As you wish, my love, but may I remind you that the brigadier is not a fractious child to be soothed, he's an old rogue who knows exactly what he's doing. Isn't that correct, brigadier?'

The brigadier winked at her.

'I'll go and prepare your medication.'

She prepared two doses, and then sealed the lid on the spare glass vial. The brigadier swallowed the dose and placed the spare vial in his pocket, nodding his thanks. 'It sounds as though Willie might need this one.' He cackled with laughter when she kissed Dominic's cheek, and he turned his attention back to the papers. After a while he gazed up at the attorney. 'I have a condition or two of my own to add, if I may.'

'What are they?' James Archibald asked, and with some impatience now they were no longer in peril.

'When I die, if I have no heirs, which seems likely at my age, what's left of the house and legacy will be turned over to charity. As for Mrs LéSayres . . . with her husband's permission—' and he offered Dominic a nod – 'I would like her to have what my aunt intended – that is, the contents of her room. It will compensate her a little for the rough treatment of her. Will you accept that on your wife's behalf?'

Dominic nodded.

'Now, with some good luck and a little speed I shall rejoin my regiment and set sail for *terra Australis*. High tide is at midnight, and I should arrive at the ship before she sets sail . . . though she'll wait if necessary. Why don't you join us, Oliver? The great southern continent is well on its way to becoming a land of plenty. I can promise you adventure, which is better than sitting at a desk polishing the seat of your chair with your arse or pouring cups of tea for the officers. The regiment could do with some fresh blood and a new officer or two.'

'My father wants me to remain in London. Besides, what should I tell my superiors?'

'A little ingenuity might be helpful. Send a note with a messenger just before we sail. Tell them you succumbed to an overwhelmingly patriotic urge to represent your country in the new colony. I will write the order and sign it, since you can't refuse a direct order from a superior officer.'

Interest sparked in Oliver's eyes.

A clever move, one that would turn the tide in the brigadier's favour. Dominic couldn't fault it.

'I might seek out that woman, Jessie . . . take her with me. I might even put a ring on the wench's finger. Do you think she'd accept such a proposition.'

He headed for the door. 'Don't take too long making up your mind, Oliver. I doubt if Willie will be fit to travel. Besides, he gives my regiment a bad name.'

Grace didn't trust the brigadier and her hand curled around the ned in her pocket. He could easily kill Dominic with the sword. She gave a scornful, 'Hah!' and when the brigadier reached for it she hurled her ned at him. The ned hit the blade, split open and showered sand all over him.

'Your woman has a good aim,' he spluttered, brushing the sand from his uniform. He dusted the blade almost tenderly, the long slice of quivering death answering with a cold, loving song as it slid back into its sheath.

Grace shuddered. How many men had fallen under its bloody onslaught? How many more would it kill before it rusted away into nothing? As long as there were wars, she supposed. She shuddered.

'If this gets out I'll never live it down.'

'It will merely add a moment to your legend,' she said, but doubted if he'd live long enough to reach his destination.

He blew her a kiss.

Grace had been about to tell the brigadier that Jessie was

already married, but she recalled that she'd made the same mistake over Dominic. She wondered about her hasty marriage. Shouldn't she have signed something? She dismissed the thought. Dominic was a gentleman, not a man to use trickery to gain his own way. She trusted him implicitly and believed in him.

'I must go to my lodging and collect my personal effects,' Oliver Tuttle said striding after him.

'Get on with it then soldier. We haven't got all day.' The brigadier vaulted on to his horse with no sign of impediment, and rode away without a backward glance.

After a moment of hesitation Oliver said, 'Good day, gentlemen, nice to see you again . . . Mrs LéSayres . . . I'd best be off then . . . things to do.'

He tipped his hat and followed after the brigadier.

Twenty-Two

It was early morning, at least nine o'clock. The day was crisp with frost, revealed and disposed of as the sky gradually lightened and the temperature grew fractionally warmer.

Alex and his estate manager had left the day before.

The Jones's family carriage pulled away from Oakford House, carrying the luggage, mainly those contents of Lady Florence's room that Grace wanted. They would change to the more comfortable King's Acres carriage at Ringwood. Sam slept on the opposite seat. He was still a child, one making his own way in the world, and in the best way he could.

Dominic rode Argus, who was quiet, having made the most of his short taste of freedom by rounding up and covering a couple of available army mares that had flirted their tails at him.

Inside the carriage, Grace was wrapped in a drowsy blanket of dreams.

They had not meant to spend another night, but the inventory needed to be checked and adjusted for the new tenants. James Archibald had recommended an agent for the house, who lived in Ringwood and Dominic agreed to take the account on to his books for the time being.

The strongbox that had been the cause of Grace's beating from Brian in the first place had been concealed in the false bottom of a trunk containing a tangle of embroidery silks and other objects related to the womanly pursuits of sewing and painting. The trunk had been searched many times without it being discovered, since the false floor of the lower section was hard to open. At the moment it was tucked in the space between the seats. Dominic expected to deposit them in the local bank, and obtain a receipt. In due course the problem of probate would be resolved.

Grace came to her senses when the carriage jolted to a halt so Dominic could settle the bill for the ale consumed by the soldiers and the yeomanry. Grace sought out the innkeeper's wife. 'What happened to my cat and her kittens?'

'I'm sorry, Mrs LéSayres I thought you'd left them, so my sister gave them a good home. She's a farmer's wife and they settled in right away. She's going to let me have one of the kittens when he's big enough to fend for himself. You're obviously a person inclined to be kind to God's creatures and I've got a dear little pup you could give a home to. Someone abandoned him on the doorstep, all cold and shivering and near to death.'

Grace's heart went out to the pup in his rough, brown fur, clutched against her bosom. He snuggled into her arms, making beguiling whimpering noises and gazing at her through anxious eyes.

When they were about to depart the pup gave a couple of yaps. Dominic gazed down at it, resignation in his eyes. 'What have you got under your blanket, for certain it's not the cat and her brood?'

'A home was found for the cats.' She lifted the corner of the blanket. 'This is a puppy.'

'Well, at least it's not a carthorse.'

'It was left on the landlady's doorstep. He's so small and sweet, look at his pretty little feet,' she said, prompting a favourable answer from him.

'I've seen feet like that before, on my brother's lurchers.'

She tightened the noose a little. 'You seem to have an interest in feet. I was never allowed to have a dog when I was a child, though I always wanted one. I took him as a gift for you. I thought you'd like him. He'll die in the cold if we don't give him a home.'

Dominic was enjoying her attempt at artfulness now. She was too honest to carry it off and was beginning to laugh. Eventually she gave in to it. 'Damn it, Dominic, I promised the pup he should have a home with us. Every man should have a dog, so tell me you like him, otherwise he'll be upset?'

'I do like him. I love him, he's the best gift I've ever received. I love you more.'

'What will you call him?'

'Baron.'

Baron sighed, and sensing he'd been accepted, he fell asleep.

Poole

It was late in the afternoon when they reached Poole. Sam went ahead to King's Acres in the LéSayres carriage with the luggage and the pup, and accompanied by the earl and his agent.

The sky deepened from blue to a deeper violet. Grace was seated in front of Dominic on Argus. The stallion walked with an easy swaying motion. The horse seemed to be settling down now, growing used to being handled. He was fussy as to whom he'd allow on his back, though.

The head groom had told him, 'Argus has a good turn of speed but he's been ill treated, I imagine. His temperament is improving. Be firm with him, but don't punish him with pain. He should breed well.'

Grace snuggled into the man she loved. 'I'm cold.'

'I'm sorry . . . I wanted to show you something.'

'I won't see much in the dark.'

'We might, or we might not.'

'You're talking in riddles.'

'I'll take a room at the inn afterwards and we'll soon find some way to warm ourselves.'

It wasn't hard to guess how.

They went uphill for a short while and then stopped. Now the sky revealed itself as a cloak of black satin sprinkled with stars that reflected in the water of the harbour. He lifted her down. 'We're standing on my land, Gracie. It was the first purchase I made when I began to make a profit. It has increased in value considerably. If you like it, we will build our home and raise our children here.'

A star streaked across the sky and disappeared beyond the horizon. Grace cried out at the fleeting miracle.

'Creating a symphony, a new star . . .' he said softly.

'When are you going to give me this poem you're composing, Dominic?'

'I don't know. There's a time for everything, and my poem hasn't quite settled into its style yet.'

She turned into his chest, held him tight and smiled into the darkness surrounding them. 'You're being a tease. Do you think that star we saw might have been your mother's star?'

'I expect she was showing her approval.'

'I love you,' she said.

He bore her hand to his mouth. 'I love you too.'

'How much?'

'As much as all those stars above us, and they're beyond counting.' There was something in his voice, a reluctance that sent a chill through her. He hesitated for a moment and then he said quietly, 'There's something I must tell you.'

The stars in the sky spun around her, peppering her happiness with a worrisome spot of decay. 'Do you not love me after all?'

'Didn't I just say I did love you, and always will.'

Dread gathered inside her. 'Then if it isn't that, perhaps you are married to another after all, or perhaps you have children and you didn't want to tell me. I don't mind. I will love your children as though they were my own – like Lady Eugenie loved you and your brother. And if you are married I will still adore you, and will do so until I die.'

He ran his knuckles gently down her face. 'Such a lot you have endured, my Gracie. Now this.'

'What is *this*? Tell me.' Fear flamed in her again. 'You're not ill, are you?'

He chuckled, and then kissed her with great tenderness. 'If I tell you I've deceived you, will you be so forgiving then.'

'Have you deceived me then?'

'Yes, I'm afraid I have . . . but it was for your own good.'

The moon went behind a cloud and stayed there.

Twenty-Three

Gracie couldn't believe what she was hearing, and her vulnerability was suddenly very apparent to her.

First she'd been Miss Ellis, and then she'd become Mrs Dominic LéSayres. Now she was Grace Ellis again.

She fell silent, near to tears. So much for her pride in using his name, in repeating the marriage vows, when she had meant every word uttered – and he had not. She had trusted him, given herself to him and told him she loved him. How many other women had he treated like this, as a means to the end?

She had given him everything she had, while he'd given her nothing but a future that would never materialize. What about the land on which he'd build their home, the children they'd share? She no longer had a roof over her head so where would she go now. His promises had all been lies.

'Gracie . . . talk to me.'

'And say what? That your behaviour is reprehensible, that I cannot trust you and you've brought me down as far as I can go.'

'There's no need to be so melodramatic, my dear. We will be married properly as soon as I can arrange it. The licence will be obtained, the banns will be properly read, and, come the fourth Sunday, our vows will be exchanged and there will be a New Year's Eve ball to introduce you to local society. This I promise you.'

'I know most of them. They are the people who turned their backs on me when I had nowhere else to go.'

'Can we not allow them that small slight, when none of us are perfect?' He kissed her ear. 'I thought you loved me . . . you said you'd love me unto death.'

Dominic was the very devil to deal with. He countered fantasy with logic and vice versa. When she was agitated he was calm. 'That was before. Will you please stop kissing me. And stop being clever.'

Laughter huffed from him. 'Oh Lord, I knew your pride would be pricked but I didn't think you'd make such a fuss. It's not that important.'

She pushed him away. 'It might not be important for you, Mr LéSayres, but you've tricked me into believing we were married, and you've made a fool out of me.'

His voice cooled slightly. 'Mr LéSayres is it now? May I point out that it's you making a fool of yourself. If you'd done as I asked in the first place and stayed safely at King's Acres instead of pursuing some hare-brained plan of your own, then there would have been no need for this conversation. Shall we drop the subject for now? If you allow time for your temper to cool you might be able to apply some reason to the subject.'

'Reason . . . hare-brained . . .' She mentally stamped her foot, and, feeling totally miserable, she turned away from him and began to walk down the hill, tears scalding her cheeks.

He caught her up. 'Where are you going, my Gracie?'

She was shivering now, and it wasn't all due to the cold. The dark void of the sky scape with its uncountable number of stars served only to remind her of her loneliness. Her life was falling apart, all her dreams scattering like seeds in the wind. 'I don't know.'

The fob watch he wore under his jacket offered him five muffled chimes and sounded like a death knell. 'Can you forgive me for being such a fool, Gracie?'

'I don't know . . . I can't think and I don't want to talk about it now.'

She didn't want to talk about it ever.

'Will you ride with me? I'll take you to King's Acres.'

Where else could she go? When she nodded he lifted her on to Argus and mounted behind her. She stiffened when her body touched against his.

It was a romantic night. There was enough moonlight to illuminate their way as it sailed out of one cloud and into another, appearing again like a cutter carving up the sea and wind. It painted the foliage with a brittle icy crystal.

Argus thundered along, his feet drumming on the hard–packed earth, faster than Dominic usually allowed. There was something wild and exhilarating about the ride, and dangerous but it was more about horsemanship than temperament. Dominic knew how fast he could go and still keep control. He and his horse were a perfect fit. Steam clouded the air around them. Grace clung on to Dominic, tighter than she wanted to, and when they could smell the animal's perspiration he gradually reduced his stride.

Soon they reached King's Acres. He handed the reins to the stable hand on duty and slid her from Argus's back. When she wouldn't meet his eyes he lifted her chin with his forefinger, so she had no choice. 'Gracie, trust me. I do love you.'

Even those words couldn't warm her, since she no longer believed them.

Vivienne came from the drawing room, pulling a shawl round her shoulders. 'Alex wasn't sure if you'd be home in time for dinner, so I told the kitchen to cook for you both anyway. It will be lovely to have a full table again.' She kissed Dominic's cheek. 'Welcome home, Dom, you look done in. Is your business over and done with now?'

'It seems so. I'll be returning to my rooms after dinner.'

'What a pity, I was looking forward to hearing of your adventures.'

He managed a grin that made Grace's stomach flutter with guilt at the twisted pain of it. 'I'll be home for the weekend, as usual.'

'Alex is in the library. Go and talk to him.'

There was so much love in this family, and Grace wanted to be part of it. She owed Vivienne an apology. 'I'm sorry, my Lady . . . leaving as I did was rude of me.'

'I admit I was a little piqued at the time, but nothing is unforgiveable. We worried before your maid found your note, but we knew Dominic would look after you.' Vivienne kissed her cheek, and then said, 'You've been crying, Gracie dear. Is there something wrong?'

'I'm, tired, that's all. The cold air has caused my eyes to water.'

Dominic removed his hat, gloves and topcoat, and handed them to the waiting footman who carried them away. 'Grace is tired and hungry. Unfortunately she has overtaxed herself these past few days, and it's been a long ride. Would you like me to carry her to her room?'

'I'm capable of managing by myself.'

'As you wish.' He gave her a short bow, and then he turned on his heel and strode off.

Vivienne looked bewildered. 'I've never seen Dominic so put about. He is not his usual self.'

Grace admitted, 'We have argued.'

'May I ask what about?'

'I'd rather not say, it all seems so stupid now.'

'Did Dominic start the argument? He has a tendency to withdraw into himself, and then let fly. He wouldn't have liked you placing yourself in danger on his behalf.'

'I see.' They walked together up to her room, and she was only a little out of breath, though it felt as if her energy was draining away.

Jancy was bustling about, unpacking her bag. She was wearing the King's Acres house colours of dark blue with white collars and cuffs, and with a white apron over the top.

When Grace lived in the house on the hill with Dominic she must buy her servants their own colours. Pale blue perhaps, since it was such a clean and neat colour.

But Dominic's word had proved to be false and her house on the hill would probably never eventuate.

Her grievances burst out of her. 'We were wed . . . and it was all lies, for we had no licence or permissions. All we did was to exchange vows. I didn't know it was an illegal marriage until an hour or so ago. I didn't expect him to be so casual about it, I suppose. He had it all planned out. Now I don't know how I feel.'

'About him?'

'About anything. Dominic made me feel so secure, yet there is something about him that's so precious and vulnerable, and . . . needful of me.'

'And now you don't love him . . . doesn't that tell you something?'

'I do love him, Vivienne. He's so unexpected . . . but I've never known him to be as curt as he was this evening. He promised we would take our vows again, and with all the legalities intact and he even showed me the land where our home was to be built. He had everything planned, but it was a diversion from what he really wanted to tell me.'

'Which was?'

'That he'd deceived me. That we were not married after all.'

'That was clumsy of him.'

'I told him I no longer trusted him, and I still don't.'

'Oh, my dear, that would have wounded him. No doubt he will think it through and reach the same conclusion. He will try to put things right between you, and he might even make a grand gesture with an ultimatum. If you want my advice, make him work a little for your favour, but don't put him in a position where his back's to the wall. Now . . . you have to sleep and regain your strength.' Vivienne turned to Jancy. 'Fetch your mistress some mutton stew and dumplings while I ready her for bed.'

'Yes . . . my Lady.'

'I'm not hungry, Vivienne.'

'You will be when you taste the stew. It's just the thing for a warm winter's evening. Cook has had it on a slow heat all day and the meat falls from the bone.'

Vivienne was right, the tasty hotpot filled Grace up and made her sleepy.

The whisper of a man's voice only just penetrated the darkening barrier of her exhaustion.

'How is she?'

'She ate most of her dinner, has warmed up and is now fast asleep. She is upset, but as far as I can see the pair of you have blown things up out of all proportion. Grace does have a legitimate grievance, but so do you. Leave her for a while, my dear.'

'How long is a while?'

'A month . . . you can see her in church on Sundays.'

'A whole month, and with the congregation commenting on everything we do and say. That will be torture. Can I see her now.'

'Just for a moment, but don't wake her.' Vivienne chuckled. 'You know, Dom, if you truly love Grace then you will easily survive a short parting.'

The recumbent Grace could picture the expression on Dominic's face, that endearing little frown of his, and she wanted to giggle.

He picked up her hand, kissed her palm and folded her fingers over the kiss. 'So be it, Gracie girl . . . Vivienne has just lit the fuse and we will see who will win this little skirmish. I know you better than you know yourself, and if I'm going to be made an ass of I'm going to do it in grand style, and do it my way.'

'How exciting,' Vivienne said. 'I knew you'd come up with an ingenious plan. Do tell me what it is.'

'Certainly not, it's none of your business.'

'It will be everyone's business by tomorrow. I know you went through with that form of marriage to protect her, dearest brother-in-law but now you must take time to court her. Surely you can think of something romantic to make her feel loved.'

'Grace does feel loved, she just won't admit it.'

Grace fell into sleep feeling somewhat annoyed . . . even if there was a grain of truth in his words.

It was not such an easy night for Dominic. He tossed and turned like a frog in a frying pan as he went over the details in his mind.

Tomorrow he would see the reverend. Over the next three weeks Dominic could post the first bann, and if nobody objected they could wed on the fourth Sunday. He had his work to do as well, and he remembered he'd offered Gracie the clerk's position and sat up in bed.

That same day he sent a pile of documents with Vivienne for her to copy. They were connected to her small legacy. She ran her finger over his signature, murmuring, 'LéSayres.' She still wore the gold ring he'd placed on her finger.

Vivienne smiled at her. 'Dominic said he'd wait for the small bundle, since he's in a hurry. You will have to sign them and he'll countersign them. The other papers are to be copied over the coming week.'

She'd just started to sign them when Eugenie came in for a chat. 'My goodness, aren't you dressed for church yet, what are you doing?'

'I've got to sign these papers.'

'Well, do hurry.'

Grace abandoned the reading of them and quickly signed the remaining papers. Eugenie took them from her and headed for the door. 'I'll give these to Dominic, you get yourself ready for church.'

Jancy came in, slightly out of breath. 'I'll fashion your hair.'

Dominic's plan regarding Grace was related to his brother, and was overheard by a passing footman. The words spread like ice melting on a pond. Servants passed the news on. Ladies began to trim their hats and men left visiting cards. Conjecture ran rife.

The following Sunday saw the homely little church packed to the rafters.

There was also a sizeable crowd waiting in the churchyard. Introductions were made. They took their places inside, squashing in where they could.

The reverend moved into the pulpit, beaming happily.

Dominic arrived, his pale trousers tucked into his boots. A ruby in a gold setting secured his snowy cravat. His jacket was a blush of dark rose that matched the gown Grace wore with the velvet bodice.

It had been one of the garments from Lady Florence's wardrobe. With an unerring eye Dominic had packed the prettiest and newest garments, along with accessories and bonnets.

'I can't afford all those gowns,' she'd protested.

'You've already paid for them with some interest from your mother's legacy. They look as though they were made for you and will do for a start. Don't worry, I'll give you a receipt.'

She blushed when all eyes turned her way. So this was his method of bringing her around to his way of thinking. Her calf muscles tensed as she prepared to take flight.

'Miss Ellis, may I?'

She nodded, her forefinger smoothing over the ring she wore.

Sweeping her a bow Dominic grinned and slid into the empty space beside her. It was a tight fit. 'Your pardon for being late, you may proceed, Reverend.'

There was a sprinkle of clapping as her heart exploded in all directions, and she tried not to smile. Sometimes she felt as if she could eat Dominic LéSayres, and this was one of those moments, with his thigh pressed warmly against hers and laughter in his usually austere face.

He kissed her hand.

Grace closed her eyes and allowed her imagination to run riot until the reverend said, and quite unexpectedly, 'I publish the Banns of Marriage between Dominic LéSayres of this parish, and Grace Elizabeth Ellis. If any of you know cause, or just impediment, why these two persons not be joined together in holy matrimony, ye are to declare it. This is the first time of asking . . .'

There was a breathless silence. She shot upright in her seat and half turned her head, to be confronted by a sea of faces full of eyes. They were curious, amused, assessing and brimming with good wishes, and if anyone objected she would kill them! She opened her mouth to protest but couldn't get the words out. She felt like an exhibit, a goldfish swimming in circles in a glass bowl. Next time she would publish her impediment and put an end to it . . . she just had to think of one.

After a few moments the reverend nodded in satisfaction. 'We will now say the Lord's prayer together.'

There was a collective exhale as she bowed her head.

She whispered, so only he could hear it, 'Not me . . . you're past redemption.'

'I thought you liked wicked men. Don't you love me any more, my angel?'

'No . . . yes . . . sometimes.'

He smiled. 'That's encouraging.'

Grace sat through the rest of the service, her eyes closed, marvelling at the lusty country voices that thrust the words of the hymns out of their mouths with a joyous sincerity that rang to the rafters.

When she arrived back to King's Acres she found a wicker basket on the chair.

'Mr LéSayres left it for you before you went to church,' Jancy said.

'Oh, how lovely of him . . . I must thank him.'

She'd barely lifted the lid when there was a hiss. A bundle of striped fur leapt at her. She managed to catch it, lifting it by the scruff of the neck like its mother would have. 'You don't have to be so fierce. Nobody will hurt you.' She cradled him against her chest and stroked his chin until he relaxed and began to purr. 'There now, Jancy will go and fetch you some milk and then you'll feel like one of us.'

'Your man left you something else,' Jancy said.

'Please remember to refer to him as Mr LéSayres.'

It was a roll of parchment tied with a red ribbon.

'What is it?'

'I don't know, Miss Ellis.'

She opened it with trembling fingers. It was the poem Dominic been writing for her.

Winter love (1)

Love should be declared in the evening
When fierce snaps of firelight ignite
Scarlet rainbows in your hair and
Mellows the bouquet of strawberries
And wine that turns a lover's kiss
Into musk in our seeking mouths.

Verse 2 follows next Sunday if you behave.

Twenty-Four

The Sunday that followed was similar, with Grace, squirming in her seat and ignoring Dominic as much as she was able considering the urgency she had to be with him. The banns were read. Nobody had objected, but why should anyone object . . . except for herself, of course?

All the same she couldn't help but look forward to the next verse of her poem.

Between Sundays they had busied themselves, making arrangements for the ball, and praying the weather wouldn't rain or snow, or do anything remotely unfriendly to spoil the New Year

festivities. The three ladies' maids were summoned, the contents
of their wardrobes tossed out and different garments tried. They
shopped for new ones and practised their dance steps.

'What will you be wearing?' Eugenie asked Grace one day.

'I have clothing Lady Florence provided for me in her will.'

'That's day wear.'

'I thought I might decorate a gown with some lace.'

'Then it will look like a day dress decorated with lace sewn
on to disguise it.'

'It will have to do because it's all I have. It was kind of Lady
Florence.'

With some heat in her voice, Eugenie said, 'Nothing that
woman ever did was a kindness to you. Thank goodness Dominic
saved you from her scheming. If you hadn't died from that beating,
you might have died from starvation.'

'Dominic grows schemes like a field grows turnips,' Grace said,
and felt compelled to defend the woman. 'Lady Florence wouldn't
have wished, or expected, any harm to come to me. She just wanted
that nephew of hers to reform. I quite liked the brigadier. He
scared me a little but there was something fearless about him.
He was also amusing, and had a lot of charm.'

'You told Dominic that?'

She nodded.

'What did he say?'

'He gazed at me as though I was a lunatic, then he pulled on
his scowly face and made me laugh.' She kissed Eugenie's cheek,
guessing that the woman's countenance was a little dented now
her small charges had grown into men with minds of their own,
and that other women would take her place. 'I do love him,
Eugenie.'

'Then why are you making him run in circles.'

'He knows why.'

While Eugenie inspected her wardrobe Vivienne took Grace
with her to the window and examined her face. 'Your skin has
healed quite beautifully, Grace, and you have such pretty hair. You
are quite a beauty, no wonder Dominic fell in love with you.'

'I have a gown and accessories that would be perfect for
her,' Vivienne ventured. 'When it arrived from the dressmaker
I discovered it was too short.'

From the depths of the book Eugenie chuckled. 'I remember that one.' She laughed again. 'My goodness, Gracie, where on earth did you get this book from?'

Giving a little cry Grace flushed to the roots on her hair. 'It belonged to Lady Florence. Dominic packed my bag and I thought it had been left behind.'

'You mean Dominic has seen it? Let's hope he doesn't expect you to put everything into practice when you're married.'

'I have not yet received any formal proposal, nor can I trust him now.'

'Oh, stop being such a mope, Gracie.' Vivienne pounced on the book when Eugenie let it go. Grace giggled when she turned a page and then burst out laughing. 'Oh, my goodness, look at that—'

A knock came at the door and the book was hastily shoved under the quilt. The kitten had been busy practising its fighting skills and had tied himself into a knot with stray ribbons. He hissed, leaped in the air, and trailing the ribbons behind him joined the book.

Jancy opened the door.

It was the housekeeper with a tea tray. She set it on the table, and then handed her a small package and another roll of parchment. A smile lit up her face. 'A messenger brought it for Miss Ellis.'

'Who's it from?'

'I can't rightly say, miss.'

Gracie knew without looking. The box inside the package contained two golden chains with tiny rubies and twinkling diamonds joining them.

The two women crowded about her. 'Isn't that lovely. Dominic has such good taste, and you can wear it in a hair arrangement as well as a necklace. What does the message say?'

She held it gently against her body. She wanted to savour it, keep every precious word for herself. 'I don't know, I haven't had time to read it yet. Go away so I can.'

'Come Vivienne, let's give Gracie some privacy. You fetch the garments and accessories you were talking about, while I pour the tea. Cook has sent up some muffins, we must eat them while they're hot.'

Grace left them and moved to the window. Gently, she broke

the seal on the parchment and unrolled it, flattening the paper in her palms.

Verse 2

> Beyond the window moonlight creeps
> Like molten silver to kiss the naked limbs
> Of the birch, frost snowflakes on the glass
> As delicate as the lace on a wedding veil
> Crushed and discarded in disarray
> You reveal me to myself.

'Oh, Dominic, you are so very worthy a man. How could I have thought you'd deceive me,' she whispered, and tears filled her eyes. She placed the precious parchment into the drawer with the first verse. She wouldn't read them again until she had it all.

She couldn't wait for Sunday to arrive, when she would see Dominic again, if only from afar.

She avoided the places where she usually could be found, the window seat on the stairs with its view over the dreaming hills to the distant sea, the library with its smell of age, leather and dust. One night she crept down there in the dead of night and buried the *Karma Sutra* in the dimmest corner of the shelves amongst the dustiest books.

Mostly Grace stayed in her chamber, where in body and mind she recovered from her injuries, due to the attention of Eugenie and Vivienne. Sometimes Vivienne brought the son of the house to visit. Little Nicholas was a delight.

The dress Vivienne carried in later that afternoon was perfect, made from a creamy satin fabric with lace overskirt. The sleeves and bodice was sprinkled with pearls. There was also a velvet cloak with a fur trim to keep the cold at bay, a hat with a fluff of feathers.

'The outfit matches your necklace perfectly,' Eugenie said.

Grace laughed. 'And now you're going to tell me it was all a coincidence.'

The two countesses gazed at each other and laughed. 'What else can it be?'

'A LéSayres plot,' she suggested.

The days had slowed and shortened as winter settled in. The

sound of the sea surging against the shore was a muted but ruthless grind of pebbles and sand. The wind sent up great sprays of water and she was carried away on the wings of a gull and across the sea, restless and whispering his name.

'Dominic.'

Sometimes she woke with a start and couldn't help but wonder how the brigadier and his regiment were surviving such a restless surging of water when they were in such a small vessel.

She was lonely despite the visits from Vivienne and Eugenie, but tried not to show it. What would she do if Dominic decided he didn't love her any more, where would she go?

The earl visited her on the third Sunday. 'Are you comfortable . . . is there anything else you need?'

'Thank you for your hospitality, my Lord, but no, there is nothing I need, and you couldn't be kinder.' An outright lie and she couldn't help but ask, 'How is Dominic?'

He indicated to Jancy to leave them, and then he sighed and gazed at her face. 'There is no sign of the beating you took now; are you able to come to my table for your meals, do you think?'

'Yes . . . my Lord.'

'Then it would please me if you did. I prefer not to have my guests hiding like mice in their holes.'

'Has Dominic asked you to talk to me?'

'Good Lord, no! Dominic considers himself old enough to conduct his own affairs. He has been busy of late.'

'Does he mention me?'

'Not very often, about every ten minutes but I think you're perfectly aware of his regard for you.'

'As perfectly as knowing his patience is not infinite. Tell him I miss his company.'

He gave a wry grin. 'Better you tell him yourself.'

'I never see him.'

'He grew up here and knows every nook and cranny. We had some fine games of hide and seek.'

'Are you telling me he's been spying on me.'

'Not at all, but he does have the ability to keep himself concealed if the need arises. Dom can read, pen words, out-shoot, fence and ride as well as out-think me at every turn. He said you were honest, so I'll be the same. Do you love my brother?'

'He's the bright star in my sky.'

Alex laughed. 'Then I'll rest easy until tomorrow.'

'Tomorrow?'

'It will be the fourth Sunday.'

Ah yes . . . she had not forgotten the banns that had been read, but rather she'd put them aside as her expectations wavered back and forth. Would he abandon her at the altar as a punishment, or would she allow him to make a fool out of her by not going to church at all.

You either love, trust and respect one another, or you don't.

It was that simple. His actions tomorrow would tell.

Grace had expected to see Dominic at the breakfast table, so she was disappointed when his place remained empty.

Alex smiled reassuringly at her, 'Dom ate earlier because he had some business to attend to.'

He'd been avoiding her.

As she shook out her table napkin a familiar roll of parchment fell out. How had he known she'd be dining downstairs? Concealing it in her lap she ate a small amount of oatmeal with stewed apples, and honey drizzled over the top. It was followed by coddled eggs, a slice of bacon and some mushrooms.

Grace heard the sound of Argus cantering off down the carriageway. Odd that she could recognize the noise his horse made. Dominic *was* avoiding her. She wanted to jump from her chair and chase after him, beg his forgiveness. Instead, she drank her tea and then excused herself.

Tucking the little scroll into her shawl she changed her mind again. He *hadn't* avoided her after all.

She wished her emotions would stay at an even level instead of dancing around all over the place. Her hands shook as she unrolled the parchment.

Final verse (3)

Love is music of the soul. Like Beethoven
A powerful thrust into the soaring
Sky exposes a quivering heartstring
Winter bright its rising crescendo

Creates a new symphony, a new star to
Begin its trajectory across the heavens.

She began to tremble. She had still not seen Dominic . . . but his precious poem had made his regard for her quite clear.

The following week everyone was walking around with smiles on their faces. Grace was bathed, her hair washed and prepared for her new role like a turkey ready for roasting.

New Year's Eve, and Grace, gowned in burnished gold taffeta that rustled when she walked, sat in the LéSayres pew.

This afternoon at the celebratory feast she would be the bride in the virginal cream silk gown Vivienne and Eugenie had bought for her. At least, she hoped so.

It was one of those perfect winter days, cold and crisp, and the sky so blue it made her eyes ache. A bright sun made the frost glitter.

Again, the church was crowded. Grace saw no sign of Dominic and knew she would die from a broken heart if he didn't arrive. This time people had come from far and wide to line the church wall for a chance to see the gentry turn out in their finery.

The vicar in his white embroidered vestment arrived and pottered around trying to look busy. He was old and bent, white-haired and pink-cheeked, like an angel, his shoulder blades indicating where the wings were folded.

There was a bustle at the back of the church and everyone turned to see who'd arrived. Grace knew from the smile Alex gave that it was Dominic.

The congregation fell quiet as his footsteps strode purposefully down the aisle. Despite his confidence Dominic's heart would be thundering in case she refused him.

He stopped, went down on one knee and held his hand out to her. 'I love you, Miss Ellis. Will you marry me now?'

She couldn't help but tease him just a little. 'You mean now . . . this very instant and in front of everybody?'

'Nobody can say we didn't have witnesses, and they've been waiting long enough to see the outcome of my petition.' His smile became beguiling, but nevertheless he gave a quiet little growl. 'I love you dearly, Gracie girl, I've done so from the first moment I set eyes on you, and I know you love me. What better reason is there to wed?'

She didn't know of one, except . . . and she gazed at the row of faces, the earl and Vivenne, Eugenie, Mr Howard, who she had only briefly met. Suddenly she had a family of her own, and she wouldn't be lonely any more.

She placed her hand in his and their fingers intertwined. She kissed his cheek.

'There is no better reason, my love. Of course I'll wed you.'

He led her to the waiting vicar whose smile was as wide, if not wider than those in the congregation.

'I do like to officiate over a wedding that isn't strictly conventional. Are you young people quite ready to exchange your vows now – and yes, young lady, I do mean now, this instant.'

A rumble of laughter went through the church.

They gazed at each other and smiling, said together, 'Yes we are.'

'Good, then it will be my privilege to take you through your vows. He opened his prayer book. '"Dearly beloved, we are gathered together here in the sight of God, and in the face of this congregation, to join this man and this woman in holy matrimony . . ."'